GRODY TO THE MAX PRESENTS:

ECHOES

A NOVEL BY
NEAL McLAUGHLIN

1st edition
© Neal Writes Things 2025

Neal McLaughlin is the author of eight novels, writer/director of the feature films "I Was a Teenage Wereskunk" and "Hillhead," and co-host of the podcasts "Golden Gab w/ Lanie and Neal" and "Grody to the Max: A 1980s Horror Movie podcast."
He lives in Boston with his three cats.

To find out more about Neal's works and to sign up for his monthly newsletter, please visit
www.nealwritesthings.com
or scan the QR code:

Cover art by Aaron Needham
www.aaronneedham.com

Hello Reader,

Echoes is the first book in a massive project I've undertaken: the Grody to the Max Series, a collection of ten horror novels, one set in each year of the 1980s. For inspiration, I'm going back and watching all the notable horror movies of each year, trying to pick up vibes, tropes, and just get a general idea of what each individual year felt like. To document this research I've also launched a podcast, "Grody to the Max: A 1980s Horror Movie Podcast," with co-host Christian Drerup (available on Apple or Spotify).

The movies I studied that became the foundation for *Echoes* were: *The Fog, The Changeling, Inferno, The Shining, Friday the 13th, Cannibal Holocaust, Prom Night, Mother's Day, Motel Hell, Terror Train, Christmas Evil, New Year's Evil,* and *Maniac.* All of these films played some type of role in the creation of *Echoes.* Some quite prominent (the female radio DJ was taken from *The Fog,* the grieving, middle-aged man alone in a haunted house is the set-up for *The Changeling*), others a bit more fleeting (the idea of having James take quaaludes came from a passing reference to the now antiquated drug in *New Year's Evil,* a character suggesting they play strip Monopoly was lifted out of *Friday the 13th*).

I don't know what's been my favorite part of the journey so far: watching the films, discussing them on the pod, or writing the books inspired by them. If just a small percentage of the joy I've experienced working on this endeavor comes across in the prose, then you should be in for a fun read!

At the time of this writing, Christian and I have already worked our way through all the 1981 movies, and I'm about halfway through the first draft of the corresponding novel: a classic 80s summer camp slasher cheesefest called *Three-Fingered Willy.* Please go check out the podcast to catch up on all that. For news and updates on when that book will be released (as well as information on all my projects, current and past), be sure to visit **www.nealwritesthings.com** – and while you're there, don't forget to sign up for my monthly newsletter.

In the meantime, enjoy *Echoes*!

Stay grody,

Neal
April 23, 2025 - Boston, MA

ECHOES

It was Kelly Riordan's twelfth birthday. Also, her last.

Kelly and Michelle held hands as they skated around the walking path that framed Jamaica Pond, jubilantly singing "Magic" out of tune. They knew every word, each of them having worn out the Olivia Newton John sides of their respective *Xanadu* soundtrack records over the past several weeks. They let go of each other's hands to let a male jogger pass between them, then rejoined hands.

They were in excellent moods. It was Friday afternoon, the horrors of middle school in the rearview until Monday morning. The weather was beautiful for late September, warm but crisp, vaguely apple-scented. Most importantly, it was Kelly's birthday.

1

When her father got home from work in an hour or so he and her mother were going to take the two girls to McDonald's then up to the Revere Drive-in to finally see *Xanadu*, a film which, despite their devouring of the soundtrack, neither of them had actually seen yet.

"You're basically a teenager now," said Michelle, when they'd reached the song's conclusion. "I wonder why they chose to call it twelve instead of two-teen. Or eleven instead of one-teen for that matter. Weird, huh?"

Kelly didn't respond.

"Hello?"

"Hm?"

"I'm wondering why the teens don't just start up right after ten. One-teen, two-teen, thirteen, fourteen… You know?"

Kelly said she didn't know, but with such disinterest she left out all the consonants, grunting a lazy flow of vowels that sounded something like: "Ah-uh-oh."

"You're thinking about *him* again," said Michelle.

"Who?"

"Oh please. You know exactly who. Travis Curtly."

"Am not." The involuntary smile and pinkening of her usually pale cheeks at the mention of this name contradicted her denial.

Travis Curtly, a seventh grader with Leif Garret hair and jeans that fit like Henry Winkler's, had smiled at her in the hall that day—looked right into her eyes and gave her a Vinnie Barbarino smile. She'd been gliding on air ever since, rendering the roller skates on her feet superfluous.

"You should invite him to the movie tonight," said Michelle.

"Stop it."

"He could feel you up in the backseat of your dad's Mercury."

"At least I have something to feel up."

"I guess, long as he likes feeling mosquito bites."

"It's more than you got, Flat Benatar."

The girls giggled. Last year, in fifth grade, boobs never crossed anybody's mind. But many girls had arrived in sixth grade having done quite a bit of growing—both upward and outward—over summer break; boobs were suddenly an obsession. Discussing, comparing, teasing, admiring. Those who didn't have them desperately wanted them. Ironically, those who did have them were finding them burdensome. The sixth-grade boys didn't notice or care. Who had time for such trivialities when *The Empire Strikes Back* had recently been unleashed on the world and needed to be endlessly discussed?

They were coming up on the boathouse, where the walking path started running parallel with Pond Street for a few hundred yards before curling back around the pond. "We should head back," said Kelly, "so we have time to get ready." Seeing *Xanadu* was a long-awaited event; wardrobe had to be considered with thoughtful and meticulous care.

They skated off the path, merging onto the sidewalk along Pond Street. Kelly's house was just a few blocks down on Lochstead Avenue.

"You still thinking white dress?" asked Michelle.

"What do you think about a disco cowgirl crossover?" said Kelly. "Kind of a *Coal Miner's Daughter* meets *Saturday Night Fever* type of look."

"Ooh, me likes," said Michelle.

They were heading down an incline. It wasn't particularly steep in the abstract, but on skates it was slightly treacherous, especially on the cracked and uneven surface of the Pond Street sidewalk. But Michelle and Kelly were eleven and newly-twelve respectively; treachery is seldom a concern at that invincible age.

3

"I was thinking my royal blue sequined blouse, white cowboy hat, white boots, and my high-waist Calvin Kleins," said Kelly.

"I love it," said Michelle. "Except the jeans."

"What's wrong with the jeans?"

"Well, like Brooke says in the commercial, nothing's supposed to come between you and your Calvins, right? So, if you're wearing your Calvins, how's Travis Curtly supposed to get his hand down there?"

Kelly belted out an eardrum-piercing shriek, originating in the overlapping space in the Venn diagram of delight and horror. "Michelle!" This big reaction caused her to stumble slightly; she had to grab Michelle's shoulder to stabilize.

"Oh don't pretend like you wouldn't let him," said Michelle.

"You're terrible!"

An acorn. A tiny little acorn was what did it. A ubiquitous and mostly useless nut to anyone who isn't a squirrel.

The girls weren't moving at a speed one might call breakneck, but it was fast enough that when the plastic wheel of Kelly's skate rolled over that fateful acorn her balance and momentum were disrupted such that she was sent careening toward the grass median strip between the sidewalk and Pond Street. Were it not for a recent rain, the grass might have slowed her down such that she could have regained control, but the wheels of her skates sunk into the saturated ground, not slowing her down but stopping her completely. Her feet stopped, but her upper body continued its forward trajectory, which at this point was trajected toward Pond Street—Pond Street and the fast-moving traffic zipping along it.

She landed in front of a Saab, which was doing precisely fifty-one miles per hour. The driver slammed the breaks immediately, but by the time the vehicle's speed had decelerated even a single mile per hour, Kelly had already been sucked underneath it, her body scraping, tearing, twisting, bending, breaking as it was thrashed violently between the undercarriage and the pavement.

The good news was she was dead before she felt anything, or was even aware it was about to happen. One second she was delighting in the idea of Travis Curtly's fumbling fingers coming between her and her Calvins, the next second everything went black.

Her body, on the other hand, did not have the luxury of vanishing from this earthly reality the way her consciousness did, and ended up faring quite poorly in the incident. It stayed in one piece after its encounter with the Saab—though pulverized, her skeleton reduced to shards and fragments—but the station wagon that came screeching and skidding up behind the Saab really did a number on her. Its left front tire rolled over her profile, eliminating any possibility that may have existed of there being an open casket. The left rear tire severed her leg at the knee, sending the amputated portion bouncing and rolling up onto the grass median strip.

They say when events such as these occur they often seem to do so in slow motion. That was not the case for Michelle. The accident was so shocking and sudden she didn't even register what had happened until her friend's severed leg landed mere inches in front of her—a disembodied shin and foot, blue and white striped sock poking out of a yellow, high-top roller skate, one blood-drenched, plastic wheel still spinning.

The poor child then screamed so loud it could be heard all the way in Xanadu.

"The challenge with writing about Shakespeare," said Professor James Riordan, "is you're going to be hard pressed to come up with a thesis that hasn't been done before. Especially with a heavy hitter like *Macbeth*. Have you considered doing your paper on *The Winter's Tale*? I thought what you said in class the other day was incredibly insightful. About the Hermione statue being something of a bridge between the urbane art world of Sicily and the more natural world of Bohemia. And how when she stepped off the podium it was a metaphor for Leontes' transformation."

Susan had in fact said nothing of the sort. She'd been talking about the merging of the two worlds being represented by the marriage of Leontes' daughter to Polixenes's son. James had been the one to bring up the Hermione statue, not Susan. He had a tendency to do that sometimes: steer class discussions back to his own ideas.

"Hear me out," said Susan. "It's about the blurring of the gender lines. Lady Macbeth makes the whole 'unsex me' speech, right? But—"

"Susan, let me stop you right there." He pointed to the wall of his office, which was a corner to corner, floor to ceiling set of shelves overflowing with books, texts, academic journals, and myriad other forms of the written word. "Go over there and pick out any three books at random. Guaranteed at least one of them will contain a dissertation on the 'unsex me' speech. It's right behind 'to be or not to be' on the list of topics freshman write their final paper on."

"I don't doubt it. But hear me out. She thinks she needs to be unsexed in order to carry out her cruel intentions, right? Like women are soft and sensitive and incapable of evilness, but if she were a man..."

"Fill me from crown to the toe top with the direst cruelty."

"Right. But here's the thing, she doesn't ask the spirits to *change her sex*, she asks to be *un-sexed*. In other words, genderless."

"So, you're saying it's not about the defining of gender roles but about the blurring of gender lines. Like when Lady Macbeth tells her husband to look like the innocent flower but be the serpent under it, combining perhaps the most vulvic and phallic symbols in the natural world."

"Let me finish. What I'm saying is it's all bullshit. Women are weak, men are strong. Women are sensitive, men are cruel. It's crap. When Lady Macbeth goes off and does her wicked deeds, she's still a woman. She hasn't grown a penis, has she? So clearly women are perfectly capable of carrying out wicked deeds."

"The play is suggesting it was the spirits she pled to that 'unsexed' her and put that wickedness in her."

"But it was always there. Right before she makes the 'unsex me' speech she tries to convince Macbeth to kill Duncan but doesn't think he has the balls. She says something about having to inject herself into him so he can go through with it."

"Pour my spirits in your ear and chastise with my tongue all the valor that impedes you."

"That's it. Talk about vulvic and phallic metaphors! A tongue and an ear? But in the metaphor, *she's* the one with the penis and *he's* the one with the vagina."

"Okay. Sure. But Susan, this isn't entirely new. The gender roles in Macbeth is well-trod territory."

"That's where *The Wizard of Oz* comes in."

Susan was a smart girl, but there were always a handful of smart kids in every class he taught. What set Susan apart was the singularity of her mind. You could talk to her for several minutes and think you were just talking to a run-of-the-mill smart kid, but then she'd drop an unexpected comment that changed the entire context of everything about the conversation that came before it.

Professor Riordan loved finding kids with those types of intellectual quirks. Specifically: girls. He'd been fucking Susan since the second week of fall semester.

"I'm listening." He kissed her neck, just below the ear. Their bodies were twisted together on the couch in his office, post-coitally naked.

"The whole plot of *The Wizard of Oz* centers around these characters thinking they need certain things, right? A brain, a heart, courage. But they all had them all along. The Scarecrow was always coming up with the ideas. The Tin Man was always crying. The Lion was always stepping up to fight. Even Dorothy, all she wants is to go home, and the means to get there were on her feet the whole time. Same thing for Lady Macbeth. It goes a lot deeper than that, but you're gonna have to wait for the paper."

James planted a purposeful kiss on her forehead and said, "I love your brain."

"Can I ask you something?"

"Of course."

"Am I your first?"

"Nope. Leslie Pettigrew. Sewell's Beach, Maine. Nineteen-fifty-seven. Stole my innocence."

"You know what I mean."

"Does it matter?"

"Well, that answers that question."

"Well, does it?"

"Everything matters. But it you're asking if I'm going to stop sleeping with you just because you've screwed other students the answer is no. I just wanted to know."

He took her hand and brought it to his mouth. He dragged his lips back and forth across her knuckles. Her hands were unblemished. Smooth. Silky. Hands weren't something he ever noticed when he was younger, but now, months away from forty, there were lots of things about the bodies of youthful females he was realizing he'd always taken for granted. Linda's hands were dry and creased. They weren't hideous or anything, at least in a vacuum, but if Linda were to lay her hands side by side with Susan's they'd look like vulture talons by comparison.

Linda was still only thirty-five and quite attractive. She was fashionable and kept in shape with regular aerobics classes. James was proud to have her on his arm at cocktail parties or campus events. But the imperfections were starting to creep in. The aforementioned hands. The creases at the corners of her eyes. The cellulite below the buttocks. Stretchmarks on her lower abdomen. Breasts that were losing their shape. Experiencing the pristineness of Susan's twenty-year-old body, untouched by childbirth and a decade-plus of extra wear, really shone a spotlight on all his wife's physical imperfections, minor though many of them may be.

"I don't have a new flavor-of-the-semester every fall and spring if that's what you're thinking. You need to understand things were a lot different when I was coming up. I got my first professor gig in 1966. Those were different times. Students and professors would go to the same parties, drink and smoke grass together, and, yes, fuck. But it's not like that anymore. That kind of thing is frowned upon now. Times have changed."

There was also the fact that in the Summer of Love he was only a few years older than the students he was bedding. He was twice Susan's age.

Susan reached down and grabbed James's Pall Malls from the floor. She put two between her lips at once and lit them both. She passed one to James. "Tell me about Lisa Pettigrew."

"Leslie Pettigrew. Why?"

"I wanna hear about your first. And since it happened before I was born I can't get jealous."

"Well, my family used to rent this beach cottage in Maine for a week every summer when we were kids, my sister Connie and I. There was this family that lived in the main house on the property, the Pettigrews. They had a daughter my age. Leslie. The first few years I didn't really think much about her one way or the other. She was around here and there. Sometimes she'd go off with Connie doing girl things. Whatever. Then one year, I think when I was maybe fourteen or fifteen, I saw her in a two-piece and my whole perspective on Leslie Pettigrew's role in my life changed.

"We developed a bit of a flirtation, in that awkward teenage way. Teasing each other. Showing off. Ignoring each other. That kind of nonsense. But nothing ever came of it. Until 1957. I was sixteen. It was our last day of vacation. It was the middle of the day and we were all out on the beach. I went back to the cottage to get something. I don't even remember what. All I know is I'd gone into my room to grab whatever I needed to grab, and when I turned around, there was Leslie Pettigrew standing in the bedroom door, stark naked."

He could smell the salt air. He could hear the waves pushing and dragging the sea rocks over one another, a phenomenon he and his sister called the Rock'n'Roll Dance Party. He could still see Leslie Pettigrew's naked body—the first he'd ever seen outside of a water-damaged black and white photo his buddy Tommy Dinapoli kept hidden behind the boiler in his basement back in Somerville.

"Wow. I didn't think teenagers were that promiscuous in the fifties." She felt around on the floor for the ashtray. Finding it, she set it down on her chest, nestling it in the top of her cleavage, and ashed her Pall Mall into it.

"Well, it certainly wasn't as free as what was about to come a decade later, but we weren't quite as buttoned up as what you see on *Happy Days*."

"So, how was it?"

"Great for me. Probably not so much for her. I think I might have lasted four thrusts, and that estimate might even be giving myself too much credit."

"Then what?"

"Then nothing. We put our bathing suits back on and went back to the beach. That was it. My family left the next day. The factory where my father worked shut down that year, so the annual family trip got nixed. I haven't been back to Sewell's Beach since. Never saw Leslie Pettigrew again." He took a long drag of his cigarette and deposited the ash into the ashtray on Susan's chest.

"Is it weird that that story turned me on?"

"I'm a bit turned on myself."

"Mm. I'd say more than a bit," she reached down between his legs, finding a steel flagpole down there. She stubbed out her cigarette, then took his from him and stubbed it out as well. She placed the ashtray back on the floor and straddled him.

They'd only just finished their last round of love making ten minutes prior. At his age it generally took him at least a half hour to be charged up and ready to go again, but that trip down memory lane had him fully primed. The image of Leslie Pettigrew naked in his bedroom door had been masturbation fuel for him for years after the incident, but over time she'd slowly been replaced by countless other images, either memories of actual sexual encounters or saucy fantasies. He hadn't thought of Leslie in at least a decade. But now he was back in that beach cottage. Sixteen-years-old. Filling his eyes with his first ever in-the-flesh naked girl. Young, dumb, and full of cum, as the saying went.

However: "We can't."

"We can, we have, and we shall," said Susan, softly biting his nipple.

"No, I've got to go. Really. It's my daughter's birthday. I'm taking her and a friend up to the Revere Drive-in to see *Xanadu*."

"Oh Jesus. Skip it. It's an abomination. She'll thank you later."

"I can't. She's been dying to see it."

"Well, we'll just have to make it quick then. You can pretend I'm Leslie Pettigrew and get the job done in four thrusts."

It took him more than four thrusts, but he made relatively quick work of it. He would have still arrived home with plenty of time to get his daughter and her friend to the drive-in were it not for a fleet of police cars and ambulances on Pond Street slowing down traffic.

Apparently, there'd been some kind of accident.

"I'm not sure I can go through with it," said Linda.

"We don't have a choice," said James.

"Of course we have a choice. We could simply not go in. We could just pull out of here. Go south. We could go to Key West. Remember on our honeymoon? Remember we said we were going to retire there?"

"We can't afford to retire."

"I could waitress. I used to waitress in college. I was good at it. And you could teach high school. Maybe write that novel you're always talking about. Let's go, Jim. I can't go in there. I can't. If one more person offers me their fucking condolences! What is a fucking condolence? What's its value? It's fucking

Monopoly money. It's worthless. Worse, it's condescending. *Oh, your daughter was killed? Here, have a condolence.* Fuck you."

"It's just a thing people say, Lin, when they don't know what else to say."

"I hate it."

They'd been sitting in the Mercury in the parking lot of St. Thomas Aquinas Parish for twenty minutes, unable to drag themselves inside. The thought of that coffin—that necessarily closed coffin that contained a hopeless reconstruction of their daughter's mangled body... It was too much to bear.

"Let's not do it, Jim. Please. I can't."

"We have to, Lin. Kelly's in there."

Guests were arriving. His uncle Edwin. Linda's cousin David, his wife Sheila, and their three kids. Professor Almendinger from the university. Their neighbors Brad and Louise. Kelly's best friend Michelle and her parents. All descending on the church like zombies in black clothing. All with a fucking condolence to offer—as if maybe with enough condolences Kelly might roller skate out of her coffin, alive and in one piece.

"I can't do it, Jim. I can't face these people." Linda started to cry.

Jim took her hand, brought it to his mouth, and gently rubbed his lips back and forth across her knuckles. He noted the stark contrast between Linda's worn, angular hands and the smooth, silk gloves that were Susan's hands. Susan's whole body was smooth silk. He'd been on leave since the accident and hadn't seen her. Had she heard? Surely word must have gotten to her about what had happened. Would she show up here?

Then he felt a wave a nausea. He was sitting outside a church, preparing to go to his twelve-year-old daughter's funeral. His wife was crying beside him, and he was thinking about the creamy skin of the co-ed he was shtupping behind her back, wondering—perhaps even hoping—she'd show up. Jesus Christ, he was a fucking monster.

He loved Linda. Susan excited him physically and intrigued him intellectually, but he didn't love her. It was just sex and giggles. He'd somehow managed to compartmentalize Linda and Susan—if he kept them separate in his mind there was no guilt. He wasn't cheating on his wife. Those were two separate lives, two entirely separate people. James was happily married to Linda, Professor Riordan was sleeping with Susan.

But on the afternoon of September 28, 1980, Kelly Riordan's twelfth birthday, the wall between those two compartments was disintegrated by dynamite. The time of Kelly's death was determined to be just after four in the afternoon. At that time, James was engaged in a second round of intercourse with Susan, an undertaking he suspected was going to render him late to take his daughter to the drive-in, but he'd done it anyway.

Intellectually, he knew it didn't make sense, but he couldn't shake the belief that if he hadn't chosen to go round two with Susan, if he'd left campus when he was supposed to have, Kelly would still be alive. Again, he knew that was ridiculous. The accident occurred in Jamaica Plain and he was all the way up in Cambridge. His leaving on time would not have changed a thing. Kelly would still have been dead before James had even left the humanities building. Misplaced guilt was warping his thoughts. He was cheating on his wife with a college student while his daughter—the product of him and the wife he was betraying—was being dragged underneath a Saab, spit out the back, and subsequently shredded by a station wagon.

"I've done something awful." There was no forethought to this admission. It just happened, as involuntary as a sneeze.

Linda looked up at him with tear-soaked eyes.

"I've been unfaithful."

Linda's sobs ceased, but otherwise her face showed no reaction one way or another to this statement, because she didn't understand what she'd just heard. "Unfaithful" sounded like a definitionless collection of disparate syllables. She was burying her daughter today. Unfaithful? Huh?

"I've been seeing someone. It's only been a few weeks. It doesn't mean anything. She's... well, she's younger and it isn't serious. But..." Why the hell was he telling her this? And why now? He regretted every word that spilled from his mouth but he was powerless to stop it. Like a tipped over jar of marbles. A train with a severed break line. A girl on roller skates going down a sloping section of Pond Street.

"Jesus Christ, Jim, are you serious? Are you seriously choosing right now to tell me this?"

"I know. I know the timing is terrible. It's just that I was—"

"What the fuck is the matter with you, Jim? Why the fuck would you tell me this?" She was less concerned with the infidelity and more so with the fact that he was telling her at all.

"It's just... I was with her when, you know, it happened. And I just... I don't know, I can't go in there without you knowing. I'm sorry. I don't know. I'm... I'm out of my mind right now. It just seemed like you should know. Something about going in there without you knowing where I was when it happened. I just... I don't know, Lin. I'm sorry. I'm just... I'm sorry."

"Oh great. Your sorry. That's even more condescending than a fucking condolence."

"I'm s—"

"Don't say you're fucking sorry again. Jesus Christ. What is the matter with you, Jim? Am I not hurting enough? Why would you tell me this right now?"

"I don't know. I had to."

He was still holding her hand, which she finally jerked away. "Who is she?"

"It doesn't matter."

"Like hell it doesn't. Who is she?"

"Just someone from the university."

"Is it somebody I know?"

"Definitely not. She's a..."

"She's a what? Besides a slut."

"Nothing. She's nothing."

"Oh God. She's a student, isn't she?"

His silent shame affirmed it.

"You're fucking one of your grad students."

He looked away.

"Look at me. Tell me you're not fucking one of your grad students."

"She's not one of my grad students."

"Well, that's a tiny relief." Then it dawned on her. "Oh no. No no no, Jim. Undergrad? You're sleeping with an undergrad?"

"She's very—" he was going to say mature for her age, but in a rare moment of restraint thought better of it and stopped himself.

"I'm going to be sick."

"Lin, I—" He made to put his hand on her shoulder but she swatted it away.

"Don't you dare touch me. Don't you ever touch me again. You soulless bastard. I don't even know you."

"Linda—" Instinctively he reached for her arm again. This time she shoved him hard in the chest.

"Don't touch me!"

The outburst turned the heads of their friends Peter and Krista as they walked from their car to the church.

"Okay, okay. I'm sorry."

"I swear to God if you say you're sorry one more time there's going to be two funerals today."

"I had to tell you, Lin. If I didn't—"

"Stop talking."

"If I didn't tell you I'd—"

"Stop talking!"

What had he been thinking? He'd been so overwrought with guilt it had seemed imperative he tell her, that this secret be out in the open. An unburdening. An exorcism. What had he expected? That she'd thank him after? Tell him how much closer to him she felt now that there were no secrets between them?

"Selfish," she said. "Selfish selfish asshole."

"I know"

"I can't. I can't deal with this. I can't deal with you."

"I know. Everything you're thinking and feeling about me, I deserve it. But we have to put that aside for a few hours. Our daughter is in there, and we—"

"Fuck you. How dare you talk about my daughter?"

My daughter, not *our* daughter. By cheating on his wife had he forfeited his paternal claim? Those dots didn't quite connect, but he'd learned a lesson or two in the last couple minutes about keeping his stupid mouth shut and didn't challenge this assertion.

She looked hard at him for several seconds, studying him, as if the answer to how and why she was going through this

19

impossibly tragic ordeal might be written somewhere in the creases of his face. "What the hell were you thinking?"

Which part? The affair? Doing so with a third-year? Telling his wife in the church parking lot before their daughter's funeral? Didn't matter, he didn't have a satisfying answer to any of it.

Linda took a deep breath through her nose, held it for several seconds, then slowly exhaled through slightly pursed lips. She opened the door and exited. She didn't close the door behind her.

"Linda, wait." He stepped out of the car and followed her. "We should—" he was going to say talk about this but that was not at all what they should do. Quite the opposite. He'd already talked too much and every word he said made it worse. But they needed to do *something*, right? They couldn't go into the church like this. They needed to find some sort of resolution, even if only a false and temporary one, something to keep some kind of face in that church. They owed it to Kelly.

There were several people, all in black, congregated on the stairs outside the church doors, finishing cigarettes, exchanging somber pleasantries with acquaintances.

They watched Linda Riordan walk toward them, looking as morose and torn up as one would expect under the circumstances.

They watched James Riordan catch up to her and say, "Linda, hold on," as he put a hand on her shoulder.

They watched—and many audibly gasped—as Linda whirled around and belted him.

It was open-palmed, but not loose-wristed like a slap. Her fingers, hand, wrist, arm remained stiff and rigid from contact to follow through, like an oar. A sound rang out somewhere between a thud and a smack that could be heard all the way in the church lobby. James, much larger than his wife, took the blow, but it turned his head and staggered him back a step.

"That's for the teenage whore!" said Linda.

Susan was twenty, but this hardly seemed the appropriate time to point out that triviality.

Linda wound up and smacked him again. Again, the crowd on the stairs gasped. Again, the *thud/smack* rang out. Again, James absorbed the blow.

"And that's for telling me about it right before I bury my daughter."

She hit him once more, this one the hardest yet. Gasp. *Thud/smack*. This was the one that would leave a hand-shaped bruise that would persist for the next week and a half.

"And that's for being a selfish asshole. You have taken the worst situation imaginable and somehow managed to make it exponentially worse. You'd have done less harm if you'd just gone ahead and stuck a knife in my heart." She turned and stormed up the church steps, the shocked crowd parting for her in a way that called to mind the Red Sea and Moses.

Most, including James, stood stunned. Slowly, hushed chatter began to occur. Several women—friends, relatives, acquaintances of the Riordans—went into the church to check on Linda. Several men—the husbands and brothers of those women—came down the steps to check on James.

"What the hell was that all about, Jimbo?" asked Tommy Dinapoli from the old neighborhood in Sommerville, whom James (Jimbo to that old crew) had known since diapers.

"She's upset," said James.

"I noticed" said Tommy. "You all right?"

"My face, yeah. Everything else, no."

"I can only imagine, buddy. My condolences."

Linda had been right: being offered a condolence felt as useful as being offered a sack of dog shit. James had a sudden urge to punch Tommy in the stomach, but of course Tommy hadn't done anything wrong. It was protocol. One offers condolences at a funeral. It's just what people do.

"Thanks," said James, and headed up the stairs into the church.

"Shit, Jimmy, it smells like John Hannah's jock strap in here."

James slowly turned his head to find Connie standing in his living room. Not that he needed to look; he could pick out her abrasive squawk and chunky Boston accent in a crowd of a hundred people speaking at once. "How'd you get in here?"

"The door, idiot. Do I look like Santa Claus? You think I came down the fucking chimney? What the hell have you been doing? I musta called like fifty times and you didn't answer. And I stood out there knocking on the door like a freakin' moron for ten minutes before I realized it was unlocked. You should lock your door, by the way. This ain't as nice a neighborhood as you think it is. What's going on with Luke and Laura?"

"Huh?"

"Luke and Laura." She pointed at the television. "You're watching *General Hospital*."

He looked at the TV curiously, as if noticing for the first time not only was it on, but there was a TV in the room at all. The truth of the matter was he'd turned it on three days ago and just hadn't shut it off.

"You look terrible."

"Well, I'm going through some shit, Con. Perhaps you've heard."

"Just because you're going through shit doesn't mean you have to smell like it. When was the last time you showered? Or eaten, for that matter? You look like hobo Twiggy."

"I had pizza."

There was a pizza box on the coffee table with a single slice gone. One could tell just by looking at it that it was several days old. A fat roach was enjoying the congealed cheese.

"We'll drive through Burger King on the way."

"On the way where?"

"To the polls, dummy. I said I'd take you, remember?"

"Jesus, is that today?"

"Go upstairs and shower. You're not going out in public smelling like the restrooms at Revere Beach. I'll tidy up down here. You got one of those radiation suits people at nuclear power plants wear that I can borrow?"

The house was indeed disgusting. In the four weeks Linda had been gone he hadn't touched a broom or cleaned a dish. He hadn't run the washer, nor had any of his discarded clothes found the hamper. He hadn't taken out the trash, nor had most of the waste materials that should have gone into it made it there. The living room was a combat zone: there was a half-full glass of orange juice on the mantel with a layer of something blue growing on the surface, mounds of cigarette butts overflowed out of ashtrays, worn socks and undershirts were draped over chairs, end tables, lamps.

On the television, a feathered-haired blonde gentleman who looked like he belonged in a yacht club was pimping the new Mazda GLC ("The more you look, the more you like!") and it's affordable—if you belonged to a yacht club—price tag of $4,195.

"C'mon, Jimmy. Up and at 'em. You'll feel much better after you check that box that says Reagan/Bush."

James didn't move from the easy chair he was slouched in. He wore a wool sweater, light-blue boxer shorts, and argyle socks.

"Nothing? No response to that? You're worse off than I thought, letting somebody under your very own roof even joke you'd vote for a republican."

James leaned forward, shook a Pall Mall from the soft-pack on the coffee table, and lit it. This simple action seemed to take an Everest-scaling amount of energy to accomplish.

"Get on that red train, Jimmy. Ronnie's gonna balance the budget, end stagflation, bring the hostages home. It's a new day in American."

"Great. I just hope you never plan to retire, cause there won't be any social security or medicare waiting for you."

"There he is! There's the brother I know. Now that you're inspired to go waste your vote on that sissy Carter, get your ass out of that chair and go get cleaned up. C'mon. Chop chop."

"You know something, Connie? Your bedside manner could use a little work."

Connie walked over and turned the television off, silencing an under-the-weather housewife who could perform her vacuuming duties much better after taking a Dristan decongestant. Connie shook out one of James's Pall Malls for herself, lit it, and sat down on the coffee table across from him. "I'm not gonna say my pain is in the same universe as yours, but I lost a niece and a sister-in-law in this too."

"Please. You couldn't stand Linda."

"Did I think she was a pretentious yuppie kook? Sure. But so are you. Doesn't change the fact that she was family. But Kelly... I loved the shit out of that girl. I used to fantasize you and Linda would get in a plane crash together so I could take custody of her."

"You always know just what to say."

"You need to learn to multi-task better. I'm not saying you shouldn't grieve—you most certainly should. You should grieve your guts out. But while you're doing that, you could also brush your teeth, change your clothes, maybe have a sandwich, and do your civic duty and get out there and vote for the Gipper."

"Do you remember the Rock'n'Roll Dance Party?"

"Sure. Radio show. Alan Freed."

"No. Well, yes, but that's not what I'm referring to. It's what you called high tide at Sewell's Beach. Cause the waves would push the rocks around and make that noise. Remember?"

"Oh yeah. Kinda. Why?"

"Nothing. It's just... the day Kelly died. I was with... well, you know."

"Your chippy."

"Jesus. Yeah, sure. My *chippy.* I keep replaying that afternoon over and over in my head, wondering what I was doing at the exact moment of Kelly's death."

"I think we all know what you were doing, which is why Linda's staying with her parents and nobody's emptied an ashtray around here in a month."

"Police said the accident happened at exactly four-oh-three, according to the smashed up clock in the Saab."

"Stop it, Jim. Why do you keep reliving this?"

"If memory serves correctly, I would have been talking to Susan about Sewell's Beach at the exact time of the accident."

"Okay. So?"

"I don't know. It seems important."

"It was arbitrary, Jimmy. You coulda just as easily been talking about the Red Sox bullpen, thinking about what you had for breakfast, or taking a fucking dump."

"But I wasn't. I was talking about Sewell's Beach."

"Again, so what?"

"In the last moment of her life, the last time she ever took a breath in her earthly body, I was reminiscing about Sewell's Beach. Now I can't stop thinking about it. Like, if I just keep thinking about Sewell's Beach I can keep her alive, like preserving that last moment in amber, you know?"

"Oh, Jimmy." She made to stub her cigarette out but there was no vacancy in any of the three ashtrays on the coffee table, so she instead dropped the butt into an empty can of Tab. She then reached into her pocketbook and pulled out a plastic bottle of pills and handed them to James.

"What are these?"

"I believe the kids call them Disco Biscuits."

He read the label. "Methaqualone? You're giving me 'ludes?"

"You need them, Jimmy. You're depressed."

"Of course I'm depressed! My daughter is dead. My wife left me."

"Which is why you need the pills."

"Why do you even have these?"

"Mother's little helper."

"You're not a mother."

"You might be surprised to hear this, but my life ain't perfect."

"Oh, I'm so sorry for you."

"I'm not trying to make a comparison, Jim, I'm just telling you why I have the pills."

"I don't need quaaludes." He tried to hand the pills back to her but she pushed his hand back toward him.

"Just try it. Take a half. Then get up and clean the house. Put on a Pink Floyd record."

"Who's Pink Floyd?"

"You hang around with college kids all day and you don't know who Pink Floyd is?"

"I'm fine, Con. Really. I don't need these."

"Stubborn and pigheaded. Just like dad."

"Ha. Look who's talking."

"Yeah, but I'm stubborn and pigheaded and right." She set the pills down on the coffee table. "I'm not gonna hold you down and force the pills down your throat, but I'm gonna leave them here for you. You may not wanna take one now, but when Reagan turns the entire electoral map red tonight, you're gonna wanna take the whole bottle. Don't do that, by the way—take the whole bottle. You'll die."

"I might welcome that."

"Okay, enough of your bullshit, Jim. Get your sad ass out of that chair, get upstairs, shower, dress, and come with me to the polls."

"Con, I'm really not—"

"Now!"

He didn't immediately comply, but in the tug-of-war between the respective stubbornness and pigheadedness their father had gifted them both with, Connie's eventually won. He dragged himself along with her to the English High School gymnasium and voted for Carter.

Connie had been right about the electoral map. Carter/Mondale won only seven states, even losing Massachusetts, albeit by a scant fifteen hundredths of a percent. But James wouldn't find any of this out until the following day. He spent the rest of election night smoking cigarettes in his chair, alone, TV off, thinking about Sewell's Beach.

"Monopoly?" said Susan. "Boring."

"It's Monopoly with a twist," said Karen. "*Strip* Monopoly."

"I'm in!" said Steve.

"Sign me up too," said Bill.

"Oh for God's sakes," said Susan. "That's ridiculous."

"I saw it in a movie this summer," said Karen. "It looked fun."

"What movie?" asked Susan. "*Debbie Does Dallas*?"

"*Friday the 13th*," said Karen.

"Oh, I wanted to see that," said Steve. "How was it?"

"Nasty," said Karen. "I loved it."

Bill stood up. "Anybody need a refill?"

The other three checked their cups and said some version of: "All set at the moment." Bill went over to the keg for a top-off.

The night before there'd been a party at Gebby, the suite they shared. Shenanigans had gone down that would have made the cast of *Animal House* blush. To show for it, there were hundreds of beer cans stacked in a pyramid in the corner of the common room, cigarette burns on the couch, shaving cream smeared all over the carpet (none of them could remember how that happened), and a quarter-full keg left over, which they were now sitting around the filthy kitchen table consuming, because beer shall never be wasted on a college campus, even warm, flat Schlitz.

"Flip the record while you're up," said Steve. Side one of Elvis Costello and the Attractions' *Get Happy!!* had run out of songs a couple minutes prior.

"Aye aye, Cap," said Bill.

There was a knock at the door.

"And see who that is," said Steve.

"Anything else I can do for you while I'm up?" said Bill. "Make you a sandwich? Polish your shoes?"

"Blow job," said Steve.

"You wish, fag," said Bill, and disappeared into the common room.

"So, what do you say," said Karen. "Strip Monopoly?"

"I can't believe you went to see that movie," said Susan. "I remember Pete Kotsanis taking me to see *Halloween* freshman year. I didn't sleep for a week after that. Every time I see sheets hanging on a clothesline I think I see that creep hiding behind them."

"Why would Pete Kotsanis be hiding behind a sheet?" asked Steve.

"Not Pete, you idiot, the killer from the movie."

"You're changing the subject," said Karen. "We gonna play or not?"

31

"I already said I'm in," said Steve.

"I'm not playing strip Monopoly," said Susan.

"Prude," said Steve.

"Why not?" said Karen. "It's not like everybody here hasn't already seen your tits."

"I think you mean her community chest," said Steve, which got the three of them laughing.

"Hey, Suse." Bill was back in the kitchen doorway. "Door's for you."

"For me? Who is it?"

"It's that literature teacher. Professor Riordan."

It was the most basic of questions, but a good one, and one to which he couldn't provide a satisfying answer.

"I don't know," he said. "I don't know what I'm doing here."

It had been immediately awkward. That kid answering the door, new wave punk and beer stench wafting out of the suite, Susan's distinct laugh coming from somewhere deep inside. Her laugh sounded different than when she laughed with him, tangled up nude on his office sofa after intercourse. With him, her laugh was the laugh of a woman on his level, or at least only slightly below it. The way she was laughing in her suite, with her peers, with the people her own age—it sounded immature. Juvenile. Whatever they were laughing at in there, he was almost certain he wouldn't have found it funny, even before tragedy had stripped him of all sense of humor.

"You got a cigarette?" she asked.

He reached into his jacket pocket and handed her the pack and lighter. She shook one out for herself and lit it. She did not, as she usually did, shake out two, put them both in her mouth, light them together, and hand him one. He found this soul crushing. Surprisingly so. Given all that happened, Susan not lighting his cigarette should have been so far down on his list of concerns it could be found somewhere near the earth's core, yet it devastated him.

"How's Jack doing so far?" he asked, trying not the think about the slight.

"Who?"

"Professor Spano."

"Oh. He's okay. Knows a ton about Shakespeare, but he doesn't have your passion. He talks about Desdemona the same way Professor Morrison talks about microbiomes."

"Yeah, that sounds like Jack."

A young woman James vaguely recognized as having once been a student in one of his British Lit survey courses entered.

"Hi, Sarah," said Susan. "We're just talking about my thesis."

"Okay," said Sarah, dismissively disinterested, the way one often is when receiving the answer to a question they hadn't cared enough to ask

This was another stomach punch for James. Why was Susan being defensive? Why did she feel she needed to explain why she was there with him? Sarah gave them an odd look. It didn't occur to him that a professor in the residence wing of campus was an exceedingly rare sight, let alone one sitting on the bench in the foyer of Gebby, smoking cigarettes with a student on a Sunday night.

Once Sarah was up the stairs and out of earshot, Susan said: "But really, what are you doing here?"

"You used to be happy to see me."

"Okay. Yeah. Sure. But... this is a little weird, no?"

"Why is it weird?"

"You know, *everything*. I mean, I haven't seen you since…"

"Since the accident?"

"Well, yeah."

"Everyone knows about that, huh?"

"Not at first. At first they just said you were on leave, no explanation. But, yeah, eventually the reason got out."

That was it? That was all she had to say about it? Thanks for the sympathy. As insulting as he found receiving condolences, not receiving condolences was doubly insulting.

"Did you know my wife left me also?"

"No. No, I hadn't heard that."

He hadn't known what to expect from her on hearing this news. *Oh, I'm so sorry about that,* or maybe, *Wow, that's great, now we can finally be together, out of the shadows.* What he had not expected was total neutrality. It would be inaccurate to say this wasn't going how he'd planned, because he hadn't planned it. He had no expectations. He just needed to see her. But regardless of expectations or lack of, this wasn't going well. And it was about to go worse.

"Do you want to go away?"

"Sorry?"

"With me. On a trip. I've been thinking a lot about Sewell's Beach. It's only a two-hour drive from here. I know it's November, not exactly beach season, but it'll be nice. Quiet."

"I…" she frantically searched for an excuse, "…have school."

"Thanksgiving is in a couple weeks. We could go then."

"I have to go home for Thanksgiving."

"Why?"

"Because… I do. It's Thanksgiving. My parents."

Jesus. Her parents. She was so young. She still had parents to answer to. Parents who expected her home for Thanksgiving.

Parents to whom she couldn't say, "Mom, Pop, I won't be making it this year, I'll be shacking up in a beach cottage with my forty-year-old English professor." How old were her parents? Probably not much older than himself.

"You're right. You're right. I'm sorry. I shouldn't have asked."

"It's okay. Look, it was nice to see you." She did a terrible job selling this lie. "I should be getting back upstairs though."

"I'm sorry. I didn't mean to put all this on you."

"No no. It's not that. It's just… we were about to start a game. They're all waiting for me."

"A game."

"Yeah."

He'd experienced the tragedy of his life—of *any* life—and she needed to go back upstairs and play fucking Candyland. God, she was young. She didn't know anything about the world. She never even knew of a world before television. She was only three when Kennedy was shot. She was far closer to Kelly's age than she was to Linda's.

James looked at her now and saw a stranger, as anonymous as the two-hundred-and-fifty faces in the lecture hall of the requisite English 101 class he had to teach once a year. It seemed impossible that just a few short weeks ago he'd had his face between this person's legs. He'd have almost found it more plausible he'd gone down on a space alien.

"Well, I guess you'd better go enjoy your game then."

She stood up. "It was good to see you though."

"Was it?"

"Don't be that way."

"What way is that?"

"Sour."

"My fucking daughter was killed, Susan!"

She jerked back, as if slapped.

"I'm sorry," he said. "I didn't mean to yell."

"It's okay. Really. I'm… gonna go now."

"Fine."

He watched her head up the stairs, this stranger, this child. The things he'd once found so attractive about her now repulsed him. Her youth didn't make her beautiful, it made her naïve, annoying, ignorant.

She stopped halfway up the staircase. She turned around, and when she did so, so too did his thoughts about her. Just like that he wanted her again. She'd changed her mind, he thought. She wanted to come to Sewall's Beach with him after all.

"James? Look, I'm sorry. Really and truly. I can't even imagine what this has been like for you. But this isn't what I signed on for, all this… life. I just, you know, thought it would be hot to fuck my English professor."

There it was. That surprise hammer Susan always tended to drop at some point in any conversation.

"Goodbye, Susan."

"Goodbye, James. And I really am sorry." Up the stairs and out of his life she went.

But at least he'd gotten his condolence.

He'd never been much of a drinker. He could nurse a single beer over an entire ballgame at Fenway. He'd order a nice glass of red with a steak dinner and drink half of it. He'd only been drunk once in his life, drinking screwdrivers in Tommy Dinapoli's basement back in the old neighborhood in Sommerville. They were thirteen, and had jacked the vodka from Tommy's mother, who drank so much of it on a day to day basis she'd never know any was missing. James—Jimbo back then—had thrown up so hard and for so long that even to this day the smell of vodka nauseated him.

But tonight he was going to drink. Drown your sorrows. That's what they say, right? And if anybody had sorrows to drown it was James Riordan.

They didn't keep much alcohol in the house. It wasn't uncommon for Linda to tie one on here and there, but she didn't drink at home. He'd received a bottle of nice whiskey from a well-intentioned colleague in a Christmas exchange a couple years ago. Not exactly being a man who spent a lot of time in the kitchen, it took him a while to find it, but he ultimately did, in the small cabinet above the refrigerator, untouched, red and green ribbon still tied around the neck.

He poured himself a shot and slammed it down. It was like swallowing flaming shards of glass. Jesus, people actually enjoyed this? People did this for fun? But he wasn't here to have fun; he was drinking with purpose. He poured himself another glass, this one he intended to sip, one flaming shard at a time.

He stepped into the living room. It was still filthy, even more so than when his sister had chastised him about it on... um... when was that? Oh, right, Election Day. That's a Tuesday. Was it this past Tuesday or the Tuesday before? Oh, what difference did it make? The living room had been a pigsty then and it was a pigsty now.

Pigsty. That's what Linda always used to say to Kelly when her bedroom was a mess. "Clean up your room, it's a pigsty in there."

James took a sip of whiskey. The effects of the shot he'd taken were already hitting him. The sharp claws that had been kneading his soul were a degree duller.

He really should pick up a bit. Empty the ashtrays. Throw out the trash. Toss the laundry in the hamper and the dishes in the sink—though who would eventually do the laundry and the dishes was unclear, since he'd never done either in his life and wouldn't even know how to begin. But one thing at a time. He took another sip of whiskey.

Maybe he should put some music on while he cleaned—or, more accurately, tidied. He went to the Victrola, one of his first purchases after getting those professor paychecks. Nineteen-sixty-five. He saw Bill Russel's Celtics beat the Lakers for the championship in the Garden. Malcolm X was murdered. U.S. troops were starting to be sent to Vietnam.

He opened the cabinet where they kept the records. At the top of the stack was Blondie's *Parallel Lines*. He'd bought it because it was Susan's favorite album and he was curious what type of music a mind like Susan's was drawn to. He gave it a listen and convinced himself he dug it, but he never gave it a second listen. He just wanted to be able to tell Susan he'd bought it and liked it, because he was cool, he was hip with what the younger generation was into.

Next on the pile was Bob Dylan's *Blonde on Blonde*. This record had a similar backstory. Nineteen-sixty-seven, the autumn after the Summer of Love. He was sleeping with one of his grad students—a few actually, but this one in particular was special. When James was a student at Amherst he'd been into Dylan, in the folk days, the <u>*Freewheelin'*</u> era, but he'd abandoned him when Bob had gone electric. But this grad student—a gal named Linda Shaughnessy who he'd accidentally impregnate a few months later and end up marrying—convinced him to give the electric stuff another shot.

Next was Buddy Holly and the Three Tunes' *That'll be the Day*, the very same copy he'd received as a gift from Connie on his seventeenth birthday, though she'd chosen it as much for herself as for him, since she played it as often if not more than he did.

This was the choice. A record that wasn't suggested to him by a woman he was sleeping with. Music from a time when the only notch on his bedpost was Leslie Pettigrew.

He removed the disk from the sleeve and made to put in on the turntable, but he needed to remove the record that was already there. It featured the MCA Records artwork of the blue sky with a rainbow coming out of the clouds. The title: "*Xanadu*: featuring Olivia Newton John."

James jerked his hand away as if he'd just accidentally grabbed a stove burner on high. This record had been playing non-stop in the house for a month before Kelly passed. James hated it. Back then, he'd have been happy to throw the damn thing in the incinerator. But now, simply removing it from the turntable seemed like an act of blasphemy. Kelly had put it there. To disturb anything from the way Kelly had left it, these shadows she left behind, would be akin to erasing her. Everything needed to be preserved. *Xanadu* on the turntable. Her room, pigsty though it was, untouched from when she and her friend Michelle had last exited it to go roller skating around Jamaica Pond. It's the same reason he'd been obsessing about Sewell's Beach, it's what he'd been thinking about at the moment she was killed. It needed to be preserved.

He sat down in his soft chair. There would be no music. There would be no cleaning.

He took another sip of whiskey. His eye fell on the bottle of methaqualone Connie had given him, still sitting on the coffee table where she'd left it. Eh, why the hell not? The whiskey wasn't doing its job. Couldn't hurt to drop a… what had Connie called them? Disco biscuits? How bad can something with a cute name like *disco biscuit* actually be? If nothing else, maybe it would put him to sleep and keep him there for a while. He hadn't had a consecutive hour of uninterrupted sleep since the night before Kelly's twelfth and final birthday.

He popped a pill in his mouth and washed it down with whiskey. Impatient, not feeling any effects after five minutes, he popped another one in his mouth.

More whiskey. Another pill. More whiskey. Another pill.

The sharp edges became so dull it was like being buried in a pile of magical pillows. The world became increasingly out of focus until it was just a hazy blob of colors that slowly faded out until James found himself floating in a vacuum of white nothingness.

The white place was pure neutrality. But when one is deeply depressed, neutrality feels like bliss.

He was pretty sure he was dead.

No complaints. Death was a welcome state. It was his first moment of peace since the tragedy.

He woke up in bed with no idea how he got there. He hadn't slept in his bed since the night before Kelly's funeral, Linda's last night at the house. The mattress felt foreign. As he became more aware he realized it wasn't the hiatus from it that made the bed feel unfamiliar, it was the fact that it actually wasn't his at all. It was smaller than his bed at home, the mattress cheaper, noisier. And what was beeping? And what was stuck to the back of his hand?

"Jimmy? Jimmy, you awake? Jesus, don't move. Don't do anything. Nurse! Nurse he's waking up."

"Connie?"

"Don't talk, Jim. Don't do anything. Nurse!"

His body ached. His mouth was cotton dry. The light in the room was blinding; he couldn't open his eyes past a squint. What had happened? Last he remembered he was talking to Susan in the foyer of Gebby, her suite building. "Am I in a hospital?"

"For God's sake, Jimmy, stop talking and moving and doing stuff. Nurse!"

"Yes, I'm here," said a female voice James didn't recognize, presumably the nurse.

"He woke up," said Connie.

The next several minutes were a series of nurses and doctors with stethoscopes, tongue depressors, bright lights in the eyes, reflex hammers, blood pressure machines. *What's your name?* James Isaac Riordan. *What's two plus two?* Four. *What state are you in?* Massachusetts. *Who's the president of the United States?* Jimmy Carter. No, wait. Ronald Reagan.

You're lucky Connie found you when she did. Another few minutes and you probably wouldn't have made it. Your heart stopped in the ambulance on the way to the hospital, but the EMTs were able to bring you back. The good news is there are no major red flags indicating you've suffered any permanent physical or cognitive impairment, but it's too early to declare a definitive clean bill of health just yet. We're gonna keep you another night for tests and observation.

It all sounded like a foreign language to James. He was still trying to piece together his memories. Susan on the stairs—*I just thought it would be hot to fuck my English professor.* Whiskey—flaming gasoline—singeing his throat. The tussle-haired Bob Dylan on the cover of *Blonde on Blonde.* The peaceful tranquility of white nothingness.

"What the hell did you do, you dumb asshole?" asked Connie, when they were finally left alone.

"I don't know."

"I came over this morning to check on you and found you on the bathroom floor, covered in your own puke."

"Really?"

"These were next to you." She held up the bottle of methaqualone.

Right, he'd taken a 'lude. Maybe more than one.

"How the hell many of these did you take?"

"I don't know."

"What the fuck were you thinking, you dumb shit?"

"You're the one who gave them to me."

"Yeah, but I told you to be careful."

"I guess I wasn't."

"Jesus, Jim. This bottle has my fucking name on it. Good thing I had the presence of mind to grab it before the ambulance showed up. If you woulda died they coulda gotten me for involuntary manslaughter or something."

"It's nice to know where your priorities lie."

"Oh, fuck off, Jim. I called the ambulance first thing. I stashed the pills in my pocketbook while they were on the way. No sense you overdosing *and* me going to jail. Then aunt Birdie would have nobody left to send two-dollar bills to at Christmas."

James laughed. "You got a cigarette?"

Connie pulled a pack of Parliaments out of her pocketbook. She put one in her mouth, then took out another and made to put that one in her mouth as well, just like Susan used to do.

"Don't do that," said James.

"You afraid of my germs? I'm your sister. We got the same germs."

"That's not how germs work, and no, that's not it. I just want to light my own."

She handed him a cigarette. "Weirdo."

"Did I really die in the ambulance?"

"That's what the doctor said."

"I think I remember it. Dying. I was conscious."

"Dying is the opposite of being conscious."

"Maybe that's not the right word. I was *aware*. Everything was white. A white place. And I knew. I knew I was dead."

"Mm-hm. And a bright light shone down, beckoning you to it. A choir of glowing angels sang, playing golden harps. A man in flowing robes and a long white beard—"

"Fuck you, Con."

"Okay, fine, you had an experience. So what? Maybe you dreamt it. Maybe you hallucinated it. Maybe you really went up to heaven and God took one look at your ugly face and sent you back. What of it? You're here now. On Earth. Alive. And you need to do something with that, Jimmy. I'm not trying to downplay what happened. It's unspeakably awful. But you locked up in that house, marinating in your own filth, overdosing on 'ludes—"

"You gave me the goddam pills!"

"I told you take half of one, not half the bottle. And that ain't the point. This isn't who we are, Jim. This isn't how we were raised. Riordan's are tough. We don't let things beat us."

"My. Daughter. Was. Killed!"

"I know! But you weren't. You're here. Nobody's telling you not to grieve, Jimmy. You're gonna be grieving for the rest of your life. But the operative phrase here is *your life*. You've still got to live it, even in the face of tragedy. But you're going the other way. You're leaning away from life."

"Boiled to death with melancholy."

"Um, okay, sure."

"It's from Shakespeare. *Twelfth Night*. Fabian says it to Toby."

"Great, not only do you try to kill yourself, now you're trying to bore me to death." She took a drag of her cigarette. "I think you should get out of here."

"They said I need to spend the night."

"Not the hospital, dummy. Jamaica Plain. Boston. You need a reset. Remember that time you broke your wrist playing street hockey?"

"Yeah."

"What did you do?"

"Went to the emergency room."

"Okay, sure. But were you out there playing street hockey again the next day? No. Cause if you were, your wrist woulda never healed. You needed to take a break, let the bone reset. Few months later you were back to playing street hockey. Good as new. Being here, it's too painful for you right now. Too many memories. Too much to remind you of everything you lost. You gotta get away if you wanna heal. Staying here is like continuing to play street hockey with a broken wrist... There. How'd you like that metaphor, Mr. English Professor? Not bad for a career bartender, huh?"

"Technically that was a simile, since you said 'like.'"

She held the pill bottle out to him. "Here, asshole. Take the rest. Finish the job."

James laughed. He dropped his spent cigarette into a little plastic cup of water on the side table. "I take your point. About getting away, not about overdosing on quaaludes again."

"Good. When does your sabbatical end?"

"I'll be back for spring semester. End of January."

"Perfect. Get a little cabin in the White Mountains or something. Write that stupid novel you're always threatening to write."

"I'll think about it."

"Good. It doesn't have to be the White Mountains either. That's just a suggestion. Doesn't matter where, just someplace you won't be reminded of what happened everywhere you look. You got a place in mind?"

"I do. Sewall's Beach."

Exasperated, Connie hung her head, resting her forehead in the fingertips of her right hand. "Jesus Christ, Jim. That's the opposite of what I'm suggesting."

But he'd made up his mind.

James awoke to commotion outside his room. A jumble of urgent voices. *Hand me this piece of medical equipment. Inject this many CCs of this medicine. His heart rate is at this dangerous level. His blood pressure is dropping through the floor.*

James got up and went to the door. In the room across the hall, he could see several doctors and nurses huddled around a hospital bed, tending to a seizing, convulsing man.

"We need to get him to the O.R.," said one of the doctors. "Oona, go find a cart."

A nurse, presumably Oona, hustled out of the room, the front of her uniform covered in blood, and rushed down the hall.

"He's crashing," said another doctor.

James closed the door to his room and returned to the bed. Hospitals were upsetting places, to say the very least. These doctors, nurses, and orderlies saw horrifying things on the daily. The most horrifying part of James's job was reading yet another bad essay from nineteen-year-old budding feminist about the mistreatment of Ophelia.

Whatever his hospital room door was made of sure did the trick; he could no longer hear anything coming from across the hall, not even muffled voices.

That poor man in the other room, that had been James several hours ago. Paramedics huddled around him, trying to save his life. And succeeding.

But was he happy about that?

He thought of the interval between his final lucid memories of being at home and waking up in the hospital. The white place. White bliss, he remembered thinking. How long had he been there? It seemed like both a blink and a lifetime, as if time didn't exist there. Had that been some form of afterlife, or just a quaalude hallucination? Either way, he wasn't sure he was happy to be back. The white place was pure contentment. Earth was hell.

His door opened. "Mr. Riordan?" In his dark room with the lit hallway behind her he could only see the nurse's silhouette.

"Yeah?"

"We need these doors to stay open. Hospital policy."

"Oh. Sorry. It's just, all the commotion out there."

"What commotion?"

"In the room across the hall. The man. He was… I don't know what was happening to him. But there were doctors and nurses and…" It was now dead quiet across the hall.

"Mrs. Hanrahan is across the hall, Mr. Riordan. And I assure you she's been sleeping like a cat since eight o'clock. You can see for yourself."

What? No. The nurse was mistaken. He'd seen it. Her shift must have just started.

Still, he got up and went to the door. The room across the hall where the convulsing man had been was dark and quiet. "There were half a dozen people in there not even a minute ago. A nurse ran out to get a cart. She had blood on her uniform. A black woman. Oona, her name was. Ask her. Ask Oona"

"Mr. Riordan, I haven't left this hall for the last two hours. Nothing happened in that room except Mrs. Hanrahan's snoring."

"But... I saw it."

"You had a dream, Mr. Riordan."

Had he? Was it just a dream? He'd certainly had vivid dreams before, but never so much so that, after waking, he continued to confuse them for reality. That was movie stuff. Nobody dreamt that way in real life. Plus, he'd closed the door. He hadn't dreamt that part, since the nurse had to reopen it. So had he also been sleepwalking?

Then again, he had just died of a drug overdose, it wasn't out of the question that could mess with your synapses. He'd spent over an hour with a neurologist earlier testing for cognitive damage. He'd been cleared, but it was possible they missed something.

"Yeah. Okay. I guess I was dreaming."

"Try to get back to sleep, Mr. Riordan."

The nurse left him and he climbed back into bed. The more he thought back on it, the less real it seemed. It still didn't feel like a dream, but there was a layer of artifice over it, a slight remove, like the difference between watching a ballgame at Fenway and watching that same ballgame on television.

Maybe Connie was right. Maybe he needed to get away for a while.

"Mr. Riordan?" the nurse's head poked back in the doorway.

"Yeah?"

"You said a black woman named Oona?"

"Yes. Does she work here?"

"Yes. Well, no. I mean, we did have a black nurse named Oona, but she quit. Over ten years ago…"

"Can I get you anything else, hon?" asked the waitress, Helen according to her nametag.

James looked down at his sunny-side-ups, home fries, sausage links, and white toast. "Can't think of anything." He stubbed out his cigarette in the tin ashtray.

"Okay, sweetie. Enjoy. I'll be back to check on your coffee in a few."

He'd eaten at the Seabreeze Diner countless times as a child with his family. He and Connie always ordered the pancakes—johnny cakes, as they were called here. The décor hadn't changed: light-blue and pink motif, black dresses with frilly white aprons on the waitresses, weathered buoys attached to fishing nets that stretched along the walls. They even had the same old jukebox, though the 45s of Rosemary Clooney, Eddie Fisher, and Leroy Anderson had been replaced by Donna Summer, Billy Joel, and Peaches & Herb. "This is It" by Kenny Loggins was the current selection.

Back in the '50s the place had always been packed, the Riordans often having to wait twenty or thirty minutes for a table, but this morning James had been able to walk right in and sit down at the empty counter, though that had more to do with the change in season than the change in era. Come Memorial Day the booths would once again be stuffed with hungry tourists, filling their sunburned bellies with greasy sustenance in preparation for a long day at the beach.

It wasn't just the Seabreeze that was quieter than what James had been accustomed to on his childhood visits to Sewall's Beach, the whole town seemed to be hibernating. In his mind, Sewall's Beach was an ever-bustling bizarre of families and commerce— he'd never stopped to consider what the town would look and feel like in the off-season. But it made sense. When ninety-five percent of your summer population flees after Labor Day, of course you'll be left with a ghost town in the colder months.

He dipped the corner of his toast into his egg yolk and took a bite. He'd done little more than nibble at things for the past several weeks, but he had a mild bit of enthusiasm for this breakfast. He'd only just pulled into town, the Seabreeze being his very first stop after the two-and-a-half-hour drive from Boston, but he already felt different. Connie had been right: getting away was medicinal. Kelly was still dead, Linda was still at her mother's for the foreseeable future, and Susan, well… All the associated feelings and emotions were still present, but they'd inched just a tiny bit into the shadows. He enjoyed the snap of biting into his slightly overcooked sausage link. He appreciated the ocean view out the window, the faint trace of salt air barely identifiable under the heavy scents of grilled breakfast foods wafting from the kitchen.

He opened that week's copy of *The Sewall County Coast Star* he'd picked up at the general store next to the Seabreeze Diner and flipped to the classifieds. There wasn't much by way of rentals. A couple ads for roommates. A three-bedroom house. A few industrious landlords already advertising vacation properties for the following summer. Nothing meeting his purposes, which wasn't surprising; it wasn't as if he was likely to find a rental seeking a tenant only looking to stay a few weeks.

"How's the grub?" asked Helen, refilling his coffee from a clear, bulbous pot.

"Terrific."

"We could always use a hand in the kitchen this time of year if you're looking for a job."

"Hm?"

She gestured at the classifieds. On the jukebox, the mechanical arm removed the Kenny Loggins 45 and replaced it with Cristopher Cross's "Sailing."

"Oh. No. I'm looking for a place, actually. Temporary. Just for a few weeks."

"Ah. Seems a bit backwards. Most people are looking to get out of S.B. for a few weeks this time of year."

"I want a quiet place to write a novel." Telling a stranger he was here to heal from a tragedy seemed a bit forward. Besides, he did intend to write a novel. His luggage consisted of a suitcase of clothes, a bag of toiletries, and a typewriter.

"Ah. A writer. Like that King guy from up Bangor. Wrote *Carrie.*"

"My book isn't quite like the stuff he writes."

"What's it about?" She leaned forward, putting an elbow on the counter, resting her chin on the back of her hand.

"Well, it's about the broken promise of the sixties. The hope and idealism. The dawning of the Age of Aquarius. You know? How Manson and Altamont tore away the curtain of the hippie dream. Then the disillusionment of the seventies. Vietnam. Watergate. Disco. And now here we find ourselves, 1980. The Summer of Love a long-ago child's fantasy, on the verge of Ronald Reagan's America."

"Ooh, I love Reagan."

"Hm." She'd completely missed the point.

"So, it's, like, a history book?"

"No. It's a novel."

"Then what's it about?"

"Well, everything I just said."

"But, I mean, what happens in it? Who are the characters? What do they do?"

"It's complicated. You'll just have to wait for the book to come out." The truth of the matter is he had no idea what happened in it, who the characters were, or what they did. All he knew was he'd been watching the American dream swirl down the toilet for the entirety of his adult life. The characters, the plot—those things were secondary, it was the sweeping statement that was important here.

"I look forward to reading it." She smiled politely, but he hadn't exactly sold her on it. She wasn't his audience anyway. Fans of that King drivel were never going to embrace his brand of literature.

"You could try Lobster Lodge," said Helen, rewinding back to the origins of this conversation. "Most of the hotels around here shut up after Columbus Day, but Lobster Lodge stays open. They rent rooms by the week this time of year for pretty cheap. Gladys—she works here nights—has been staying over there. It's just down that way, other end of the beach."

"Oh, thanks. I'll definitely look into that."

"Glad to help. You can repay me by dropping off a copy of the book when you finish it."

"Deal."

She stood back upright and went toward the kitchen, turning back and flashing him a smile before she disappeared behind the swinging doors. She was flirting with him for tip. It was quaintly charming. Her most effective flirting days likely tailed off in the Eisenhower era, but he appreciated her commitment to the game.

He felt good. At least, as good as one can hope under his specific circumstances. He'd been talking about this novel for years, but the idea always felt like it was still too green on the vine. But now, with the election of Ronald Reagan, he felt like it was finally ripe—like he could finally start writing.

He smiled, puffing a short breath of laughter from his nose. Twenty-four hours ago the thought of simply writing a check exhausted him—now he was excited to write a novel! The bad feelings were inching further into the shadows.

Christopher Cross ended. There was a five-second pause while the machine switched disks, then the next song started up. James threw down a ten-dollar bill and left the diner without finishing his breakfast or waiting for his change.

The song was Olivia Newton John's "Magic."

He momentarily considered just heading back to Boston, but what good would that have done? Things were going to remind him of Kelly. *Xanadu* was a phenomenon and "Magic" was playing everywhere. He was bound to hear it from time to time. Running back to Boston, where *everything* was going to remind him of Kelly, was counterintuitive. This was something he needed to get used to. Maybe even embrace. It seemed impossible, but there just might come a time where hearing "Magic" would put a smile on his face, conjuring fond memories of his daughter dancing around the living room to the record album, singing along into a hairbrush.

But for now, as long as he was in Sewall's Beach, he'd keep his dial tuned to Cool 89.9, a local radio station specializing in exclusively fifties fare: early Elvis, the Flamingoes, the Marcels, Chuck Berry—not the kind of music likely to sneak any painful memories up on him. He quite liked the DJ, finding her calming, not like those bombastic DJs on WBCN or WXCS back home. Her voice was smooth and steady, a shade or two above a whisper, honey-tinged, like a light steam wafting off a mug of tea.

"You're listening to Cool Eighty-Nine Point Nine, mixing sound waves with ocean waves, sending classic tunes across the sandy dunes and into your ears. I'm Betty on the Beach. We've got some Buddy Holly coming up, but first, here's an old favorite from the Platters that I know all you beach babies remember well." And in faded the string intro of "The Great Pretender."

Through the windshield, the sign for the Lobster Lodge came into view. When Helen had recommended it the name was unfamiliar to him, but as soon as he saw the massive sign out front—a painting of a lobster, its claws open and arranged such that they created the L's in both Lobster and Lodge—it all came flooding back to him.

In fact, a lot of things came flooding back to him driving along the beach. Many things had modernized, and the heavy foot and automobile traffic prevalent along the strip during his childhood visits had migrated south for the winter, but it was still recognizable as the Sewall's Beach of his youth. The information kiosk designed to look like a lighthouse. The giant wooden cut-out of a chocolate/vanilla swirled ice cream cone hanging over the front of Coney Island. The faded Coppertone ad featuring the little dog pulling on the young girl's bathing suit. The outdoor amphitheater that held free concerts where, in 1955, a fourteen-year-old James Riordan had his mind blown by a doo-wop showcase, headlined by a then-unknown Frankie Lymon and the Teenagers.

The cruel jukebox had brought James's pain back out of the shadows, but the nostalgia of the Sewall's Beach strip was gently pushing it back toward the darkness, aided by Betty on the Beach and her selection of Buddy Holly's "Every Day," which dissolved in at the conclusion of "The Great Pretender."

He pulled into the Lobster Lodge and parked. It was a four-story, horseshoe-shaped motel, curled around a swimming pool. He had to walk through the pool area to get to the lobby. There were a few dozen chaise lounges set up around the pool, but the pool had been long since covered for the winter. One lone, elderly woman, bundled in a heavy wool sweater, sat on one of the chaises, smoking a cigarette. She nodded at James as he walked by. He nodded back.

Then he heard the scream. Male, from above. He looked up and saw a flailing body, all skin and swim trunks, rocketing toward the ground. James jumped back just in time to avoid being crushed by the human meteor. Body *splatting*, skull *thunking*, neck *snapping*, bones *cracking*—all in unison, combining to make one horrifying sound, a human body being instantaneously pulverised by the convergence of gravity, velocity, and concrete.

The man, just a boy really, lay on the ground, dead as a stump, limbs bent in impossible angles, skull broken apart like the shell of a fumbled egg on a kitchen floor, blood and brains leaking out like whites and yolks.

Then, like the aftershock of an earthquake, an empty aluminum Budweiser can *tinked* on the ground next to him and rolled toward the edge of the pool.

James began to scream.

The elderly woman shot up from her chaise. "Sir! Sir, are you alright?"

Of course he's not alright! thought James. His brain matter is splattered all over my pants.

"Sir?" she reached him and put a hand on his shoulder. He then realized she'd been talking to him. Why the hell would she be concerned with *his* welfare when there was a shattered boy on the ground?

But there wasn't. The boy who'd fallen was gone—or, more likely, had never been there at all.

"Did- did you see that?"

"See what? I saw you walking, then you just start screaming bloody murder."

James looked at the ground again. No body. No blood. No brains. He looked up, as if maybe he'd see the mangled body floating back up to where it had come from, but of course he saw nothing but motel and gray sky.

"Come sit," said the woman, leading James toward her chaise.

He sat down and felt his pockets for his cigarettes, but he'd left them in the Mercury. He gestured toward her Virginia Slims sitting on the little white table next to the chaise. "May I?"

"Of course," she said, handing him the pack and a book of matches. "Are you feeling okay now?"

"I don't know." He lit the Virginia Slim. He looked ridiculous smoking the long, narrow thing, but vanity wasn't a priority at the moment. "I think I... had some sort of spell."

"I'll say. I thought you stepped on a rusty nail."

It had seemed so real. Well, no. Maybe it hadn't, now that he was thinking about it. It wasn't in his imagination; he definitely saw it, but at the same time, it hadn't exactly seemed real either. Like a hologram. Like a visual representation of a memory projecting itself over the real world. Only this wasn't a memory that belonged to him.

It reminded him of the experience he'd had in the hospital, the medical emergency across the hall that turned out to be a... dream?

The quaaludes. The fucking disco biscuits. It was a delayed hallucination, like an acid flashback. Or maybe it was a result of his overdose—of being legally dead for several seconds. The doctors had thoroughly checked him for cognitive impairment, but it's possible they could have missed something, right? Case in point, he'd just watched a man fall from the sky—saw it happen with his own two eyes, heard the pulverization of bones, felt the brain matter splat against his shins. And yet, there was no body there. It clearly had not happened, despite what his senses had signaled to his brain.

There was obviously a rational explanation. Delayed quaalude hallucination or brain damage. Here's hoping it was the former.

Okay. Deep breaths. That was unpleasant, but nothing to lose your head over. Like Connie said, the Riordan's were tough people who didn't let things get to them. "I'm fine," said James. "Really. Thank you. Just a spell. Nothing to worry about."

"If you're sure."

"I'm sure. Thank you for the cigarette."

"You're welcome."

James stood up, feeling a little dizzy as he did so. He resumed his way toward the lobby to check in, as if nothing had happened, as if he hadn't just hallucinated a man violently dying in front of him.

As he got closer to the spot, a wave of anxiety hit him. He was certain it was going to happen again, that body was going to splatter on the concrete in front of him. Don't succumb to it, Jimmy, he thought to himself. We're tough. We don't let things get to us.

His foot inadvertently kicked something, sending it clattering across the concrete. He looked down to find the empty Budweiser can, the same that had followed the body to the ground, rolling toward the edge of the pool.

He would not be staying at the Lobster Lodge after all. He turned on his heel and got the ever-loving hell out of there.

A salmon pink cottage with green shutters. The yard, as it were, that surrounded it was sand, covered in long tufts of wispy beach grass. A flagstone walkway led to the front door, next to which, nailed to the side of the cottage, was a license-plate-sized piece of driftwood with the words "The Seagull's Nest" etched into it.

While the property itself was pretty much as he remembered it, the context around it had changed. For starters, he was older and a physically larger human being, which made the cottage seem smaller than it had when he was a child. Also, it was close to a quarter century since he'd last been there; the salt air and more than a dozen nor'easters had weathered it some. And, of course, time of year was a factor. He associated the cottage with heat, clear blue skies and a blinding sun, the laughter of children, the smell of grilled hot dogs and sunscreen. Here in mid-

November it was cold, gray, quiet save for the sounds of the ocean and the squawk of an errant seagull who'd missed the memo about migrating south.

He walked around to the beach side of the cottage. It was perched, as all the properties were along this stretch, on a four-foot plateau above the beach, each cottage with its own private, wooden ramp or staircase to access the beach. James remembered as a child he used to forego The Seagull's Nest's staircase, opting to get a running start and leap off the cliff, one closed-fisted arm extended in front of him like Superman, beach towel tied around his neck like a cape. As a child, that had seemed like a remarkable act of derring-do. As an adult, the treacherous "cliff" was little more than a short, seagrass covered hill he could now easily step down with one long stride if he chose.

James stood on the edge of the cliff and watched the ocean. It was hightide, which meant it was time for the Rock'n'Roll Dance Party, a title Connie had come up with in the summer of '54, named after the popular Allen Freed radio show. A strip of sea rocks stretched the length of the beach up near the top, ranging in size from marbles to golf balls. At high tide, the waves would push and drag these smooth, round rocks over one another, creating a satisfying symphony of clunks and clatters. The Rock'n'Roll Dance Party. It was a distinct sound James had never heard anywhere else. It was a sound he may very well have been hearing in his mind at the exact moment his daughter was--

No. He wasn't going to dwell there. Connie was right, it was arbitrary. He could just as easily have been thinking about *Richard III* or fried chicken or dandelions at the time. The fact that he was thinking about Sewall's Beach, hearing the hightide Rock'n'Roll Dance Party—it meant nothing. Because here he was now and so what? Kelly was still buried, her body sown back together to the best of the embalmer's abilities. Nothing had changed.

Stop. Get out of the spiral. Be present.

The present came with its own concerns, specifically the fact that he might have brain damage. Though the further away from the Lobster Lodge he got, the less real his vision felt. It had been some kind of disassociative episode, clearly. A spell. A waking dream. As for the beer can that seemed to have materialized from this vision, it had to have been there all along. It was already lying there on the concrete and he'd manifested it into his vision. Hopefully it was just a one-time thing, a reverberation from having overdosed, from having been literally dead for a few seconds. If it happened again he'd make an appointment with a neurologist, but for now he wasn't going to worry about it.

And then, it did happen again. It wasn't a violent vision this time. Quite the opposite. It was a young girl, standing on the beach, facing the water, hands cupped behind her ears, listening. It was as if she just appeared there. Then again, maybe she wasn't a vision at all. He'd been quite off in his own world, and her beige dress did make her blend in with the sand; it wasn't impossible that maybe he just hadn't noticed her until now.

James took the stairs down to the beach and walked toward the girl. "Hey there," he said, but she didn't hear him over the wind, waves, and clattering rocks. Either that or she didn't respond because she wasn't there at all.

But no. When he raised his voice and called to her again, she turned around and acknowledged him. "Hello," she said. She was indeed real. A curly-haired redhead with freckles, probably eleven or twelve. Kelly's age.

"What are you doing?" asked James.

"Listening. It feels good in your ears. Try it."

James stood next to her and cupped his hands behind his ears like she was doing, as if extending the ears so they may corral more sonic waves. It did bring an immediacy—an intimacy—to the sound, as if the rocks were gently clicking against each other inside the ear canal as opposed to on the sand several yards away.

"Neat," said James. Then, "Aren't you cold?"

The temperature couldn't have been any higher than the mid forties. She wore just a sleeveless dress, no shoes. "No."

"You sure?"

She didn't respond.

"I'm James."

"Elizabeth."

"You live here?"

"Yes."

"I used to stay in this house." He pointed up to the cottage. "Every summer when I was a kid."

She turned and looked at the Seagull's Nest. "That's a bad house."

"Why do you say that?"

"It just is."

Before he could further enquire about this seemingly arbitrary dislike of his former dwelling, a small stream of blood trickled down her forehead from beneath her curly bangs, settling in her eyebrow.

"Ooh, sweetheart, you're bleeding."

Elizabeth swiped a finger through the thin trail of blood, making a smear. She inspected her finger, confirming she indeed was bleeding. Without a word, she broke into a sudden sprint down the beach.

"Hey!" James called after her, though what he would have said or done if she'd stopped he had no idea. But it was a moot point because she did not stop. Within seconds she was just a little beige speck in the distance, indistinguishable from the sand.

She must live down that way, thought James. Running home to get patched up by mom. Must have been a preexisting wound, hidden under her bangs, that had somehow reopened.

"Yoo-hoo!" chirped a woman's voice behind him. He turned to see a middle-aged woman heading down the stairs to the beach.

"Hello," said James.

"Is there anything I can help you with?" She was on the heavy side, her bulges contained by a tight, light-blue and white striped aerobics outfit. She was exuberantly friendly.

"Nothing. Just looking around."

"No problem. No problem. It's just, this is a private section of the beach. And you parked in my driveway. Not that I mind, per se."

"Oh. Apologies. I didn't think anybody would be here. I used to stay in this cottage when I was a kid and… well, I guess I've been feeling a bit nostalgic."

"This cottage? The Seagull's Nest?"

"That's the one."

"Well then, you must have rented from my dad."

"Wait a minute. You're not…? Are you Leslie Pettigrew?"

"Nope. Used to be Leslie Pettigrew. Leslie Kilgore now."

No way. Not possible. Leslie Pettigrew was petite and young. Okay, sure, obviously time changes people, but Leslie had been only one year older than him. This woman had to be in her mid-fifties. But now that the connection had been made he did see the resemblance. Strip away a few decades, several dozen pounds, and if you squint *juuuuuuust* right you could kind of see the shadow of Leslie Pettigrew buried deep below the surface of Leslie Kilgore.

"Although I'd happily give that Kilgore name right back to the son of a you-know-what who gave it to me if it wasn't such a logistical hassle. Divorced." She held up her left hand and wiggled her bare ring finger at him, as if it needing proving.

"I don't suppose you remember me. James Riordan. We stayed here every year from... oh, maybe 1950 or so to 1957."

"Jeez, I'm sorry—" and she genuinely did seem sorry, "—but we've had hundreds of families stay here over the years."

"I had a sister, a year older than me. Connie. You two used to chum around."

"Like I said, we've had hundreds of families stay here."

You once snuck up on me, nuded up, and took my virginity, he didn't say.

Jilted! How could she not remember? That had been a seminal moment in his life. He must have said a combined thousand Our Fathers and Hail Marys in the following couple years, asking God to forgive him for sinning with himself while replaying that moment. And she didn't remember? Did she strip down and screw every boy who stayed at the Seagull's Nest?

"Hm. Well, anyway, I'm sorry to have intruded. I just wanted to see the old place."

"Please, see to your heart's content. I could show you around if you'd like."

"Oh no, that won't be necessary. I just wanted a look and I've looked. Plus, I'm sure you'll be wanting to get back to your exercise."

"Exercise? Me? Not on your life."

"Oh, I just thought..." He looked her up and down, indicating her aerobic attire would suggest he'd interrupted some, you know, *aerobics.*

"What? You assume since I have the body of a Charlie's Angel that I must be a fitness nut? This is God-given, James Riordan." It was unclear if she was being self-deprecating or self-delusional.

They walked up the stairs and through the tall beach grass behind the cottage. "So, where you coming from?"

"Boston?"

"You came all the way up to Maine just to see me and my little cottage? Color me flattered. Joking. Joking."

She was reminding him more and more of the Leslie Pettigrew he once knew. He could have described her breasts, the curve of her hips, and the shape and thread count of her pubic hair in precise detail, but the truth of the matter is he'd remembered very little of her personality. But it was coming back. She may have looked a lot different, but she was still that ten-year-old who marched confidently over to their car when they pulled in that very first year, introduced herself, and asked if they needed any help with their luggage—still that bold seventeen-year-old who'd yanked down his bathing suit, grabbed his erection, and walked him over to the bed like a dog on a leash. Leslie Pettigrew—er, Kilgore—had been and still was pleasant, flattering, and just plain easy to be around.

"No. Though it was certainly part of why I chose it. My—" *daughter passed away* he was about to blurt out. Something about Leslie was so inviting—nonjudgemental. She may have taken his virginity from him (though she'd since forgotten where she put it), but she was still essentially a complete stranger, not a person who needed to know all the intimate details. "I'm on sabbatical. I'm writing a novel."

"Ooh! So exciting. Just like Stephen King. He lives right up there in Bangor, you know."

"So I've heard. It's not really that kind of book. It's about…
well, it's a little more intellectual than a psychic high school girl."

"Telekinetic. Carrie wasn't psychic, she was telekinetic."

"I haven't read it."

"You should. He's wonderful. I'm reading his new one now.
It's about a little girl who starts fires with her mind. It's called
Firestarter."

"Clever title."

"So, where you staying while you write this intellectual
opus?"

"Oh. Well, a waitress at the Seabreeze recommended the
Lobster Lodge. But I—"

"Jeez Lou-*ise*! Who over there recommended that place to
you?"

"I think her name was Helen."

"Ah, that checks. Helen Long. Three kids, three different
fathers, all out-of-towners. Summer people. She's probably got a
soft spot for the place because all her kids were conceived there."

"Yes, well, I stopped by and decided it may not be for me. I
don't suppose you have any recommendations."

"Just so happens I do. The Seagull's Nest."

"You're serious?"

"Why not? I put it up for a winter rental but most years I don't
have any takers, like this one. S.B. doesn't have a lot to offer in the
winter. There's only so many intellectuals on sabbatical looking
for a quiet place to write the great American novel. I absolutely
insist. How's fifty dollars a week sound? Stay as short or as long
as you like, just so long as you're out by Memorial Day, unless
you want to pay six or seven times that rent."

"Leslie, I don't know what to say."

"A bad sign for one who calls himself a writer. Joking. Joking."

70

"That's very kind of you."

"Nonsense. It's a few extra bucks in my pocket. And it'll be nice to have a man around here for a little while."

"Well, I'll be honest, I've always been far more comfortable around a typewriter than a toolbox. I'm afraid I won't be much use if you've got a leaky faucet or a squeaky hinge."

"Oh there are plenty of other uses for a man." She gave him a sultry wink. A moment of awkwardness passed between them, James unsure if she was serious, before she settled his confusion with a big smile and a friendly slap on his bicep. "Joking. Joking. C'mon. Let me show you the inside, see if it'll suit your needs."

The interior of the Seagull's Nest was much like he remembered it, but like everything else in Sewall's Beach—with the notable exception of Leslie Pettigrew—it had seemed much bigger when he was younger. The main room was about six-hundred square feet of cheap, ugly-colored furniture and beach décor, like generic paintings of rocky cliffs, or jars of shells and sea glass.

The kitchen wasn't a separate room, rather a refrigerator, stove, sink, and counter space ran along one side of the main room. The same yellow, formica kitchen table he'd eaten countless bologna sandwiches on as a child was still there, smaller than he remembered of course. The big silver toaster, floral patterned bread box, the copper coffee percolator—they were all still there, each one a nugget of nostalgia shimmering through the waters of his childhood.

"I had a bizarre conversation on the beach with a young girl before you showed up," said James. "Red-headed girl, said her name was Elizabeth."

"Don't know her," said Leslie. "Probably a winter renter."

"Could be. Anyway, she said this was a bad house. Any idea why she might have said that?"

"I can't imagine. This is a wonderful house."

"Hm. Well, she was certainly odd. Just fooling around probably."

The main floor also consisted of three bedrooms: a master with a queen bed, and two others, each with a set of single bunk beds and a third bed, a twin. James only poked his head into the master and the one Connie used to sleep in, but he walked all the way into his old room. He stood looking at that twin mattress, the most formative space—when averaged by square-foot—of his entire life. And here he was, twenty-four years later, in that very spot with the very girl who'd been responsible for that formativity, though oh so much had changed.

He turned. Leslie Kilgore nee Pettigrew stood in the door, in the very spot and pose she had in 1957, only this time she had a bit more on her body, namely sixty extra pounds and an aerobics outfit. But she had the same smile. It was distinct. Specific. *Hey there, little guy, I'm about to fuck the innocence out of you.* If he cropped out just the space under her nose and above her chin she was identical to the girl who'd shocked him with her nudity that day. Was she remembering? Experiencing déjà vu? Was being in the doorway with him in that room triggering her memory?

"Not much has changed, huh?" Was she referring to the cottage itself or this exact scenario?

"It's remarkable."

"Only thing left is the leisure room." She waved him along and left the doorway, unceremoniously breaking the link to the past. She didn't remember; it had just been a meaningless smile in a doorway.

The leisure room was the entirety of the second floor, though smaller in total area. The open space for the staircase, protected by a banister, trimmed down one side of the floor plan, the opposite side had a wall coming down from the slanted roof, creating a triangular crawlspace on the other side of it, accessible by little wooden cabinet doors. The ocean-facing wall, a large pentagon, perpendicular to the stairs and crawlspace, contained an enormous, round window, from the floor to the edges of the peaked ceiling, the muntins between the panes arranged such that they looked like a spider's web—gorgeous at sunrise, creepy in the moonlight.

The majority of the space was taken up by a heavy oak table in the center of the room. Along the walls were sofas and chairs. A thirty-two-inch Zenith console television sat against the wall opposite the round-window wall, old by the day's standards, but new since he'd last been to the cottage. There was a large bookshelf stuffed with paperbacks, magazines, puzzles, boardgames—many of which were the very same from James's childhood days here. He vividly remembered playing Park and Shop or the Pop-Up Store Game with Connie at the big oak table. He remembered that Hop-a-long Cassidy puzzle, already missing several pieces in the mid-fifties. He remembered—

"Oh my God."

"What is it?"

He went to the bookshelf and pulled out a hardcover copy of Ray Bradbury's Fahrenheit 51, library spine label at the base of the spine. "I think this was mine. I accidentally left it behind in 1957. I had to pay twenty-five cents to the Somerville Library for losing it." He opened the book and sure enough, "Yes. Look here." He showed her the inside cover, "Somerville Library" stamped in red ink.

"You're welcome to take it. Maybe the library will refund your quarter. Joking. Joking. So, what do you think? You gonna do your typing at the Seagull's Nest?"

James imagined his typewriter on that big oak table, the clacking of the keys harmonizing with the clattering of the Rock'n'Roll Dance Party on the beach outside that huge, round window. It was a writer's dream. "Definitely."

"Oh good. I'm so glad. I hate to think of you staying at that awful Lobster Lodge. Didn't used to be such a bad place, but ever since the accident it's taken a real turn."

His blood chilled. "Accident?"

"A kid died there. Few years ago. Maybe 1975 or so. College boy. Fourth of July. Having a party with his pals. Drinking. Drugs. Who knows what else? Thought he could jump from his fourth floor balcony and make it to the pool. Well... he didn't make it."

"This is Betty on the Beach, coming to you with more from the shore. Next up, the big voice of Little Richard, begging his girl Lucille to come back where she belongs. Cold, cold-hearted Lucille, can't you see Richie still loves you?"

James killed the engine as the opening shuffle of "Lucille" began. He stepped out of the Mercury and headed toward the Pape Family IGA. If he was going to be staying at the Seagull's Nest for the next few weeks he was going to need groceries. He couldn't very well eat every single meal at the Seabreeze Diner, the only restaurant in town that stayed open past Columbus Day. The problem was: he had no idea how to cook. He was useless in a kitchen. He couldn't even make a proper sandwich, always adding too much lettuce or not enough mustard or an improper ratio of ham to cheese. Linda had prepared all his meals. But there was no Linda. Not right now. Probably not ever again.

Not knowing how to cook, he also didn't know how to shop. His mother had toted him along to Star Market now and again when he was a kid, but he couldn't recall the last time he'd been in a supermarket. He didn't even know enough to grab himself a carriage on the way in. There was a wall of produce, a wall of meat, a wall of dairy, and all manner of dry and processed goods in the center, none of which he knew what to do with. Overwhelming was an understatement. *Hyper*whelming? *Super*whelming? *Mega*whelming?

It didn't help that his mind was elsewhere. The bomb Leslie had dropped on him, the college kid falling to his death from the fourth-floor balcony, had rattled him to say the least. But he was an academic; there had to be a rational explanation. Best he could figure, he'd somehow heard about the death back when it happened. *The Globe*—or, more likely, the *Herald* had run a story about it. It had caught his attention at the time because it happened in Sewall's Beach, a place he was connected to. He'd filed the story away deep in the recesses of his mind where it remained forgotten for several years. Then, earlier, being at the scene of the event, it jogged his memory. That combined with the methaqualone in his system and—boom—he had a vision. Perfectly rational explanation.

Did he believe it? No. Not entirely. But was it plausible enough to settle his anxiety? Just barely.

Groceries. Not nearly the existential crisis of witnessing in the present an accident that occurred in the past, but still something that had to be overcome. James, after fifteen minutes of *mega*whelming shopping paralysis in which he did not select a single item, finally started filling his carriage (once he realized he needed one). Eggs, bread, spaghetti, sauce, numerous cans, boxes, and bags of food stuffs. He had no idea what he was going to do with any of it, but that was a bridge to be crossed later. He was a smart guy. How hard could it be to fry an egg? Boil a potato? Turn on the oven and stick a Hungry Man frozen dinner in it?

He was perusing an endless wall of cereal when out of nowhere a wave of nausea came over him—a different type of nausea than any he'd felt before. It wasn't centralized in his stomach like usual, but rather all throughout his body, like were he to vomit it wouldn't just be the contents of his stomach but everything inside of him: his toe bones, the tendons in his hands, his shoulder muscles, his eyeballs—everything. One big heave and he'd turn himself inside out. And though the feeling was located inside his body, he felt as though the source of it was coming from without, not within. More specifically, behind him.

He turned. A man was staring at him. Well, *facing* him anyway. The man could not have been staring at him because his face was covered by an opaque white veil, flowing down from underneath a black derby hat. He held a mobility cane. The man was blind, if not medically so than certainly blinded by the curtain over his face. And yet he stood stalk still, facing James, penetrating him with eyes that weren't in evidence.

The full-body nausea intensified. James wanted to back away but he couldn't move—couldn't breathe.

A plain-looking, middle-aged woman came to the veiled man's side, holding a cylinder of oatmeal. She noticed the staredown—if one can be stared down by a man with hidden eyes—occurring between James and the man, then looked at James and frowned disapprovingly, as if James had done something wrong, as if it hadn't been the veiled man who'd bewitched him. She took the man's arm to lead him away but he didn't budge. She then took his hand, palm out, and made several shapes, touches, movements with her own hand against his. "Come on, Edgar," she said, though in all likelihood, given the tactile sign language she was performing, Edgar couldn't hear her. She tugged the crook of his arm again. This time he went with her.

As they passed, the force of motion caused the veil to billow toward Edgar's face. It was slight, but it was enough that it should have been stopped by a nose, a brow, a chin, some part of a face. But it didn't. No features stopped its inward flow.

There was no face underneath the veil.

James remained frozen, watching the couple walk down the cereal aisle. The further they got, the more his nausea dissipated. When they were several yards away, Edgar turned his head to "look" back at James, the motion causing the veil to once again sink into the void where the contours of a face should have been.

They rounded the corner out of sight. The spell was lifted. The nausea was entirely gone. James could move again—breath again.

Still, he stood there for another several minutes, trying to process what the hell he'd just seen, and what the hell had just seen him.

"You can't cook pasta like that," said Leslie. "Half of it isn't even in the water. One side is gonna cook and the other side'll still be raw. You either need to break it in half or get a bigger pot. Also, you want to wait for the water to boil before you put the spaghetti in. And for cripe's sake, who's going to eat all this? You expecting the whole U.S. Navy?"

"It doesn't look like that much."

"It expands when it cooks. The entire cast of *M*A*S*H* couldn't finish all this." She was still wearing the same aerobics outfit from earlier, but she'd since thrown on a large, gray Salve Regina sweatshirt over it.

"Oh. I've never actually cooked spaghetti before."

"You don't say."

James grabbed a handful of the raw spaghetti leaning out of the top of the small sauce pan he'd chosen and lifted it out of the water.

"What do you think you're doing?"

"I'm going to put some of it back in the box. You said—"

"You can't put those back in the box. Once they're wet you just have to go ahead and cook them. Move out of the way, let me. You're liable to hurt yourself."

She'd stopped by to drop off some fresh towels and see how he was settling in. And good thing she did because clearly he wasn't settling in well, at least as far as navigating a kitchen was concerned. "Jeez Lou-*ise*, James, the burner is on low. Water's never going to boil with the burner on low. Criminy, if I hadn't come over when I did or you might be standing here till 1981 still waiting for your spaghetti to cook." She held up a jar of Ragu." Is this what you were planning to put on it?" He nodded affirmative. "Anything else? Just plain, jarred Ragu?" He shook his head. She sighed dramatically and said a single word as if it summed up all the inherent problems in the known universe: "Men."

She pulled out the pasta, shaking off as much water as she could, and set it down on the cutting board, fanning it out so it wouldn't stick together. She filled a larger pot with several inches of water and set it on the burner, cranking the heat to high. "I'm going to run next door and get some seasoning for this canned sauce of yours. You're going to keep an eye on this water, wait for it to boil. You know what boiling water looks like?"

"Yes, I know what boiling water looks like."

"It's when the water starts bubbling up. If that happens before I get back you can throw in the spaghetti. But not before it boils, mind. And stir it a couple times with this wooden spoon here, so it doesn't stick to the bottom of the pot. Got it? Need me to repeat any of it?"

"No. I got it." James didn't generally enjoy being patronized, but coming from Leslie he didn't mind. Even the sarcasm felt non-judgmental. And besides, he deserved it. He was useless in the kitchen and had no problem admitting it.

She was gone for five minutes, during which James hovered over the steaming pot, eager to prove to Leslie and himself he was up for the task.

He flipped on the radio, a single-speaker Sony transistor on the counter beside the bread box. Captain and Tenille's "Do That to Me One More Time" was playing. He turned the dial down toward the lower frequencies till he found Gogi Grant's "The Wayward Wind" on Cool 89.9, finessing the nob back and forth a hair each way until he found the sweet spot where he picked up the station with no static.

The water reached a boil and he threw in the pasta, then stirred it with the wooden spoon so it wouldn't stick. He liked having a job to do, menial though it was. It took his mind off things like dead daughters, fleeing wives, falling for college students, being stared at by faceless men...

Leslie returned with her arms full of food items—having procured much more than just the seasoning she'd said she was going for. She set the items on the counter, took the spoon from James, and stirred the pasta. "Look at you! Managed to get the pasta going *and* turn the radio on, you little multi-tasker."

"It was touch and go for a moment there, but I somehow managed to keep the roof from caving in."

"There's hope for you yet." She cut the ends of a white onion and began to peel it in the sink under a stream of cold water. On the radio, Betty of the Beach changed the record to Ricky Nelson's "Poor Little Fool." "Betty on the Beach, huh?" said Leslie.

"I find her soothing. And the music feels fitting to the location. This is the stuff that was popular when I used to come here as a kid. I even remember listening to a lot of this stuff with you. You had a portable, used to bring it down to the beach."

"I remember that radio. A little red thing, wasn't it?"

"That's the one. I distinctly remember hearing Tennessee Ernie Ford sing 'The Ballad of Davey Crocket' for the first time on that thing. Begged my father to buy me the 45 for weeks after. My mother finally made him get it for me just to shut me up."

"You have a terrific memory, James. I don't think I'd have thought of that radio ever again if you hadn't just brought it up. And I certainly would have never thought of Tennessee Ernie Ford. You guys are neighbors, you know."

"I'm neighbors with Tennessee Ernie Ford?"

"No. Sorry. I should have provided a segue between one thought and the next. You're neighbors with Betty on the Beach. Well, technically *I'm* neighbors with Betty on the Beach, but so are you now, long as you stay here. C'mere, I'll show you."

She led him out the sliding back door that opened to a small patio on the beach side of the cottage. The night air was frigid and thick with the scent of salt and seaweed. Low-tide waves lapped the beach in the distance, the ocean invisible save for hundreds of glints of moonlight reflecting off it. "See the red light up there?" Leslie pointed to a tiny red light floating in the sky a mile or so down the beach. "That's the radio tower, up on top of the bluff. She lives in a little cabin at the base of the cliff. That's where she broadcasts from."

"You don't say." There was something magical about the idea of this mysterious woman down the other end of the beach, sitting in her cabin, completely invisible but for the little red light high above her, spinning records that were presently coming out of the little speaker on the radio in the kitchen and into his ears.

"Yup. Set up shop over there, oh, about ten years ago, I guess. Got her own little private beach down there, enclosed by rocky cliffs. You can only get to it by this long staircase from the top of the bluff. Or by boat, I suppose, if you were so inclined. On a clear day you can just see it from here, depending how good your eyesight is. She just sits in there all day and plays those old records. It's just her. That's the whole station. Betty on the Beach. No other DJs, no advertisements, nothing. Day and night, Betty on the Beach."

"Fascinating." Something was stirring in him. He could use this in his novel. A radio DJ, cooped up in isolation, playing nothing but oldies, clinging to the days before JFK and MLK were assassinated—before Vietnam, Watergate, gas shortages. No longer willing to participate and engage with the present and whatever horrors Reagan was about to rain down…

"Not really my kind of music," said Leslie. "I don't mind it. I grew up to it, just like you, but ever since I saw *Coal Miner's Daughter* last spring I can't listen to anything other than Loretta Lynn or Patsy Cline. Did you see that movie. It had that Sissy Spacek in it, same girl who played Carrie from the Stephen King book. Ooh! I need to stir the pasta."

Leslie managed to turn a box of Prince spaghetti and a jar of Ragu into quite a tasty meal, doctoring the plain, thin, generic sauce with ground beef, garlic, onion, basil, oregano, and parmesan, and tossing the spaghetti in olive oil, salt, and pepper before ladling the sauce over it. Betty on the Beach supplied the soundtrack to dinner and their youth. Conversation flowed, mostly from the lips of Leslie, who had a tendency to overshare.

Her family was from Providence, the Sewall's Beach house having been a summer home. She'd gone to Salve Regina University out of high school, and subsequently married a young man she'd met there, Kent Kilgore, the only son of a prominent family who sold medical equipment to hospitals. After ten years of mostly unhappiness that yielded no children ("Not for a lack of his trying every gosh darn chance he got!") they divorced. He immediately got remarried to a secretary at the company who gave him a son just eight months after he'd asked Leslie for a divorce ("I was never great with numbers but you don't have to go to MIT to see that that's some fuzzy math!"). She moved into the summer house in Sewall's Beach full time and spent the last eight years mostly reading paperbacks and watching TV ("The season premiere of *Dallas* is next week! Who do you think shot J.R.?... What? Of course you have a theory—*everybody* has a theory!).

"But listen to me, going on and on and on," she finally said, after getting through the story of her life from the cradle up to eating a spaghetti dinner at this very moment. "How about you? I see the wedding ring."

He and Linda weren't divorced, nor had she asked for one yet. She'd just packed up, moved in with her parents, and refused to take his calls. He wasn't sure what ring protocol was in that situation. The truth of the matter is he hadn't thought much about it. The ring was just part of his body at this point, like a fingernail. The fact that he was still wearing it symbolized nothing.

"Yeah. Just like you. Met her in college."

"Aw. Sweet." She may not have thought it was quite as sweet if James shared the fact that when they me in college he was a professor and she was one of his grad students. "Kids?"

"One. Daughter. Kelley. She's twelve."

"Aw. That's such a fun age."

He wouldn't know. He'd spent fewer than ten minutes with her as a twelve-year-old, just long enough to give her a pair of roller skates for her birthday on his way out the door in the morning.

Richie Valens's "Donna" faded out, Santo and Johnny's "Sleepwalk" faded in.

"And where are they while you're up here?"

Dead and estranged, respectively. "Boston. One needs solitude to write a book."

"And they don't mind that dad runs off to the beach for a few weeks while they're stuck in the big city?"

"No." Nothing he'd said so far was a lie, unless one considers misleading by omission to be a form of lying. His daughter being killed, his wife leaving him, and the fact that a few days ago he'd literally died of a quaalude overdose—one would say those were significant details of his backstory. But he didn't want to open that part of his life with Leslie. Not yet. If one were to grade on a curve, considering the darkness he'd been in for the last several weeks, one could almost say he was enjoying himself this evening. Being in the Seagull's Nest with Leslie, listening to the music of his youth—it took him back to a time before the tragedy. He didn't want to tarnish that feeling by introducing the horrors of the present into it.

"Well, they sound very supportive."

Time for a subject change. The first thing that came to his mind was: "I saw something strange in the grocery store today."

"Judging from your food incompetence, I'd expect everything in a grocery store would look strange to you. Joking, joking."

"No, you're not wrong. But this was a person. A man. He had a white sheet over his face. He was—"

"Edgar Monahan."

"Yes! The woman with him did call him Edgar."

"That's his sister, Ingrid. She takes care of him."

"You know them?"

"Not really. Nobody around here *knows* them, but we all know *of* them. They keep to themselves. Edgar can't talk, and Ingrid... well, she's not exactly friendly. Hard to fault her for her crankiness though, having to give up everything to take care of her brother. I don't even think she's thirty-years-old yet, but she looks like she's in her fifties. Poor thing."

James had been so focused on Edgar he hadn't clocked the woman's age, but now that he was thinking back on it, she definitely looked a lot older than thirty. "What's their story?"

"Locals. I didn't know either of them very well. They're a good chunk younger than me. But this is a tiny town—from September to May anyway—so you pretty much know everybody to some degree. Eddie got sent off to Vietnam in... oh, jeez, 1969 maybe? Came back six-months later wearing that veil. A grenade exploded next to his head, blew his face clean off."

"Jesus."

"I know. Terrible. Terrible. You'll likely be seeing more of them. Ingrid takes him for walks on the beach lots of afternoons."

James felt a chill, envisioning the ocean breeze blowing Edgar's veil deep inside the concave space where his face used to be.

Betty on the Beach let them know it was going to dip below thirty overnight, so make sure to throw an extra blanket on the bed. "And while you're all bundled up on this cold night," she said, "Let's hope there aren't any tears on your pillow." Little Anthony and the Imperials' "Tears on My Pillow" then faded in.

Leslie cleaned up the kitchen. He tried to help, but he was just getting in the way and creating more of his mess, so she thanked him for the effort and told him to go sit back down. They said goodnight around 9:50, because Leslie wanted to get home to watch *Hart to Hart*. She invited James to join her but he declined.

He flipped off the radio, silencing "Little Star" by the Elegants, turned off the light in the main room and went to the master bedroom, where his parents had slept in the old days. Out the window, he could see the distant red light of the Cool 89.9 tower, a few hundred feet beneath which sat Betty on the Beach, choosing the next golden oldie to spin. He closed the curtain and undressed for bed.

Other than the hospital, it was the first time he'd slept in an actual bed since Linda left. He was drifting within seconds of his head hitting the pillow, the muted, rhythmic crashing of distant waves his lullaby.

Something woke him.

The room was pitch black, save for the dark-blue rectangle of the bedroom window, its closed curtain dimly glowing with outside starlight. James didn't know where he was at first, but his bearings soon came to him. Sewall's Beach. The Seagull's Nest.

What was it that had woken him? A sound. The clank of something hitting the floor above him. It wasn't remarkably loud, perhaps the equivalent of someone dropping a golf ball, but in the dead of night, and with it occurring right over his head, it was enough to jar him out of his already tenuous sleep.

Of course, it was entirely possible there'd been no actual sound in the external world. That happened to him from time to time when falling asleep. He'd be drifting off, in the liminal space between dream and sleep, when some bang or shout from the sleep side of his consciousness would startle him fully awake. Though that tended to be a falling asleep phenomenon; he couldn't recall ever having been woken from a dead sleep by such an occurrence.

James listened. Was he now hearing the soft beats and creaks of footsteps about him? His house in Jamaica Plain was a hundred-year-old triple decker. The plumbing, the vents, the wood, the old nails that held it all together—that house was always creaking and groaning, especially in the colder months. Had he been there he'd have thought nothing of it, rolled over, and gone back to sleep. But the Seagull's Nest was more modern with fewer stories to tell. A bump in the night in Jamaica Plain could have been caused by any number of things—a slight change in temperature contracting the metal of a heating duct two floors up perhaps. A bump in the night in Sewall's Beach, in this small, intimate cottage, could not be explained away as easily.

James got out of bed and went into the living area, flipping on the light as he did so. All was as he'd left it. Still. Quiet. But wait... *was* it quiet? The outside sounds were louder in this room, with several windows and a sliding glass door facing the ocean, but over the whistling wind and the whooshing waves he could just make out what sounded like voices coming from above.

He strained his ears, concentrating, trying to isolate the voices from the beach sounds. If his ears could be trusted, there were two voices. One was that of a child, distressed, crying perhaps. The other was speaking regularly, but it was difficult to discern any tone or demeanor, let alone actual words. It was closer to a muffled hum than a discernable collection of consonants and vowels. That is, if there were actual voices at all; it was possible a recipe of wind, water, and the reverberations of a recent quaalude overdose were combining such to bake up the illusion of voices, an aural version of a trick of light and shadow. It wouldn't have been the most egregious hallucination he'd suffered in the last twenty-four hours.

He went to the base of the staircase and listened. The voices were clearer from this auditive vantage point, but only by a fraction of a degree. This time, however, he thought he could make out some actual words. They were extremely muffled, reminding him of a game he and Connie would play as children at the public pool. They would both submerge, one of them would say something underwater, and the other would have to try to decipher what they'd said. It was an amusing game. The hit rate was about fifty percent, but when they got it wrong the mishearings were sometimes close, like Connie mistaking "Howdy Doody Time" for "How you doing, Con?"--or wildly distant, like James mistaking "Frank Sinatra" for "fake baloney."

If the words he'd just heard coming from the leisure room were said in his and Connie's old game, his guess would have been: "Hold still."

The television. Of course. That was it. A power surge, faulty wiring maybe, had caused it to turn itself on. It was one of those old horror movies—a Hammer *Dracula* picture perhaps—the UHF stations liked to run in the middle of the night. Surely that was it.

But wait, if that was the case, where was the accompanying light? There was no door at the top of the staircase; the top landing of the steps was the leisure room itself. If there was a TV running there would be flickering light coming from the open space above him.

"Hello?" he called up the stairs. There was no response, nor did the voices stop. If anybody was up there, they weren't concerned with James in the slightest.

And who would be up there? And why? What possible reason could there be for anyone to have broken into this unremarkable beach cottage in the middle of November and make hushed noises in the leisure room? It was absurd. Either the "voices" were a conspiracy of elements from without or a manifestation of compromised brain wiring from within, but either way there was nobody upstairs. James intended to prove it with his eyes—though those had recently shown to be untrustworthy as well—then go back to bed. Up the stairs he marched.

He flipped on the overhead light from the switch on the wall at the top of the stairs. The room was empty, save for the furnishings and accoutrements that belonged there. The voices, if they'd been there at all, had ceased, and he was left hearing only the wind and ocean, which in all likelihood was all he'd ever been hearing.

He was about to turn the light back off when something on the floor next to the table caught his eye. Some sort of tool? He went over and picked it up. It was about six inches in length, half of that being a round, wooden handle, the other half being a jagged steel blade, but curved, crescent-like—like a cylinder cut down the middle the long way. He recognized this tool. It was a kitchen utensil. A corer. His mother used to have a similar one she'd use to dig the cores out of apples when she made apple pie. This was what had woken him. It had fallen off the table and clanked onto the floor above his head.

But what had knocked it off? There was no draft in the room, and even if there had been, the corer was too heavy to have been blown off the table. Furthermore, he'd been in this room earlier when Leslie showed him around, and neither of them had noticed a corer sitting on the edge of the table. Then again, neither of them had exactly been looking out for one either.

He took the corer with him and headed back downstairs, flicking the light switch off as he went. He dropped the corer into the silverware/utensil drawer in the kitchen and went back into the bedroom. As he lay in bed, he could swear he once again heard the voices coming from above—muffled, sporadic. But he knew that couldn't be. There was nobody up there. Just the sounds of the great Atlantic tricking the ears, he told himself.

He didn't really believe it though.

A coffee percolator is a befuddling machine to an individual who's never used one. There were only three interior components—a metal rod and two serrated metal cups, one deep, one shallow—but James couldn't for the life of him figure out how they fit together or where inside the kettle to put them. Which is why, when Leslie popped over in the morning to check in on him, she found him hovering over a pot of boiling coffee beans, waiting for the water to turn brown. "My stars, it's more hopeless than I thought," she said.

"At least I got the water boiling this time," said James.

"Small miracle, that. You have to ground the coffee, James. You can't brew beans."

"I figured they'd dissolve."

On the radio, Betty on the Beach was letting her audience know it was going to be unseasonably warm today, perhaps getting up to the high fifties.

"And look how many beans you put in there! If you drank a cup of coffee this strong you wouldn't fall asleep till 1990. And to think they put you in charge of young minds!"

"You don't need to know how to make coffee to teach *The Great Gatsby*."

"Maybe not, but you need to know how to drink it to stay awake while you're reading it. Joking. Joking."

She showed him how to measure out the beans and use the grinder, then demonstrated how the percolator components fit together, which seemed remarkably intuitive when she did it. They took a seat at the yellow Formica table and waited for the coffee to brew. Betty on the Beach transitioned from the weather report to "Teenager in Love," the lesser-heard Craig Douglas version as opposed to the more commonly known Dion and the Belmonts recording. Leslie told James all about Jonathan and Jennifer Hart's adventure-of-the-week from last night's episode of *Hart to Hart*. Apparently, Jonathan, played by the dashing Robert Wagner, had suffered amnesia. In his attempt to recover his memory he began to believe he had a mistress and that he might have killed her. Or something like that.

"Robert Wagner, eh?" said James. "I remember him from westerns and war pictures when I was a kid. He's doing TV now, huh?"

"Now? He's been on TV since the sixties. *It Takes a Thief. Switch.* Now *Hart to Hart*. Where've you been?"

TV was not his medium. He hadn't grown up with one. He didn't even own his first set until 1963, the first year of his grad program, which he'd purchased so he could stay up to date on the

Kennedy assassination aftermath. Much of the modern world had transitioned to color by that point and he was able to get a used black and white set for relatively cheap. He'd held on to that set till the late sixties when Linda finally made them upgrade.

"I'm just not much of a TV watcher. I find the stories to be a little trite."

"Trite, eh? Okay then, what's your novel about. You still haven't told me."

"Nobody gets amnesia, I assure you of that."

"Okay. Now you've told me what it's *not* about…"

"Alright. So. Well. It's about the broken promise of the sixties. The whole *smile on your brother* thing, you know? How we went from the Summer of Love in 1967 to this moment we're in right now."

"Which is what?"

"You know. We've gone from grass to cocaine. The Beatles to Olivia Newton John. Bob Dylan is putting out Christian albums for crying out loud."

"I never much liked him. He sounds like he has a chronic sinus infection."

"That's not the point."

"I assume not, but I'm not sure I'm seeing the point."

"How did we get from Kennedy to Reagan?"

"Well, Kennedy died. Johnson dropped out. Nixon resigned. Ford and Carter got voted out. Did I miss any?"

"I mean in mindset. In ideals. The contrast between Kennedy's America versus Reagan's America."

"I don't know what Reagan's America is yet."

"Well, when you try to collect your first social security check in twenty-five years and you can't cause he's done away with it you'll have a pretty good idea."

"I was paying fifty-five cents a gallon for gas last summer in Carter's America. Can't be any worse than that."

"I'm just trying to make a juxtaposition."

"I don't know what juxtaposition means, and I still don't know what your book is about. All I know is nobody gets amnesia."

"It's about disillusionment. That's the most succinct way to put it."

"Okay. So what happens in it? I mean, you can't just have a bunch of people without amnesia walking around being disillusioned, right? They gotta do something."

"I haven't worked that part out yet. I start with the theme, then the plot and characters grow from there." At least, he hoped that was how it was going to work; he'd never written any fiction longer than a short story, and the last time he'd done that was in college.

"Okay, well, you're the author. You take cream? Sugar?" The percolator had stopped hissing and gurgling, indicating the coffee was ready.

"Both."

Leslie prepared the beverage and brought it over to him. "So, how was your first night? I mean, other than the extraordinary dinner obviously. Joking. Joking." She sat back down at the table. Craig Douglas passed the baton to the Big Bopper for a little "Chantilly Lace."

"That was a highlight, no question."

"You slept okay? You had enough blankets?"

"Now that you ask, I don't suppose you heard any strange noises last night up in the big house."

"Such as?"

"Well, voices, I guess. Maybe a child crying. I don't know. It was vague. It sounded like it was coming from the leisure room but I checked and there was nobody up there, of course. I don't know. I'm sure it was nothing. A combination of outside sounds maybe. I just thought I'd ask if you'd heard anything."

"Can't say as though I did. Of course, when I'm out, I'm out. The Big Bopper could sit on my head and I'd sleep through it."

"Mm. Well, like I said, probably nothing. Oh, also…" He got up and went to the silverware drawer. "Ever seen this before? It was up on the table in the leisure room." He sifted through the drawer.

"What is it you're looking for?" she asked after several seconds.

"Um…" He dug through the drawer but the corer was nowhere in sight. "An apple coring tool. Found it on the floor. I threw it in here last night but now it's…" He started removing items from the drawer and laying them on the counter.

"I'm not gonna pretend to know the entire inventory of this place down to every last fork, but I don't remember any apple corer being in here."

James removed everything from the drawer, then put them all back item by item. The corer was not there.

James felt a sense of accomplishment when he set the Ben Franklin bag full of writing supplies on the passenger seat. A couple reams of typing paper, a pack of yellow legal pads, some pens, a bottle of liquid paper, etc. It made him feel like a novelist, even though he hadn't yet written a word. But he would. As soon as he got back to the Seagull's Nest. It would be good for him to focus his mind intensely on something.

He scanned the shops in the mini-plaza. Pape's IGA, Ben Franklin, Mike's Barber Shop, Laverdiere's Drug, a Fitness Room, Sewall Credit Union. Did he need anything else before heading back? He couldn't think of anything. His eye fell on a pair of pay phones outside the IGA. He should call Connie, let her know how he was faring.

He exchanged several dollars for coins at the credit union, unsure how much a long distance call to Boston would cost from here, and knowing Connie certainly wouldn't accept a collect call. He had to feed over a dollar into the slot before the call finally went through.

"Yuh?" Connie had been answering the phone that way since they were kids. It used to drive her father crazy.

"Con, it's me. I made it. I'm in Sewall's Beach."

"Congratulations."

"You'll never guess where I'm staying."

"Well, I suppose you're gonna have to tell me then."

"The Seagull's Nest."

"Is that supposed to mean something to me?"

"It's the name of the cottage we used to stay in. Remember? There's a sign on the front. Anyway, I swung by just to see the old place, and guess who came out of the big house next door."

"Rosie Ruiz."

"Leslie Pettigrew! She's still there. Looks a lot different, but still the same ole Leslie. Rented me the place till spring semester starts in January."

"January! Jesus, Jimmy, I meant get away for a week or so. What the hell are you gonna do in Maine for two months?"

"Write my novel, mostly."

"Hm."

"What's that supposed to mean?"

"It means I'll believe it when I see it. Everything else good?"

"Of course not, Connie, but I'm up, moving around, doing things. I slept most of the night last night. Ate breakfast. Showered. Now I'm out running errands. It's been a while since I can say I did anything like that, basic though it may be."

"Good. That's good. I'm glad you've reintroduced the barest minimums of what it takes to keep yourself alive."

"Yeah. Hey, listen, I got a question. About those pills you take."

"I barely take them, Jim. Doctor prescribed 'em to me cause sometimes I don't sleep good. It's not like I'm some 'lude-head.'"

"Well, when you have taken them, you ever have any side effects?"

"Like dying for a little while and waking up in a hospital twenty-four hours later? No, cause I never washed down half a dozen of them with a bottle of whiskey like a fucking maniac."

"That's not what I mean. I'm talking about, like, hallucinations. After the fact."

"No. But again, I never ate 'em like M&Ms the way you did."

"I think the doctors might have missed something, Con. I'm seeing shit. Really seeing things. And hearing things too. Yesterday I saw a young man fall off a balcony and hit the ground right in front of me. I blink my eyes, gone. Never happened. But I saw it, Connie. With my eyes, not my imagination. Last night I woke up hearing voices upstairs. I go check, nobody's up there. But I find this apple corer on the table. So I throw it in the kitchen drawer, no big deal, right? But this morning, gone. Nowhere to be found. Just gone. I don't know, Con. I feel like I'm losing my mind a little bit."

"Okay, slow down. Let's not assume you've gone crazy just because you lost your potato peeler."

"Apple corer. And there's been other stuff too. This man in the grocery store—"

He was interrupted by the operator, letting him know he needed to insert another twenty-five cents if he wished to continue the call. He plunked a quarter into the slot.

"Jim?"

"Yeah?"

"Listen to me. You know why I have those pills?"

"Because sometimes you can't sleep."

"You know why I can't sleep?"

"Why?"

"If you tell anybody I told you this I swear to God, Jim…"

"Tell anybody what"

There was a long pause, followed by a heavy sigh. "Stress, okay? Anxiety." It would have been easier for Connie to confess she'd killed a dozen children and buried their bodies in the backyard.

"Okay. So you have stress."

"I'm not talking about everyday stress, Jim—worrying about paying the bills kind of stuff. I'm talking total overwhelm, out of the blue, for no reason. My heart races. I can't breathe. I start imagining all kinds of crazy shit. A few months ago I ended up in the emergency room thinking I was having a heart attack. Turns out there was nothing physically wrong with me. It was all in my head. That's when they gave me the 'ludes."

"Jesus, Con."

"I'm not kidding, James, you tell anybody this and I'll take you out. You won't even see it coming. Just a quick shot in the back of the head like fucking Whitey Bulger does it."

"Jesus Christ, Connie. Colorful. I'm not going to tell anybody."

"Better not." A pause, then: "Mom had it too."

"What?"

"All her life. Hid it well. Had to raise a family, you know? And anyway, what other option did she have? Dad would have just told her to stop acting hysterical. Point is Jim, it runs in the family.

We ain't as tough as we let on. You're going through some unimaginable shit, and it's making your mind do funny things."

"You really think that's it? This boy falling, Con, it seemed so real. I mean, I *saw* it happen in front of me."

"You'd be surprised at the shit a messed up mind can make you think you see. I once thought I saw a flock of birds fly under my car on Storrow. Slammed on the breaks. Nearly caused a pile-up. But when I looked in the rearview—no birds. And if you ever tell anybody that story I'll—"

"Yeah, yeah, I'm not gonna tell anyone."

"Whitey fucking Bulger, Jim."

"I'm not going to tell anyone."

The operator interrupted again to let him know another quarter was required to continue the conversation, but he was out. He said a quick goodbye, she insisted once again she'd murder him if he told anybody about their conversation, and they were cut off.

He set the Smith Carolla on the black table in the leisure room and spread out his purchases on either side of it. He sat down, loaded a sheet of paper into the typewriter, and lit a Pall Mall. Here we go. This is what it's all been about. The novel that had been inside him all his life was finally going to come out.

He put his fingers on the keyboard.

And there they sat, unmoving.

He just needed a push, that's all. Like that rusty, mustard-yellow Oldsmobile his father used to have when they were kids. Every now and then James, Connie, and both their parents would have to get out and push. When the car was rolling fast enough, Bill Riordan would hop in and get it started, then the rest of the family would follow. Once that baby was running it chugged along without any problems, it just needed that initial push to get it going. That's what James needed: a push to get it going. Something—anything—to get the fingers moving.

Once upon a time.

He of course had no intentions of starting his novel this way; what he was writing was as far from a fairy tale as you could get. Quite the inverse, really.

It was a dark and stormy night.

The notorious, universally agreed upon worst opening to any novel ever.

Call me Ishmael.

Melville. Classic. A man and a whale. Maybe that was a metaphor James could use in his novel: Ahab representing man in general, the whale representing disillusionment.

It was the best of times, it was the worst of times.

Dickens. Yes. Dickens excelled at sprawling explorations of the current state of society. Old Chuck was something to aspire to. In fact, if he remembered correctly, there was some Dickens on the bookshelf up here in the leisure room, wasn't there? He was pretty sure he'd read the Seagull's Nest's copy of *Great Expectations* one summer. And there might have been a *Bleak House* and a *Nicholas Nickleby* over their too if memory served. He stood up to check.

No. Sit back down. You're procrastinating. You can peruse the bookshelf for Dickens later. Right now: type.

Outside, high tide must have been approaching, because he could hear the first clicking and clacking rocks of a forthcoming Rock'n'Roll Dance Party. He clicked and clacked along with it on the keyboard, rattling off more famous first lines, channeling the greats, as if by funneling their words through his fingers, some of their greatness may be left behind to fuel his own. He reached the end of the page with Hamlet's opener—*Who's there?*—two little words that arguably posed the central question of the entire play. He tore the sheet of paper out of the typewriter and set it beside him for inspiration. He fed in a new sheet, primed to fill this one with originality on par with the geniuses he'd just plagiarized.

But nothing came.

It was the time of day. Early afternoon. He'd always fancied himself a morning writer. Get up at dawn. Coffee. Cigarettes. Sunrise. Prose. Early afternoon was no time to write. Early afternoon was time to nap. Maybe he'd cozy up on the sofa with one of those Dickens books he hoped to find on the shelf, catch a few winks listening to the waves and the clacks of the sea rocks rolling over each other.

He stood up from the table, intending to go to the bookshelf, when something outside the spiderweb window caught his eye. Down on the beach below, same spot as yesterday, same dress, hands cupped behind her ears.

Elizabeth.

James wasn't generally one to poke into other people's business. And while he didn't exactly dislike kids per se, he didn't take particular interest in them either. Even his own. He loved and adored Kelly, but he hadn't been nearly as engaged with her life and interests as he could have been. He never went out of his way to ask how her day was. He never tried to understand her moods, quirks, proclivities, and interests.

And now it was too late.

Had he never had an adolescent daughter, or if Kelly had still been alive, he probably would have never talked to Elizabeth in the first place. But the small rations of paternal energy he possessed hadn't been used in weeks and were building up, and Elizabeth was an outlet to release some of it.

He met her down on the beach. It had been a pleasant day for late November, as Betty on the Beach had promised, but at this point in the afternoon the sun was favoring the Pacific more than the Atlantic, and the temperature had dropped considerably. James was wearing a corduroy sport jacket over a thin cardigan sweater and was still chilly, yet Elizabeth, barefoot, in only that sleeveless beige dress, didn't seem affected at all.

"Hello, Elizabeth."

The girl turned to look at him, hands still cupped behind her ears. She smiled at him. "Hi."

"James. We met yesterday."

"I remember you."

"Aren't you cold?"

"Always."

"Don't you have a jacket or a sweater or something you could put on? Shoes?"

"Not anymore."

"What do you mean by that?"

"I used to have lots of things. Now I just have this."

"I don't understand. Where did all your things go?"

"I don't understand either."

James occasionally thought Kelly was a space alien—that Martians had stolen his human daughter and replaced her with one of their own. What other race would listen to the *Xanadu* soundtrack on repeat while cutting up magazines to make collages of Scott Baio? But she had nothing on Elizabeth in the oddity department.

"How's your head? Did you go home and get yourself all patched up yesterday?" Her curly red bangs still hung down over the spot where the blood had been trickling yesterday.

"It doesn't matter. It'll just happen again."

"How so?"

"It just does." She spoke of it as if bleeding from the forehead was as common as a recurring bloody nose.

James was reminded of Tessie Prather from the neighborhood. Her father had been killed in World War II back when she was a baby. She was raised by a single mom. Pretty normal kid. Then, when Tessie was about ten or so, mom remarried and Tessie changed. She got quiet, and when she did speak it was vague and cryptic. She started showing up to school with bruises and sprained wrists. Each new malady, according to her, was due to a fall. Strange. She'd never been particularly uncoordinated before, now suddenly she was taking an injurious tumble several times a month. James and his peers noted the changes, but, being kids, they never questioned it. It wasn't until James was an adult, thinking back, that it became painfully obvious Tessie Prather hadn't just suddenly become clumsy—that the onset of her chronic injuries coincided with the arrival of her new stepfather.

James obviously couldn't assess Elizabeth's situation on the limited information he had, but something wasn't right in this kid's life.

"I'm going to run inside and grab you a sweatshirt, okay?" He'd brought an old Amherst sweatshirt to laze around the house in; he could spare it for the girl.

"It won't do any good."

"It will keep you warm at least."

"The rocks keep me warm. Everything's okay when the rocks are singing."

"Singing rocks. I like that. My sister and I used to call it the Rock'n'Roll Dance Party when we were about your age, after an old radio show of the same name."

"Alan Freed."

"That's right. How'd you know that? That show hasn't been on the air in twenty years."

"I don't know. Sometimes I just remember things. Sometimes I don't.

"Hm. Okay. Well, anyway, I'm going to run inside and grab you a sweatshirt before you catch your death, all right? Be back in a minute."

He went inside and grabbed the sweatshirt from his suitcase— gray with maroon lettering reading "University of Massachusetts at Amherst." As he stepped out of the bedroom he heard a woman's voice call: "Elizabeth? Where are you?" The girl's mother calling her home in all likelihood. This would have made perfect sense had the voice been a shout from some distance, another cottage along the beach perhaps, but that was not the case. It sounded as if it came from inside the Seagull's Nest, up in the leisure room.

Out the sliding glass door he saw Elizabeth running down the beach, the same direction she'd gone yesterday, assumedly answering her mother's call. James's ears were clearly playing tricks on him. The mother was not in the leisure room. Of course she wasn't. What sense would that make? She was at a neighboring cottage, calling her daughter in, hopefully to put on a damn coat and some shoes. Maybe the synapses between James's ears and brain were misfiring, confusing the origins of sounds in his mind. Or maybe there was something about the acoustics of the cottage and the beach that caused sounds to carry in strange ways. This could also explain the voices he'd thought he heard last night. Maybe Elizabeth and her mother were staying just a couple houses down and for some reason sounds originating there bounced around the landscape in such a way that made them seem as if they were coming from upstairs.

Plausible? Sure, why not? James was a professor of English literature, not physics.

He stepped onto the patio to see if he could see which house the girl was staying in, but by the time he got out there she was nowhere to be seen, indicating whichever house she was in, it must be close. James wanted to try to keep an eye on the place if he could. If his suspicions were correct, the girl might not be safe. He thought of the whimpering and crying he'd heard the night before, and the woman's voice—*Hold still*. If that had indeed carried over from where Elizabeth was staying, he didn't like the implications.

He walked a short distance down the beach, as far as he thought Elizabeth could have run in the time between him seeing her take off and him stepping out onto the patio and finding her gone. He didn't see any signs of life—no clues as to which house she might be staying in. In fact, all the houses he passed looked pretty closed up for the winter. Oh well. Next time he saw Elizabeth he'd subtly try to get more information from her, though if the two prior conversations were any indication he suspected he wouldn't be able to get much.

He headed back inside to pick up where he left off, which was to find something by Dickens and fall asleep on the couch reading it. Back up in the leisure room, as he walked past the table, the Smith Carolla mocked him, fresh sheet of paper primed, glaringly empty of prose. Next to it was the sheet on which he'd written all those first lines of notable works. But it wasn't as he'd left it. The perimeter of that sheet of paper was stained dark red.

Huh.

James moved closer. The whole area around the head of the table where he'd been sitting was wet. He hadn't brought any liquids up with him, so it couldn't have been a spill. He looked up at the peaked ceiling to check for signs of a leak but all seemed normal up there. It wasn't possible to discern what the liquid was, the table being black, but the edges of the paper told the tale.

Red. Blood red.

James picked up the typewriter, which sat in the middle of the mess. Blood, or whatever it was, dripped from the corners as he raised it up. Jesus. What the hell had happened up here? And how?

He gently shook the typewriter until it stopped dripping, then carried it downstairs. He had big places to go in this vehicle; he couldn't have whatever had spilled up there gumming up the works. He wet a sponge and carefully wiped off the bottom. Whatever had spilled up there—or dripped or leaked or appeared out of nowhere—was thick and sticky. Beet juice? A melted popsicle?

No. It was blood. James may not have been a custodian in an emergency room, but he'd seen enough blood in his lifetime—schoolboy scrapes, teenage brawls, that time he sliced open his hand on the lid of the aluminum can while packing down the garbage—to recognize it when he saw it.

An animal? Had a wounded animal gotten into the house, found its way up onto the table, bled for a while, then found its way back out? Seemed more than a bit absurd. For starters, blood would be trailed across the floor if that were the case. Unless it was a bird. A bird flew in, landed on the table, bled, then flew away.

And if you believe that one there's a bridge in Brooklyn...

There had to be some explanation. He'd missed something. He was going to go back up and find an empty bottle of fruit punch he'd forgotten he brought up there, empty on the floor, having tipped over, spilled, and rolled off the table.

It's a great bridge, sir. A magnificent bridge! And it can be all yours for only...

He went back up the stairs. The room was as he left it, which shouldn't be at all surprising under normal circumstances, being that he'd just left it three minutes ago. But these weren't normal circumstances. The last time he'd left and returned to this room he'd come back to find half a pint of blood on the table with no apparent origin.

But as he reached the top of the stairs and could now see the room with the advantage of his full height, he realized it wasn't exactly as he'd left it. The sheet of paper with all the first lines typed out on it no longer had the red-stained edges. In fact, as he got closer he saw the table was bone dry. No spill. No blood. He ran his hand across it, thinking maybe he'd find it damp or sticky, like this type of wood might have a particular way of quickly absorbing liquids. But no. Nothing. Dry.

Either the world's stealthiest and most talented maid had snuck up and cleaned while he was downstairs, or the blood had never been there at all.

He thought back to what Connie had told him earlier. *You'd be surprised at the shit a messed up brain can make you think you see.* Was that really possible? Could his depression be causing this? Making him see things that weren't there? What was happening felt a little more extreme than that. There was blood on this table. He was certain of it. He'd washed it off his typewriter. Could stress really make him imagine all that?

But now that he really thought about it, yes, the blood had been there, but differently. Like the falling boy. He'd seen it, that was not in dispute, but there was also something a little uncanny about it, like a matte painting on a movie set. It was there, but in

111

some inexplicable, subtle way it didn't quite match the rest of the scenery.

James was both a street kid and an academic, neither stratification coming with a proclivity for believing in ghosts, but he still entertained the idea that the Seagull's Nest may be haunted. That would explain a few things in a tidy way. But even if he allowed his natural skepticism to let its guard down and accept that as a possibility, it didn't explain the falling boy. That had happened miles away from the Seagull's Nest.

If there was a haunting it wasn't in the cottage, it was in his brain.

He picked up the sheet of paper with the first lines.

In my younger and more vulnerable years my father gave me a piece of advice I've been turning over in my mind ever since.

It is a truth universally acknowledged, that a single man in possession of a good fortune, must be in want of a wife.

Lolita, light of my life, fire of my loins.

Unhappy families are all alike; every family is unhappy in its own way.

He went down the whole page to the Shakespeare quote at the bottom: *Who's there?*

But wait a minute. Those weren't the words on the paper. It was a two word sentence, but not the two he remembered writing. And it wasn't a question but an imperative. Nor was it a first line of any piece of literature he'd ever read. But he had heard it before. Last night. Coming from this very room.

Hold still.

"Hold still!"

James's eyes snapped open. Those two words had been playing over and over in his head since that afternoon, and now here they were in his ears, coming from above.

He sat up in bed and listened. Just like last night, he heard the whimpering of a child and the muffled voice of another individual. He focused his listening—really concentrating. After the fact, he'd been able to convince himself the voices he'd thought he'd heard upstairs the previous night actually came from an entirely different cottage, the soundwaves somehow floating across the beach such that they seemed to be coming from the leisure room. But now, in the moment, that seemed ridiculous. There was nothing but floor/ceiling between him and the voices.

Or perhaps Connie's theory was correct. Maybe it was all the emotional strain causing his senses to hear and see things that weren't there. But that too seemed ridiculous now that he was in the moment. The voices were tangible. They were in the house, not in his imagination.

But how did he know for sure? If the mind was so powerful as to actually make him hear voices, how would he be able to discern if what he was hearing was actually real or not?

This is what it must feel like to lose your mind.

He closed his eyes. *Focus. See if you can shut them out. Try to separate the real from the imagined.* He tried to focus his hearing on the ocean waves. It must have been high tide because he could also hear the clicks and clacks of the rocks. The Rock'n'Roll Dance Party. He listened intently, trying to isolate just the ocean and the rocks, thinking maybe if he could connect strongly with the real, the fake would fade out.

The child shrieked.

"Hold still!"

James's eyes shot open. He turned on the light next to him, half thinking the change to the environment would quell the voices, but they continued. He got out of bed and went into the living area. The voices were slightly clearer out here, drifting down the stairs from the leisure room. The cries and whimpers of the child. The muffled voice of whoever insisted the child hold still. And yet, there was also something slightly unreal about the voices. He was hearing them in his ears, not in his mind, that wasn't in dispute, but there was something just a bit uncanny about them. One degree removed from reality. Like hearing an audio recording as opposed to the real thing.

He tried to catch his bearings. This same thing had happened last night, and when he went upstairs there'd been nothing there.

Similarly, that afternoon he'd clearly heard what he thought was Elizabeth's mother calling to her from up there, and again he'd found the place empty. Why should tonight be any different? Whether these were ghosts or figments, James just wanted them to stop.

He went to the stairs, pausing at the base. Every hair follicle on his body tingled.

The cries of the child were almost crystal clear from this spot, with the opening to the leisure room directly above him. From here the whimpers sounded less muffled and more stifled, as if there was something preventing the child from crying out with all the gusto he or she would like to—like their mouth was covered.

James took the first step. Then the second. Each step taking him closer to the inevitable horror awaiting him above: either somebody was up there abusing a child, or there was nothing at all up there, which meant he was truly losing his mind.

Third step. Fourth step.

"Hold still! We've got to let the demons out!"

He froze, his head just inches below the spot where the ceiling of the living room became the floor of the leisure room. It was a woman's voice, urgent, but controlled.

Not audible was James's breath, because that had stopped. He could hear his own heart, however, slamming against his ribcage at a dangerous rate and pressure, fit to burst—as if one were to crack the tiniest opening in it blood would erupt out like a vigorously shaken soda can.

Hold still! We've got to let the demons out!

On tip-toes, James could see above the floor line, through the slats in the wooden banister protecting individuals in the leisure room from falling into the staircase. It was dark, save for the moonlight coming in through the spiderweb window on the oceanside wall. That window was in his line of sight, but the bottom half was blocked by the large table in the center of the room. But that wasn't the only thing causing an obstructed view of the night sky outside. Silhouetted in the top half of the window, standing at the head of the table, was a woman.

James ducked his head down. Mother of God! He reflexively put his hand over his chest, as if to keep his heart strapped in, like a mother extending her arm across to the passenger seat to protect her child when she unexpectedly hits the brakes.

Next door. He needed to get next door and call the police. There was no phone in the Seagull's Nest, but Leslie had kindly offered him the use of hers any time he needed it—though the middle of the night likely hadn't been what she'd had in mind when she said "any time." Still, these were extraordinary circumstances—and certainly Leslie would want this intruder reported immediately, being her property and all.

He got halfway down the stairs and paused. His Boston upbringing stepped in. What would his father, God rest his soul, have done in this situation? If Bill Riordan had woken up to find an intruder in the leisure room, he'd have marched right up there, fists balled tight, ready to bash in a nose and/or knock out a few teeth. The last thing he would have done was flee to the neighbor lady. James had been a relatively sensitive kid, choosing the Somerville Library on Walnut Street over the boxing gym just up the road in Winter Hill where Tommy and the rest of the neighborhood kids hung out, but he was still a Somerville kid, and that came with a level a scrappiness, even if you preferred *Robinson Crusoe* to Sugar Ray Robinson. And not for nothing, he'd only seen a silhouette, but it was clearly a woman up there. Was he about to go running, screeching, and fleeing his home like a skittish housemaid who'd seen a mouse in the kitchen rather than confront a woman?

Of course, that wasn't the whole story though, was it? Given everything else that had been happening there were heavy odds this woman was a manifestation, the realization of which might be more frightening than if Sugar Ray Robinson himself had broken in looking for a fight.

"Hey!" he called. No response. He could still hear the whimpering of the child, though the other individual—*Hold still! We've got to let the demons out!*—was, for the moment, silent.

He went back up the few steps he'd retreated, far enough that his sightline was again above the floor of the leisure room. All was the same: the woman, silhouetted in the spiderweb window. He could make out no features, nor could he describe exactly what she was doing, but she was standing at the head of the table doing *something*. Her position and movements reminded him of how his dad used to stand at the head of the table on Sunday dinners and carve the ham or—on very special occasions—the roast beef.

From his vantage point he could just see the bottom of the table, and only the vague, dark shape of it at that, but it didn't take too creative an imagination to assume the whimpering child was on top of it. What the woman was doing to him or her to cause such distress, however, was less clear.

"Hey!" he called again.

"Stop squirming," was the response, though not to his exclamation. The table was shaking, as if the child who was presumably strapped to it was violently struggling.

James marched up the remaining steps and flicked the light switch.

On the one hand, it was a relief to find the room empty, on the other, it was the worst possible outcome. He really was going crazy—or, at the very least, was suffering major cognitive impairment from his accident. His overdese. His death. He had seen the woman. He'd heard her—heard the cries of the child. Unequivocally and empirically.

At least, his damaged brain had convinced his eyes and ears they had.

He scanned the room. It was an open space with nowhere to hide, save for the crawl space, but there hadn't been time to get there in the two seconds between him having seen the woman's silhouette and turning on the light.

He inspected the table. Nothing out of the ordinary. No indications that a distressed child—or a Sunday dinner ham—had been there any time recently. In fact the ash tray and the writing items he'd left there were still there, completely undisturbed.

He went over to the crawl space and crouched down by the cabinet door that accessed it on the oceanside of the room. He and Connie used to goof around in there when they were kids—there being few things as exciting to a child as a secret tunnel. There was nothing remarkable about it; it was just a dusty, triangular hallway, about four feet tall at its peak, sloping down at a forty-five degree angle until it reached its vertex. When they were little they thought it was just the bee's knees to enter through one cabinet door, sneak down the crawl space, and pop out the other door, as if they'd just pulled some inexplicable magic trick. *Look, Ma! I was just on that side of the room—abracadabra—now I'm on this side!*

Usually, that which scares us as children becomes silly in adulthood: the monster under the bed or the boogeyman in the closet, for example. Rarely is it the other way around, but here was such a case. He'd opened that cabinet door and jubilantly entered the crawl space at least fifty times in just the summer of

'49 alone, their first year staying at the Seagull's Nest, when he was eight years old, without a speck of fear. Yet here it was, 1980, him weeks away from his 40th birthday, and his hand trembled as he reached for the nob, imagining the door about to burst open on its own at any moment, releasing a geyser of shrieking ghosts.

He tapped his knuckles against the door. "Hello?"

Nothing. Of course there was nothing. If the phantom woman hadn't responded when he called out to her when she was visibly standing in front of him at the head of the table, why would she respond to him now when she was hiding in the crawl space? Which raised another question of logic: why would she hide in the crawl space at all? She clearly didn't seem concerned about him.

James laughed. Not a *funny-ha-ha* laugh, an *I-can't-believe-the-absurdity-of-the-situation-in-which-I-now-find-myself* laugh. He heard Connie's voice in his head. *Riordan's are tough. We don't let things get to us.* He heard his father's voice. *Open the door, sissy boy.*

He did. No geyser of spirits burst forth, just a rush of cold air. He poked his head inside. Like so much else in Sewall's Beach, he was taken by how much smaller the crawl space was than he'd remembered. As a child he could run up and down the space, maybe having to duck a bit as he got older, but now he doubted if he could even crawl down the aptly named space without scraping his back on the splintered roof slats lining the diagonal ceiling at steady intervals.

Regardless, it was empty. He couldn't quite see all the way down the other end, but he could see far enough. There was nothing. No sound. No presence.

He closed the cabinet door and gave the room one last look around, as if he could have possibly missed anything. All was as it should be. He went back to the top of the stairs and put his hand on the light switch when a thought occurred to him. It was when the room was dark that the woman was visible to him. As soon as he'd turned on the light she'd vanished. Was that how it worked? Did some kind of otherworldly physics make them visible in the dark but not in the light? It was absurd, of course, but James had driven past absurdity several miles back.

He flicked off the light, a large percentage of him expecting the woman to materialize at the head of the table again, to hear the muffled cries and whimpers of the child. But no, nothing but darkness and silence, save the moonlight and the sounds of the beach below.

With the light on, the spiderweb window had reflected the interior of the room back at him. With the light off, he could see the night sky, clear and speckled with stars, like glowing flies caught in the window's web.

James went to the window and stood in front of it, looking out. The moon, the stars, and a few outdoor lights from residences provided enough light to get a clear enough picture of the basic scene: a layer of sand, moonlight-glistening ocean in the middle, topped with an expanse of blue-black sky, gibbous moon floating above it, orange, slightly filtered through a mesh netting of thin cloud cover. Down the beach to the south he could see the red light of Betty on the Beach's radio tower.

James would call the doctor in the morning and let him know about the side-effects he'd been having. The visions. Hallucinations. But for now, all was right again at Sewall's Beach.

He turned to leave, to go back downstairs and see if he could clear his mind enough to fall asleep, when something stopped him. As he was turning away he could swear he caught a glimpse of...

He turned back around. Sure enough. In the minimal light provided by both natural and man-made means, he could see her silhouette, standing on the beach, hands cupped around her ears, maximizing the auditory sensations provided by the Rock'n'Roll Dance Party. Elizabeth.

Everything's okay when the rocks are singing.

What the hell was she doing out there at this time of night?

James descended the stairs, went through the living area, and out the sliding glass doors, stepping out into the nearly freezing November night in just his bare feet and pajamas. From this lower vantage point the girl was below his sightline, but as he marched closer to the stairs leading down to the beach, more and more of the beach becoming visible with each step, he still couldn't see her.

He stood at the top of the stairs and scanned. No Elizabeth. Had she been there at all? Had he even seen and spoke to her earlier that day? Or yesterday? Or had she been just another apparition, another rumbling aftershock from his temporary death? Christ, was he even at Sewall's Beach? Or was he still in his chair in his filthy living room in Jamaica Plain imagining this entire thing? Maybe the paramedics had never brought him back at all. Maybe he was dead, and this was… certainly not heaven, but not quite hell. Purgatory, he believed they called it.

Regardless, James Riordan's world was teetering on the edge of reality, arms flailing, desperately trying to swing its balance toward the safety of the land.

He climbed back into bed. There were no more incidents that night, and in a few short hours, the sun began to peak its dome over the Atlantic ocean, filling the bedroom with the brown-orange light of dusk, James not having slept, not even having shut his eyes, barely even blinking.

James had enough self-awareness to realize he was a cliché: an English professor who talked a lot about the novel he was going to write, but never actually writing the novel. He'd had a few false starts over the years. He had a handful of moments where he got so far as to sit down in front of his Smith Carolla, spool a sheet of paper around the platen, and place his fingers on the keys. There was even a time or two when his tortured poet's brain freed itself enough to send signals to those fingers causing them to type out a dozen words or so, only to seconds later tear the sheet of paper from machine, crumple it, and shoot it into the waste basket like John Havlicek. Cliché. Pathetic cliché.

There was always an excuse. His job. His wife. His child. Susan. His own perfectionism. But the glaringly obvious excuse, the one that would sneak into his head for fleeting moments before he shunted it off to the bottom of his brain with other unwanted thoughts, was he was not a novelist. Novelists write novels. That's the definition. Seemed like every time he turned around, there was a new Stephen King novel for the curator at Arlington Books to stick in the window. That hack upstate could fart out a book or two a year and James couldn't get down more than a handful of words? Unacceptable.

No more excuses. His daughter was gone. His wife was gone. His mistress was gone. He was on hiatus until late January. Even his perfectionism—a person who's cheating on his wife with a woman half his age at the moment his daughter is being killed, then decides the goddamn funeral would be the ideal time to tell his wife all about it… How perfect can that individual be? All that was holding him back before had been removed. He was free. Yes, obviously he would give up that freedom in a blink to have just five more minutes with his daughter, but the situation was what the situation was, and he intended to take advantage of it. What else did he have?

And—who knows?—maybe it would distract him enough to keep the ghosts at bay. He'd had too much time to dwell on the recent horrors of his life, and those dark thoughts were manifesting themselves through his other senses. If he could just stay busy. If he could just occupy his mind. If he could just write his novel.

He sat at the yellow Formica table in the kitchen, nibbling burnt toast with butter and too much jam, sipping coffee that tasted like and had the consistency of spent motor oil. But hey, he'd prepared it himself and it was edible and drinkable, if only just barely, so that was something. His Smith Carolla sat in front of him, still downstairs from when he'd brought it down to wash the (imaginary?) blood off it yesterday. He loaded a fresh sheet of paper—that gleaming white canvass of limitless potential, like the six strings of a guitar, infinite melodies contained therein, just waiting for a musician to pick, pluck, and strum them out. It was a romantic sight indeed, this artist, this genius, about to take his first step of a journey that would change the world.

Thirty minutes later, little had changed. There were now three crushed cigarette butts in the ashtray. The coffee mug and the plate where his toast had been were now empty, but so was his canvas. Not a word.

Words. Words words words. How many words was he going to need? He knew the average novel had about 250 words per printed page. His novel was going to be an epic, so he was figuring on about 600 pages, that ought to be enough to communicate his profound message about... well, you know... hippies, Vietnam, Reagan. He scratched out some math on the notepad beside him. One-hundred-and-fifty-thousand words. That seemed like a lot. If he kept up his current pace of zero words per half hour he'd be done... (quick math)... never. He needed a schedule. Goals. There were roughly sixty more days until his hiatus ended. One-hundred-and-fifty-thousand words divided by sixty days... He needed to write 2,500 words a day to bang out a draft of his epic novel before it was time to leave the Seagull's Nest. He could do that. He used to routinely bang out 10,000-word term papers in a single evening back at Amherst. The journey of 600 pages starts with a single word.

And yet, the paper remained blank.

The yellow Formica table was the problem of course. Who could be expected to get any work done at a yellow Formica table?

His original plan, when he'd decided to do his great work here at the Seagull's Nest, was to write at the big table in the leisure room overlooking the ocean. That was a creative space. That was a place to pen an opus.

But that place was haunted by a ghost lady and a whimpering ghost child.

Did he believe that? No. The prevailing theory of quaalude flashbacks was still the one that made the most sense. He intended to go into town and call the hospital at some point that morning, but he at least needed to get down a thousand words or so. This novel, the idea of it, was all he had. Kelly, Linda, Susan, his sanity perhaps... all gone. It was a mortal imperative he wrap himself up in this novel. Without it he had nothing.

But he couldn't be expected to write it at this damned yellow Formica table. This was a table for eating baloney sandwiches. John Updike wouldn't even write a shopping list at this table, let alone a novel. Hell, Stephen King probably wouldn't even lower himself to writing—if you could call it that—at a table like this. It should shock nobody that the paper was still blank, that the great artist's fingers refused to dance across the QWERTY in this stale environment.

Ghosts be damned. He picked up the heavy Smith Carolla and carried it back upstairs.

There is something about the sun that washes away fear, like a disinfectant. A kid will have no problem crawling under his or her bed in the daytime, but when the sun goes down they believe wholeheartedly a child-eating monster has taken residence in that space. It is not dissimilar with adults and their own versions of monsters-under-the-bed. With the morning sunlight beaming through the spiderweb window, the events of last night seemed distant, in both time and reality, as if it hadn't actually happened to him but rather was something he'd seen in a movie. Had he really seen that woman standing over the table? Really heard the cries of the child? Yes, he had. He wasn't trying to convince himself otherwise. But at the same time, they didn't seem quite real either. Much like with the convulsing man in the hospital room, or the falling boy at the Lobster Lodge, what he saw and heard felt like it was layered over the actual world, like a double exposed photograph. It was there, but it didn't quite match its surroundings.

Which only served to further stamp what he already believed: hallucinations.

He set the typewriter down on the black table and sat himself in front of it, perpendicular to the spiderweb window, which cast a beam of orange sun over the workspace, like a spotlight on Hamlet during his existential soliloquy.

He looked out the spiderweb window, half expecting to see Elizabeth down there, but there was only empty beach, save a lone man a ways down throwing a piece of driftwood to a chocolate lab. The sky was gray/blue, ribboned with hazy strips of yellow sun-reflected cirrostratus clouds. The ocean was calm, almost still, a blank canvas in its own right, full of underwater mysteries and seafaring adventures. Way off to the south, where the beach gave way to stone cliffs curving slightly toward the ocean, James could see the radio tower for COOL 89.9. Below it, if he squinted, he could just barely make out the little cabin in the alcove of the cliff, where Betty on the Beach sat spinning her oldies.

Right. The DJ character he'd thought about the other night with Leslie. He'd forgotten about that. It was a way in. As much as he hated to admit it to himself, his critics—Leslie and Helen the waitress—were absolutely right: his novel needed characters and a plot. Right now all he had was an idea, a theme, and he barely even had that. This theme needed to play itself out through the machinations of plot and story, through the actions or inactions of characters. He'd had none of that. But now he did. A radio DJ.

He sat down at the table, put his fingers on the keys, and then, in a forty-eight-hour stretch of time which contained some of the strangest events he'd ever experienced, perhaps the strangest occurred: He started typing.

A stack of papers sat beside the Smith Carolla, all covered in ink, stamped in horizontal rows of staggeringly brilliant prose. The bell dinged, James yanked the current sheet of genius out and added it—upside-down so as to keep everything in its proper order—to the top of the pile. He inserted another sheet into the top of the machine, spun the platen knob to feed it into position, and immediately started clacking the keys again. The process was seamless and almost instantaneous, like a concert pianist turning the page in a book of sheet music without missing a single eighth note.

It was the first time he'd written—*really written*—since Amherst. It felt good. Natural. And most importantly, as long as his fingers were moving, he wasn't thinking about the horrors of his life—the actual or the manifested.

However, while writing may have kept the horrors from permeating his mind, it offered no such protection for his body. He'd been typing for... he didn't rightly know. Three hours? Four? Rear end never left chair. Not for a glass of water. Not to pee. Not to stretch his legs. Not to pace the room momentarily while working through a plot obstacle. Never. He'd been in the zone. Possessed. Like the story was floating in the atmosphere and he was merely a conduit through which it flowed into the typewriter and onto the paper. But something stronger than the muse had infiltrated. He suddenly felt sick—uniquely sick in a way he'd only felt one other time in his life, two days ago, in Pape's IGA when he'd seen the faceless man.

It wasn't nearly as severe as it had been the day before, but it was the same feeling, no question. Nausea, not confined to the stomach but distributed throughout the body, like all five million of his pores might vomit.

He turned toward the window, part of him already knowing what he'd see out there. Sure enough, down on the beach stood two figures, a man and a woman, bundled up for the cold weather, the man with a white curtain hanging over his face. Edgar and Ingrid Monahan. There was no mistaking it this time, the nausea had come first, a bellwether letting James know the faceless man was near.

James stood up and went to the window. His legs were unsteady, half from having not left a sitting position for several hours, half from the uncomfortability of seeing this pair of siblings again. They were a hundred or so yards away from where he stood in the window, but from what he could tell they seemed to be in some sort of heated conversation. Not with words, however. They were aggressively signing to each other, the same tactile sign language James had seen Ingrid use in Pape's IGA, taking each other's hands in turn and communicating through touches and movements. Edgar would occasionally point in James's direction. The distance was too great to confirm by sight alone, but James was beyond-a-doubt certain not only was Edgar pointing at the Seagull's Nest, he was pointing directly at the spiderweb window in which James now stood. Ingrid kept shaking her head no, despite the fact that Edgar couldn't see her, as she aggressively signed into his hand.

This continued for a minute or so before Ingrid, seemingly losing the argument, threw her hands up in defeat and walked toward the Seagull's Nest, leaving her brother waiting behind on the beach, staring up at James — that impossible, eyeless stare from behind an opaque veil.

James went down the stairs, through the living area, and out the sliding glass door to the back patio, extra hustle in his step, wanting to meet Ingrid outside before she could come to the door, which James believed was her intention. He didn't want her in the cottage; there was something unholy about these Monahan siblings.

James met Ingrid at the top of the stairs to the beach. "Hi," he said. "Can I help you?"

Ingrid looked him up and down. "So, it *is* you. My brother was right, as usual." She didn't appear the least bit surprised. Annoyed perhaps, if she showed any emotion at all.

"I'm sorry?"

"My brother said you were staying here. Sure enough, here you are."

"Do I know your brother?"

"You saw him the other day in the grocery store. And he saw you. And he saw you again, just now."

"I was under the impression your brother couldn't see."

"I was under the impression you didn't know him."

"I don't. It's just… I assumed. The veil."

On the beach, Edgar hadn't moved. He stood stalk-still, staring at James, his veil rippling in the gentle ocean breeze.

"He can see."

"And he saw me through the upstairs window, from all the way down there? And recognized me from the grocery store?"

"He doesn't see that way. My brother has no eyesight, but he is not blind."

"I'm not sure I understand."

"I think you do. The same way you saw him before you actually saw him."

"I don't know—"

"Sir, you can drop the ignorant act with me. I saw the way you were looking at him at the grocery store. I see the way you are looking at him now. You are not the first, okay? I've been forced by my brother to have this conversation with several others. If it were up to me I wouldn't be standing here right now, but Edgar, my brother, is a bleeding heart and always wants to help when he finds another one."

"Another one what?"

"Another like him. You feel the sickness, yes? And you felt the sickness in the grocery store as well, but probably much stronger then, because of the proximity."

James was too stupefied to reply. He was feeling it still, perhaps a little stronger than when he'd been up in the leisure room, but still not as strong as in Pape's IGA.

"Don't ask what it is because I don't know. Edgar doesn't know. Nobody knows. It just is. It just happens to people like you."

"What d—?"

131

"Sir. Please. I don't know. Whatever questions you have you're going to have to seek answers on your own. I'm only up here because Edgar absolutely insists I give you a message. He suggests you leave this house. He says it's not good for you. He says it echoes."

"Ma'am, I'm sorry but I haven't understood a thing you've told me since you showed up."

"You're new. It's always the new ones that feign ignorance. Denial, I suppose. You've seen the echoes, sir. Maybe you call them something different. Many refer to them as visions. Edgar calls them echoes. You are free to call them anything you choose. You are even free to continue to pretend you don't know what I'm talking about. I've been tasked by Edgar to suggest you leave this house and I've done it. Good day to you, sir." She turned and descended the stairs.

"I've seen them!" called James. "I've seen the echoes."

Ingrid stopped in the middle of the staircase and turned around. "I know."

"Please. What are they? What's happening to me?"

"Sir, I've told you: I don't know."

A million questions logjammed in his throat. "Why is...? Is there...? Can't you tell me *anything*?"

For the first time, the sternness melted from her face briefly enough for James to detect a whisper of what one might call sympathy. "No. Good luck to you, sir."

Ingrid turned and descended the remaining steps to the beach. She rejoined her brother, let him hook her arm and they continued walking. James didn't move, just stood watching them head north along the shoreline, his nausea fading incrementally with every step away from him they took.

He was convinced. Ingrid, cryptic and unhelpful as she was, had hit enough nails on the head that she needed to be taken seriously. She called out the sickness. She called out the visions. Echoes. Hell, Edgar had even sightlessly "seen" James from a couple hundred yards away on the beach. James understood none of what was happening, but the Monahan siblings had proved reliable enough to be heeded. If they said he should leave the Seagull's Nest, that the house was no good for him, he believed them. He had plenty of mounting evidence of his own, but that interaction confirmed it.

He may not have understood what was happening, but at least now he knew he hadn't been imagining it all.

Then again, maybe he was imagining the Monahan siblings too.

No. That couldn't be. They were real. Leslie had confirmed it.

Was Leslie real? Had he imagined her too?

Stop. This was a dangerous spiral. If he started to question the reality of every single aspect of his life he'd be in a room with rubber walls in no time. The Monahans were real. Leslie was real. The visions—the echoes—were not. He could tell them apart. In all cases—the hospital, the Lobster Lodge, the voices in the leisure room, the blood—there'd been an undefinable element of facade to all of them, like they were part of a separate reality laid over the actual one. He didn't feel that with the Monahan's or Leslie.

Regardless, he had to leave. Warning given, warning heeded. Thank you, Edgar Monahan. He didn't know exactly what the echoes were, where they came from, what they meant, but he knew the Seagull's Nest was full of them, and he was getting out.

He went back upstairs to grab the Smith Carolla. He saw the stack of paper next to it, full of words, hundreds upon hundreds of them, double-spaced genius. Tangibly it was nothing but paper and ink, but it was oh so much more. It was pride. Satisfaction. But not quite. The feeling he got when he looked at the stack of papers was unlike anything he'd ever felt before. The closest comparison he could make was when he first looked upon the bloody, wrinkled, blue raisin that was Kelly seconds after she'd slid from the birth canal.

Despite his intentions to leave, he sat back down and started typing, picking up right where he'd left off before Edgar Monahan had walked by and sensed him—before they'd sensed each other.

He typed. Words. Sentences. Paragraphs. Pages. Each strike of a typebar against the paper pushed the badness further from his mind. There was nothing else, just him and the words. Kelly,

Linda, Susan, the echoes… none of it mattered. None of it existed. It was just him and the words. It was pure contentment.

It was like he was back in the white place.

Knock knock.

Type type type type…

Knock knock knock.

Type type type…

"Yoo-hoo? James?"

Type type type type type type…

"James, are you all right?"

Type type t—

"Hm?" It was like waking from a dream. He was up in the leisure room, at the table. It was dark outside, the room illuminated only by whatever light crept in through the spiderweb window, which wasn't much at all.

"How can you even see what you're doing?"

Leslie was at the top of the stairs. James, as lucidity trickled back into his consciousness, now recognized he'd been hearing her knock and call to him for the past minute or so, but it was so deep outside his bubble it hadn't fully registered.

"Hm?"

"I said how can you even see what you're doing? It's pitch black up here."

It was a fair question. James could see the black stripes of words on the paper in front of him, but couldn't make any of them out, even if he leaned forward and strained his eyes. "I guess I was just so in the zone I didn't even realize it had gotten dark."

Leslie flicked on the light. That fully broke the spell. James was back in his body, back in his consciousness. The muse that had possessed him for however many hours skittered off into the shadows.

"Sorry to just barge in like this." She wore a hot pink aerobics leotard over black leggings. "I knocked and knocked and when I opened up the door a crack and called inside I heard the typing but you weren't responding. I thought maybe something was wrong."

"It didn't occur to you that perhaps I was just working?"

"Well. Sure. But… well, all the lights were off and… I kept calling and… You know, I'm starting to think this is what my ex-husband was talking about when he said I have a problem with respecting boundaries. Wow, you've been busy."

The stack of filled pages next to the typewriter had more than doubled in size. All in all he must have written about fifteen thousand words. And judging from the overflowing ashtray he'd smoked about that many cigarettes. He was aware he'd been sitting and working for a long time, but simultaneously it seemed like just seconds ago he'd come upstairs to grab the typewriter, intending to pack up and leave the Seagull's Nest. "Yeah. I guess I have."

"I shouldn't have interrupted you. Again, I'm sorry. It's just, I picked up some fresh scallops at the Bedrock Lobster Pound and I thought maybe you might be hungry. But I shouldn't have imposed. I'll leave you back to your work."

Now that the spell was broken he was feeling all the minor physical maladies of one who's just been upright in a wooden chair typing for several hours without a break. His ass was numb. His back stiff. His wrists sore. His bladder throbbed. He'd eaten nothing since the burnt toast and jam that morning—unless one counts several dozen Pall Malls as food—and his stomach was letting him hear about it. "No. That's okay. I'm done for today. I'd love some scallops."

"I remember you now," said Leslie. She'd put jeans on over her leotard. Bobby Darin was singing "Mack the Knife" on Cool 89.9.

"What do you mean?" James put a piece of baked asparagus in his mouth.

"I remember you." She took a sip of red wine. "From when we were kids."

"You do?"

"Yup. It was the face you made upstairs, when I walked up and surprised you. It reminded me of… well, I'm sure you remember."

Now that it was out in the open, James felt embarrassed. He hadn't known any better at the time, but now, as an adult, the memory of his four-thrust performance was downright shameful.

"I probably shouldn't have done that to you. You were just a kid."

"You're only a year older than me."

"Yeah, but it seemed like much more at the time. I was almost eighteen, you were barely sixteen. And girls mature faster than boys. I took advantage of you."

It occurred to him Susan was barely older *now* than Leslie was *then*. "I assure you, you did not."

"I don't know what came over me that day, James. I'd never done anything like that before. I mean, I'd done *it* before, but to seduce somebody like that, and with your whole family right outside on the beach!"

"Leslie, I promise you, you have nothing to be ashamed about. If I may be totally candid it was one of the highlights of my life."

"Really?"

"In a way, it's the reason I came back here." A naughty smile shone on Leslie's lips, and it occurred to James she might have misunderstood—she might have thought he came back hoping to rekindle that momentary inferno. "I hadn't thought about this place in a long time. Then, a few weeks ago, I was telling that story to—" *my twenty-year-old mistress* "—a friend. Couldn't get this place out of my head ever since. Now here I am."

"I'm very flattered." James's attempt to clarify his comment hadn't totally worked; a hint of her naughty smile remained.

"Dinner was remarkable," he said, intentionally moving away from the subject. "Thank you again for cooking."

"Oh, my pleasure. It's nice to have somebody to cook for again. My late husband always took that for granted."

"Well, his loss is my gain." Damn it. He did it again. He'd said something else that could be construed as flirtatious. "You really are a wiz in the kitchen," he added, lest there be any misunderstanding of which of Mr. Kilgore's losses he intended to accept as his gain.

"Do you mind if I use your bathroom?"

"Technically it's your bathroom."

"Yes, I suppose that's true. I'll be right back, then we'll clean up."

James remained at the Formica table. He lit a cigarette. Betty on the Beach's smooth voice let him know that it was going to be a cold one, especially if you live on the water, so you may want to throw an extra blanket on the bed tonight. She then put on Tennessee Ernie Ford's "Sixteen Tons."

James felt good. He hadn't forgotten his real world troubles—or his imaginary ones depending on how you categorized the echoes—but he was recognizing the wins in his life as well. Coming to Sewall's Beach was the right move. Just a few days ago he was so depressed he could barely dress himself, now here he was, having dinner and pleasant conversation with an old friend. Even the eating dinner part would have been unthinkable a week ago, let alone doing so with company.

But the real victory was the writing. He almost couldn't believe it. He half expected that the next time he went upstairs he'd find that stack of papers to be blank, the whole experience having been imagined—an echo. But he knew that wasn't the case. He'd written those pages. They were real. And he couldn't shake the feeling the Seagull's Nest had something to do with his productivity. Specifically the leisure room. It could have only happened there.

"Sixteen Tons" got staticky. Passing plane maybe? Thick cloud cover? But with Betty on the Beach's radio tower being so close, that kind of physical interference seemed unlikely. Regardless of why, the static increased until he could barely make out the song playing underneath it. He got up to adjust the antennae. That didn't help. He adjusted the radio dial ever so slightly to the left, then to the right, but to no avail. Cool 89.9 was totally overtaken by static.

Then, abruptly, it went away all together. But not just the static, all sound from the radio. But wait… maybe not all sound. He could hear something coming from the speaker. A voice. Soft. Almost imperceptible. He turned up the volume nob but it had no effect. He leaned his ear to the speaker. It was a child. Whimpering. Crying. The same sound he'd been hearing at night coming from the leisure room.

Suddenly, loud, a woman's voice screamed: "Hold still! We've got to let the demons out!"

James jerked back from the radio. "Sixteen Tons" was playing again. It had never stopped playing.

Which wasn't to say James hadn't actually heard what he heard. He had. But it was separate from the physical world. Hovering slightly above it. The more echoes he experienced, the more he was able to tell the difference. He wasn't going crazy. The visions were real. Kind of. And knowing Edgar Monahan had them too—it validated the situation for James—made it more acceptable.

Which isn't to say it wasn't still chilling as hell to hear a woman screaming about demons through a radio.

Enough was enough. It was time to heed Edgar Monahan's advice and leave the cottage. But the echoes weren't just confined to the cottage. He'd seen them other places. And what about his novel? Would he be as prolific in another setting? Would he be able to write at all? Silly as it was—but, really, hadn't the criteria for silliness gotten a little warped in the past few days?—he felt certain his productivity was inextricably linked to the leisure room.

The echoes seemed harmless, right? Edgar Monahan lived with them. If staying here meant keeping the creative juices flowing, seeing and hearing a few phantoms here and there might be worth it, no?

He turned around. What he saw there might have been more shocking than what had just occurred with the radio: Leslie Kilgore nee Pettigrew was standing in the doorway of the bathroom, in the same pose she stood in twenty-five years ago when James had turned around to find her in his bedroom doorway. And just like in 1957, she was stark-ass naked.

Time hadn't been kind to Leslie's body. The face of Leslie Pettigrew James remembered from his childhood was still discernable in the face of Leslie Kilgore, but the same could not be said for her body. The smooth perfection of the seventeen-year-old that had charged his fantasies for years afterward was nowhere to be found in what now stood before him. Parts of her that used to tightly hug her frame now hung down in flabs and rolls. And not just the parts one would expect. The tight leotards she always wore packed it all in, when released from its restraints, gravity seized her excess flesh and pulled it toward the earth like a bulldog's jowls.

Leslie was a great gal. Kind and easy to be around. But her days of turning heads in a two-piece were long since behind her.

James's face must have betrayed his revulsion, because Leslie's face went from sultry to horrified. "Oh my God." Of all the places on her body that were exposed, she covered her mouth. "You find me hideous."

"What? No. I…"

"You should see your face right now, James. It's as if you're looking at a monster."

"No. I'm just… you surprised me is all. I wasn't expecting…"

"No. You were surprised in 1957. That's not surprise on your face, it's disgust." Not bothering to go back into the bathroom and put her clothes back on, she walked over and sat on the couch.

"It's not that, Leslie. It's just… well… we just met."

"We've known each other for thirty years. And we've done it before."

"Okay, well, sure. But there was quite a gap in there. And like you said, we were just kids when we did it that first time. Entirely different people."

"Well, clearly my body is entirely different, since you now find it so repulsive."

"Leslie, your body is perfectly fine. It's not that…" It was exceedingly awkward to discuss her body while it remained on full display in front of him. Given the specific situation, one would

141

think the first thing Leslie would want to do is cover up and hide the source of this bodily shame, but she continued to sit there with everything hanging out, as if she was oblivious to her own present state of undress. It also didn't make the scene any less awkward that Johnny Horton's "The Battle of New Orleans" was playing on the radio in the background.

"It's your wife, isn't it? I just so happens I try to seduce the only faithful human man on earth. Oh I'm a fool. Such a fool." She buried her face in her hands and began to sob.

The situation was as surreal as anything else that had happened in the house since he'd arrived. He momentarily entertained the thought once again that Leslie might not even be real, that she might be an echo, but that sense of being just off the surface of the physical universe he'd felt with the other visions wasn't present here. Leslie was decidedly real. And decidedly naked and crying on the couch.

With as much trepidation as he'd ascended the stairs last night to face the source of the voices, he went to the couch and sat next to her. He put a hand on her shoulder. Her skin was soft. Smooth. He may have been judgmental of the optics of her flesh, but it was pleasing to the touch. "Leslie, I haven't been completely honest with you. I'm not married. Well, technically I guess I am, but we're separated. It's part of the reason I came here."

Leslie pulled her face out of her hands and looked at him, a little shocked and disgusted herself. "Is that what you say to make me feel better? That you're not even married and you *still* don't want to sleep with me?"

"No. Leslie, it's... There've been a lot of things in my life recently that... Let's just say I haven't been happy for a while. I came here to get away from my life. For a distraction."

"I see. And the last thing anybody would want to do to distract themselves is have sex. It's okay, James. I get it. It's one of the many short-ended sticks we women are handed in this world. Our bodies don't hold up as well as men's. Look at you. You probably have the same body you had when you were twenty-five. It doesn't work that way with us. Between gravity and babies they really do a number on us."

There was little Leslie could have done about the former, but it was James's understanding she hadn't had any children.

"I know what you're thinking. Just because I don't have any kids doesn't mean I've never been pregnant. I have. Three times. Made it into the late stages each time. Once even carried the poor thing to term. Nothing to show for it except a ravaged body, a divorce, and a broken heart."

"Jesus, Leslie, I'm so sorry. I didn't know."

"Well, it's not the kind of thing you advertise."

He put his arm all the way around her and rubbed her bare shoulder. Her nakedness, while still a distraction, was becoming less so. Her disregard of it was infectious. If she felt no indignity at the fact that she was stark raving nude—she herself fully aware her body wasn't likely to be featured in the underwear section of the Montgomery Ward catalogue—why should James be uncomfortable? And besides, the intimacy of her sharing her three failed pregnancies took priority over the fact that he could see her nipples.

On the radio, the Diamonds were singing "Little Darlin'."

"I never got a chance to know any of them. Never got to see any of them grow up, even for a day. But that doesn't make you love them any less."

"I lost one too," said James.

"No."

"Yes. My daughter. Recently."

"Oh my God. No."

"On her twelfth birthday."

"No. Oh James, how horrible!"

Now it was James's turn to put his face in his hands and sob, and Leslie's turn to comfort him.

He hadn't talked about Kelly's death, even to Linda. He acknowledged it of course, he accepted people's well-intentioned but insultingly useless condolences, but he hadn't talked about it. He did so now. He told Leslie how she was killed right down the street from their home, wearing the new roller skates he'd given her that very morning as a birthday gift. He told her that while it was happening, he was in the arms of a mistress—though he left out the fact that she was his undergrad student. He told her how he'd chosen perhaps the most inappropriate time imaginable to tell his wife about the affair, and in the retelling realized for the first time that perhaps his subconscious had done that on purpose. Telling Linda about the affair—having the affair at all—might have been clues he wasn't totally happy in his marriage and wanted out.

And Leslie told James about her pregnancies. About miscarrying twice in the third trimester before finally giving birth—"Third time's a charm they say"—to a bundle of joy who lived for forty-five minutes outside the womb. Leslie never even got to hold her. She told James how after each one, her body, mind, and marriage deteriorated a little more. She told him how after the third one she and Mr. Kilgore slept in separate rooms and never touched each other intimately again. He started sleeping with his secretary—"What a dull cliché. Can you even believe it?"—and barely even tried to hide it.

All the while Betty on the Beach spun the music of their childhoods: Elvis, Sinatra, doo-wop. All the while Leslie Kilgore nee Pettigrew had all her bits exposed. She got up to refill her wine a couple times, even used the bathroom once, where her garments were still strewn on the floor, and never put on a stitch of clothing. After a while it started to feel completely natural. There was something about the easiness of Leslie that made the fact that she was sitting around naked feel totally commonplace. In fact, the more he got used to it, the more James started to like it. She wasn't ever going to be mistaken for one of Charlie's Angels, but suddenly that very unconventionality made her more appealing. The more time she spent prancing around in the buff in front of him, the more the manufactured notions of what he'd always taken for granted as "female hotness" began to shed. Leslie Kilgore nee Pettigrew was sexy.

At some point they were kissing. Without segue, neither having made the first move, it just sort of happened. Soon he was as naked as she was—hands re-explored bodies they hadn't touched in twenty-five years. He led her to the big bedroom, but she pulled him to the smaller one he used to sleep in as a child, where they'd first done what they were about to do. She winked at him and said, "For old time's sake." The Everly Brothers singing "All I Have To Do is Dream" was the soundtrack to their reenactment of their steamy teenage affair.

They giggled like teenagers at the fact that he barely lasted longer than his four-thrust performance in 1957, Leslie saying, "The data collected on you so far isn't promising. Joking. Joking." He excused it by pointing out he hadn't released in several weeks. The chain of thought that emerged from that revelation led him to remember that the last time he'd had sex was in his office the day Kelly died—perhaps at the very moment, for all he knew.

He couldn't let himself think like that. Kelly was dead. It happened. It wasn't going to unhappen. And whatever he'd been doing at the time wasn't going to unhappen either. Dwelling on it wouldn't change it. He needed to start compartmentalizing the different emotions associated with the tragedy and putting them in their proper places. The sorrow could stay, but the guilt needed to go.

It took less than ten minutes for James to be charged up and ready to perform again. The Maguire Sisters were singing "Sugartime." He lasted through numbers by Frankie Avalon, Boyd Bennet and his Rockets, Elvis Presley, Doris Day, and tomorrow's weather report from Betty on the Beach.

When it was finally over, Leslie's data now averaged out in his favor.

He wasn't scared anymore. Well, yes, he was scared of the *fact* of the echoes and what it might mean for his mental state, but he wasn't scared of the echoes themselves. He believed them to be harmless. In fact, all evidence would suggest they didn't exist corporeally, at least not in this world. He could see and hear them, but they couldn't see and hear him. They posed no physical threat. At least that's how he, with his limited knowledge of the phenomenon, interpreted things.

So when he awoke in the middle of the night to the voices—it was now becoming routine—he was not frightened. In fact, he was curious.

Leslie was beside him in bed, the two of them squeezed together on the little twin in the small bedroom, being too exhausted to move to the larger bed in the other bedroom after their back-to-back sessions. He shook her softly. "Leslie… Hey. Leslie."

She stirred. "Mm."

"Leslie. Wake up for a second." He felt a little bad waking her, but he couldn't pass up this opportunity to have another set of ears confirm or deny the actual existence of the voices.

"What's wrong?" Sleepily. Less than half awake.

"Do you hear anything?"

"Mm."

"Leslie." He gently shook her again. "Listen. Do you hear anything?"

"Like what?"

"Just tell me what you hear."

The whimpering of the child and the intermittent mumblings of the woman were muffled but unmistakable. It wouldn't take high-tech surveillance equipment to pick them out; anyone with reasonably functioning ears would hear them.

"The ocean. The wind. Mr. Ouelette's American flag rippling."

"That's it? Nothing else?"

"James, what's going on? Are you okay?"

"Yes. Fine. Go back to sleep."

And she did. Gladly and immediately.

He wasn't particularly surprised, but it was now clear that whatever was happening, whatever an echo was, it was only present for him. Well, him and Edgar Monahan. And "other people like them," whatever that meant.

Out of bed, through the main room, up the stairs. The whimpering. The mumbling. The occasional "Hold still." Just like the previous two nights. Up the stairs. As he approached the point where his line of sight passed from the main room's ceiling to the leisure room's floor, his nerves heated up.

The whimpering.

"You've got to hold still."

One step. He could now see just above the floor line. The woman's feet in front of the spiderweb window, silhouetted in front of the night sky, her upper body blocked from view by the underside of the table.

Another step. Then another.

"Hold still, dammit."

Another step. He was nearly at the top and could see the full woman now, standing at the head of the table, leaned slightly over, doing something that once again reminded James of Bill Reardon carving the Sunday dinner ham. Only it wasn't a ham on the table and she wasn't carving. From what he could tell by the limited light supplied through the window, it was the whimpering child on the table, arms and legs extended like a starfish. It thrashed around but had limited mobility, James deducing that he or she was somehow secured to the table.

"We have to let the demons out!"

James knew what this was. He and Linda had gone to see *The Exorcist* several years ago when it had gripped the nation. Linda wanted to sleep with the lights on for weeks afterwards, but James thought it was ridiculous. Not only had he secretly renounced his Catholic upbringing nearly two decades ago (though he still went through many of the motions to keep his heresy from his family), but the film defied logic. Okay, sure, maybe the demon could make the girl levitate, he could suspend his disbelief enough to accept that, but if her head spun around 360 degrees her neck would snap and her head would loll forward like a ball on a string. And where did all that vomit come from? That much liquid wouldn't fit in her entire body let alone her digestive system.

But silly movie nonsense aside, what James was seeing play out before him in darkness was an exorcism.

"Hey," he said to the visions. He didn't expect a response nor did he get one.

He took a step closer.

Then another.

His typewriter, stack of papers, ashtray, and other items were still on the table, undisturbed by what was happening, like the two scenes were playing out in the same space but in separate dimensions. The typewriter was where the child's head was, but James wasn't seeing them both at the same time, as if one were superimposed over the other. It was more like he was looking at two photos, one of the writing table, one of the exorcism, and they paradoxically existed in the same space and time while simultaneously being completely separate of each other. It defied physics and rationality. Were he to try to explain it—and he probably should, to a shrink—he would not have been able to.

"You've got to hold still."

James was only a few feet away from the woman now. He was scared. Terrified, actually. But that fear, like the visions, also seemed to exist on a separate plane of reality. In the same way the woman and child were both there and yet not there, so was his fear.

The woman was fiddling under the child's chin—tying something there perhaps? James, with his adjusting eyes, now saw the child was a little girl, based on her a long dress and curly locks. Judging from the muffled nature of her cries, he also deduced she was gagged in some way, though it was too dark to make that out visually. She thrashed as much as her restraints would allow.

James reached out his hand—fascinated, the way a small child might reach for the television screen the first time they see one, thinking there are actually tiny people and sets inside the box.

"Stop it!"

Startled, James pulled his hand back, but the woman, in whatever alternate space she existed in, be it within or without James's mind, was completely unaware of him.

He reached for her again. He had to know. Would his hand connect with solid matter? Would it go right through her? Would he somehow simultaneously feel her and not feel her, the way his other senses perceived the visions as being both there and not there at the same time?

Closer. Inches. Centimeters.

At the moment of contact she disappeared. Not only did she disappear, but *everything* disappeared. Not just everything associated with the vision—the echo—but literally everything.

He was floating in the white space again.

"There you are." Leslie's voice, from nowhere and everywhere all at once. "What the heck are you doing up here on the floor."

The real world faded back in. He was in the leisure room. On the floor. It was daylight.

How the hell had that happened? Not even two seconds ago it had been the middle of the night. He'd reached out to touch the echo woman. He'd been in the white place barely long enough to register where he was, and now it was morning?

"Are you sick or something?"

He turned his head. Leslie was crouched over him, still bare-ass naked, her sagging breasts dangling inches from his face. He considered the question. He didn't feel sick. Not physically anyway. Mentally, that was a whole other story.

"No." He sat up. "I'm okay."

"Then what are you doing up here?"

"I… I was feeling inspired in the night and came up to write," he lied. "I guess I, uh, fell asleep."

"There's a perfectly good couch over there."

"I must have passed out while I was working and slid out of the chair."

"The chair's on the other side of the table."

"I don't know what to tell you, Leslie."

"Artists are strange people." This coming from a woman who'd been shamelessly parading around wearing nothing but earrings and pubic hair for the last twelve or so hours.

"I don't deny it," he said.

"So this is the great artist's work, huh?" Leslie had stood up and was running her thumb up the corner of the stacked pages of James's manuscript, flipping through the sheets of paper like a deck of cards.

"So far." Ah, his manuscript. His fingers began to itch for the keyboard.

"Can I read it?"

"You want to read it?" He picked up his soft-pack of Pall Malls from the table, shook one into his mouth, and lit it.

"I just asked if I could, didn't I?"

The typewriter was pulling him toward it—or perhaps it was the muse pushing him. He walked over and sat down in front of it as absentmindedly as he'd just taken and lit the Pall Mall.

"So?" said Leslie.

James began to type. He didn't even need to reread the last few sentences he'd written the day before to refresh his memory, he just jumped right in.

"Hello?"

"Hm?" James had entirely disappeared, swallowed by his work. Cigarette dangled from his lips, fingers clacked at the keys, eyes stared not quite at but through the paper.

"I asked if I could read what you've got so far?"

"Mm."

Leslie took this ambiguous grunt as a yes. She picked up the manuscript. James didn't object. Didn't even notice.

"Well, I guess I'll be heading back next door."

Nothing. *Clackity-clackity-clackity-clackity...*

"I really enjoyed last night."

Clackity-clackity-clackity-clackity...

"I'm going to put a lit sparkler in my bum and run around the room pretending I'm a rocket."

Clackity-clackity-clackity-clackity-DING! James tore the sheet out of the Smith Carolla and cranked in another in one fluid motion. *Clackity-clackity-clackity...*

"Artists are strange people." She snatched the new sheet of paper from the table, added it to the pile, and descended the stairs, finally reapplying her clothing and leaving the cottage, calling out a "Goodbye" up the stairs before departing.

James didn't notice. He was possessed.

It was the crying of the little girl that finally snapped him out of his writing trance, which judging by the pile of prose-filled papers next to him had lasted several hours. These writing sessions from the last couple days had been transportive, out-of-body experiences. The world around him ceased to exist, as did time. When he came to he had only vague memories of having been in the chair, hammering the keys like a concert pianist, cranking cigarette after cigarette. It was like waking from an intense afternoon nap. Or returning from the white place.

The crying was different this time. It wasn't the desperate, muffled whimpers of a gagged child struggling for its soul, it was more commonplace this time. Just a run of the mill child crying.

He scanned the room. He was alone. No child. Was the crying coming from downstairs? No, it was closer than that. She was in the room. But where?

The crawl space.

He was filled with a sense of new intrigue. For the past three nights he'd seen or heard some version of the little girl strapped to the table while the woman prepared to perform what James now believed to be some demon exorcising ritual. But this was new. The plot had thickened—or at least gone in a new direction.

He stood up and went to the wall. He crouched by the cabinet door and put his ear up to it. The was no mistaking this is where the crying was coming from. There was also no mistaking it was an echo. He was becoming quite good at discerning them now, recognizing the shifted reality of their sights and sounds.

He opened the cabinet door. Slowly. While he'd developed an intellectual curiosity for what was happening, there was also a part of him under the surface that was rightfully terrified. Visions of swinging open that cabinet door and a fully possessed, demon-faced little girl ala the *The Exorcist* bursting out of the crawl space and sinking her fanged teeth into his cheek passed through his mind. But there was nothing on the other side of the door but darkness and dust.

He poked his head into the door, a little at a time, exposing more and more of the crawl space as he did so. The crying was far more distinct in here. If there'd been even a fraction of doubt this is where it had been coming from, that doubt was now entirely removed.

While certainly dark, James was at the end of the crawl space by the spider web window, which let in enough light to just barely see. About ten feet down the triangular hall, James saw her. She was leaned against the wall, hugging her knees to her chest, rocking back and forth, trying unsuccessfully to stifle her cries. She was the same size as the child on the table, same curly locks. No doubt the same girl. But in this light, James recognized her as more than just the shadowy, struggling child strapped to the table. He recognized the red hair. The beige dress.

"Elizabeth," he said.

Elizabeth didn't respond. Because echoes never do.

But wait a minute... He'd spoken to her twice before. If he could see the echoes but the echoes couldn't see him, and Elizabeth was an echo, why had he been able to talk to her on the beach? Furthermore, while there was definitely an otherworldly quality to the Elizabeth he'd met, he hadn't felt the sense of removal from reality with her the way he was feeling now.

"Elizabeth!" As if saying it louder might permeate the divide between worlds. It didn't.

A shaft of light spread against the sloped wall at the far end of the crawl space on the other side of Elizabeth. The door on the opposite side of the room had opened. A woman, no doubt the woman from the previous visions, poked her head in. In the dim light, James could see she too had fair skin and red hair, just like Elizabeth.

"Elizabeth! Come out of there." The woman crawled through the door.

Elizabeth, terrified, scampered onto all fours and speed-crawled, sobbing, panting, toward James.

James, remembering how touching the echo last night had sent him to the white place, jerked his head out of the crawl space and rolled away from the door, lest Elizabeth should come exploding out and crawl through him.

But that didn't happen. No Elizabeth. No Elizabeth's mother — who James fairly confidently assumed the woman to be. All was quiet. He leaned back over and peaked in the doorway. Nothing. He poked his head back and looked down the shaft. Darkness and dust. The door at the other end was closed again. Nobody. Nothing.

James leaned against the wall. Was it time? Had he had enough? Should he finally heed Edgar Monahan's warning and get out of the Seagull's Nest? What he was experiencing was well beyond normal, he knew that, and yet he seemed to be leaning in to it as opposed to running from it, like any rational thinking human would do.

He got up, went to the table, and lit a cigarette. He looked down at his manuscript output for the day so far. That was the reason to stay. The manuscript. It was this room that was responsible for his prolific output, he was almost certain of it. When he was anywhere else he barely even thought about it— hell, last night at dinner, when Leslie had asked him about it, he could only remember vague generalities about what he'd written so far. But up here in the leisure room it was all encompassing. The typewriter was an extension of his body, the words came out of him as naturally as if he were singing "Jingle Bells" or "Happy Birthday to You." Even now he found himself sitting down at the Smith Carolla without thinking about it, the way he often found himself autopiloting a cigarette in his mouth and lighting it without consciously deciding to do so.

He set his fingers on the keys. Outside, he could hear the clacking of the Rock'n'Roll Dance Party, a sound not entirely unlike a typewriter itself. Out of the corner of his eye he saw her, down on the beach, through the spiderweb window. Elizabeth. Same beige dress. Hands cupped behind ears, listening to the rocks.

As recently as yesterday he might have questioned the improbability of this. She was just in the crawl space, how could she possibly now be down on the beach? But probability was not a factor when it came to the echoes.

But was Elizabeth an echo? What he'd just seen in the crawl space certainly had been, but the Elizabeth on the beach, both when he'd spoken to her before and looking at her now, did not have that echo quality he was becoming increasingly better at discerning.

Down the stairs, through the main room. He opened the sliding glass door to the patio, and it took that wave of November cold hitting him to realize he was still dressed only in his Jockey shorts. He'd thrown them on last night when he'd gotten up to investigate the leisure room and hadn't been back downstairs since. He went to the small bedroom and quickly threw on yesterday's clothes that had been discarded there, half-expecting Elizabeth to be gone when he reemerged. But she was still there.

Out the door, across the patio, down the stairs to the beach.

"We meet again," he said to the girl.

She turned around. "Seems we do."

"I really wish you'd put more clothes on. It's terribly cold out here."

"It wouldn't change anything."

She definitely wasn't an echo—or if she was she lacked the defining qualities of the other echoes he'd experienced—but there was still something off about her. Not being cold in forty-degree weather while wearing just a light dress ranked low on the list of this girl's oddities. Higher up was the fact that she'd just appeared out of nowhere in his crawl space then disappeared just as quickly and reappeared on the beach.

"Where do you live, Elizabeth? I assume you're staying somewhere on the beach?"

"I'm not really sure."

"You're not sure where you live?"

"I don't remember things as well as I used to."

"But surely you must go somewhere when you leave here."

"Surely I must."

"And you don't know where that is? Where did you come from just now?"

"I just come out to listen to the rocks."

"Yes, but from where? Where were you before you came here."

"I don't know."

She was very matter of fact in her answers. Not defiant. Not irritated. Not upset in any way, as if having no idea where you came from or where you'll end up was the most natural thing in the world.

"Do you remember when we first met?"

"No. I do remember you, but not when we first met."

"It was only a couple days ago."

"I don't know what that means anymore."

"You don't know what what means anymore?"

"You should really listen to the rocks, mister. Everything's okay when the rocks are singing."

"Sure." He stood next to her and cupped his hands behind his ears like her, gathering up the sound of the Rock'n'roll Dance Party and guiding it directly into his ears.

Personalitywise, Elizabeth was nothing like Kelly (which says little, because personalitywise Elizabeth was nothing like any human James had ever met), but physically she reminded him of his daughter, if only in the fact that they were both girls of about the same age. But Kelly was always forthcoming with

159

information—too much so, James felt at times. The kid would ramble on and on about the most trivial aspects of her life as if they were as dire as the Iran hostage crisis. He'd taken that openness for granted—was even annoyed by it at times. What he wouldn't give just for one more minute of Kelly's enthusiastic ramblings.

Elizabeth, on the other hand, was not exactly a fountain of information. One needed dental tools to get anything out of this kid. But James was determined to try, partly because he was deeply intrigued, but another part of him, on some level, was surrogating. There was nothing at all he could do for Kelly, but maybe if he could help Elizabeth…

"The day we met," his hands were still cupped around his ears, "I told you I lived in that house behind us. You said you didn't like that house. Do you remember that?"

"I don't like that house. It's a bad house."

"Why do you say that?"

"It just is."

"Did something happen to you there?"

"I don't want to talk about that."

"But something did happen there?"

"I said I don't want to talk about that."

"Okay. You're right. We won't."

So something definitely did happen to her there, not that James was surprised; he'd watched it happen three nights in a row. Her mother strapped her to a table, crying and struggling, and performed an exorcism on her.

"I wish you'd talk to me, Elizabeth. I'm worried about you, standing out here every day in the cold in just this little dress. And the same one every day, too. Don't you have any more clothes?"

"I think so. I did once."

"And where are they now?"

"Where everything else is, I guess. Gone."

"See, I don't know what that means, Elizabeth. To talk to you, it's like you don't own anything, don't live anywhere, and don't remember anything. But surely you must eat and sleep somewhere. Somebody must take care of you. Your mother, maybe?"

Elizabeth spun her head toward him, uncupping her hands from her ears. The look of remove on her face was replaced by one of stone seriousness. "Don't mention mother."

"Did she hurt you? Is she still hurting you?"

"Stop." From behind her red locks, blood trickled down her forehead into her brow, just like it had the other day.

"You're bleeding again."

Elizabeth touched the blood and checked her finger to confirm James's statement. "Oh no," she said, and just like the first time, she broke into a sprint south down the beach. "Elizabeth! Wait!" James took off after her, but it was instantly futile. The girl was much faster than him, and her lungs hadn't sustained the damage of the hundreds of thousands of Pall Malls James had inhaled since he was a young teen. He was winded before he'd run ten yards. He stopped and watched her become smaller and smaller, her beige dress and pale skin blending with sand till he could no longer discern her from her surroundings.

In a vacuum, it had been a remarkably strange interaction, but in the context of the last handful of days it barely registered on the oddity scale. The abnormal—perhaps even the paranormal—was the normal now.

He arrived back at the Seagull's Nest just as Leslie was dropping by, fresh aerobics outfit on, yellow with horizontal black stripes, making her look like a bumblebee. She carried the stack of papers James barely remembered telling her she could read.

"I read it," she said.

Of all James had seen and heard in the last few days, this might have been the most frightening. His manuscript, his opus, his baby—somebody else had read it. Somebody else had thoughts about it. To an artist, the muse is the most powerful force, but at a close second is the critic—capable of building or destroying universes with a single thumb depending on whether it was pointing up or down.

They went inside. James had become so accustomed to Leslie's naked body prancing around the cottage he half-expected her to shed her leotard upon entering, but alas she remained covered. She made coffee. They sat at the yellow Formica table. Elvis sang "(Just Let Me Be) Your Teddy Bear" on Cool 89.9.

"I'm not entirely sure I understand it," said Leslie.

"Oh." This was not starting off promising. Then again, Leslie was a devout devourer of Stephen King novels, which had to be taken into account when considering her literary opinions.

"Well, the DJ storyline. It's okay and all. Young girl working at the college radio station. Being taken advantage of by that awful professor."

"I don't know if I saw it as her being taken advantage of. She's just as willing as he is."

"That shouldn't matter. He's twice her age and in a position of power."

"She's an old soul, and he's got a young spirit."

"She's a kid and he's a pervert."

"She's twenty-years-old."

"I'm not saying there's anything illegal going on, I'm just saying it's icky."

Icky. Now there was a solid piece of literary criticism. Not even his lowest performing student would ever use the adjective icky in an essay, and if they did he'd stop reading immediately and give them an F. "Rochester was twenty years older than Jane Eyre, and that's considered one of the greatest love stories ever written."

"I don't know what else to tell you, James. The writing was good. I liked the world of a college campus in the days after the Kennedy assassination. I like the Susie character. I just thought the professor was a bit of a creep."

"Hm." Cleary she was projecting her own life into the pages. She was having a hard time separating James's perfectly acceptable fictional affair from the fact that Mr. Kilgore had left her for his much younger secretary.

"But that aside, I'm not sure what the other storyline has to do with anything. I'm sure you're going to bring them together somehow, but right now it feels like two entirely different books."

Other storyline? There was no other storyline. There were other characters and digressions, but it all orbited around Susie. "You mean about the roommate who joins the John Birch Society?"

"No. The whole other storyline. About the mother and daughter. Although I'm honored you chose to set it here at the cottage."

Huh? There was no mother and daughter in the novel, and certainly no scenes set at the cottage.

"Like I said, it's like two different books."

And it was indeed two different books: one James remembered writing and one he didn't.

It took a little while to get rid of Leslie, but once he did he devoured the pages of his manuscript, both the stack Leslie had read and his output from that morning.

The DJ story was as he remembered. Susie O'Brien, a good Catholic girl from a conservative family whose biggest problem in the world is when the ice cream float at Woolworth's soda fountain is so thick she can't get it through the straw. Then she sees President Kennedy's head get blown apart and at the same time so does her naivete.

She takes a work study cataloguing record albums at the campus radio station where she's introduced to the likes of Phil

Ochs, Joan Baez, and Bob Dylan, and suddenly her Leslie Gore and Beach Boys 45s seem a little trite. Her supervisor at the radio station, the handsome music professor Mitch Saxon, takes a shine to her, and she in turn takes a shine to him.

One day in mid-December, while the students were clearing out for winter break, the station found itself in a last-minute bind to fill the 5pm to 8pm slot on Sunday night. Susie, who just happened to be there at the time, volunteered; she'd been around the station enough at this point to know the lay of the land enough to step in. Saxon, who hadn't yet gotten her dress off but really hoped to do so someday, allowed it against his better professional judgement, female DJs still being an extreme rarity in 1963.

Susie was a natural. Smooth, informed, funny. The phone lines blew up. Who was this remarkable DJ and when and how could they hear more of her? After the show, Saxon asked her if she'd like to be promoted from cataloguer to full-time Sunday night disc jockey. She accepted and rewarded him for the opportunity with a session of closed-mouth kisses, breast fondling, and even a bit of petting over the underpants on the ratty sofa in the backroom of the radio station.

That was all he'd written of that storyline so far. As far as his memory was concerned, it was all he'd written period. He was shocked to find that, intercut with Susie's story, was another story—a story he didn't remember writing, but at the same time felt closely familiar, like rewatching a movie he'd seen as a kid.

It concerned an eleven-year-old girl named Alice and her mother, who was only ever referred to in the text as Mother. They were on the run from something or someone, moving around the state of Maine, staying in cheap boarding houses, motels, or winter rentals, never for very long, Mother bouncing around to different waitressing jobs.

The story opens with the duo renting a single room in the home of a widow in Lewiston. Mother arrives for the late-shift at the diner where she works and is informed by a fellow waitress that a man had been there earlier looking for her. Mother asks the waitress to describe him, which she does. Mother is horrified. Without a word of explanation she sets her apron on the counter and leaves the diner, never to return. She hurries back to the widow's house, looking over her shoulder every step of the way. She collects her daughter, packs in a hurry, abandoning all non-essentials, and they're gone.

Flash forward an untold number of weeks or months. They are living in a beachfront winter rental that's described exactly like the Seagull's Nest, right down to the crawl space in the leisure room. We learn that Alice suffers from crippling migraines and tinnitus. Mother, rather than taking her to a doctor, insists she needs to "fight them. Don't let the demons take over like they did your father."

Alice doesn't know how to fight them. How does one fight a headache and ringing in the ears? No matter how many Rosaries she says—Mother's suggested remedy—she gets no release. The demons remain.

The only thing that helps is at high tide, the push and pull of the ocean drags a field of smooth beach-rocks over itself, creating a pleasing cacophony of clicks and clacks that's soothing to the ears, especially when she cups her hands behind them, creating a makeshift, miniature auditorium for each ear. She calls this phenomenon the singing rocks.

And, as she's fond of saying, everything is okay when the rocks are singing.

"I'm looking for this address." James handed the torn out phonebook page to the gas station attendant.

The man looked at the circled entry. "Edgar Monahan?" There was no "R" anywhere in the vicinity of his pronunciation of Edgar.

"You know him?"

"Ayuh, everybody round here knows Ed. What you need to see Ed for? Or is it Ingrid? You going out there to see Ing?"

James didn't feel it was any of this business, and even if it was, Ben (according to the name patch on his navy-blue jumper) would never have believed him. "Just need to talk to them. That's all."

"Massachusetts."

"I'm sorry?"

"I seen your plates when you pulled in." He pronounced "pulled" as "pult."

"Okay."

"Just saying." What exactly he was just saying was entirely unclear; his tone was neutral.

"So, the address."

"Ayuh."

"You know where it is?"

"Ayuh."

"Could you direct me there?"

"You family or something? Ed don't do any talking, and Ing don't like to if she can avoid it. Used to. I went to school with Ing, you know. Lively gal. Pretty too." He pronounced it "purdy." "We used to go together a little bit. Nothing serious. Burgers and milkshakes, that kind of thing. Dances. She was quite a dancer. Knew all the new moves before anyone else. She was something back then. But after what happened to Ed… Now she's something else. Gave up her whole life to take care of Ed." The pump handle snapped off, indicating the tank was full. Ben replaced the nozzle in its holster at the pump and returned to James's window. "Seven oh six."

James handed Ben a ten and six sticky pennies he fished out of a small compartment in the arm rest on the door.

"You tell Ing Ben Nosek says hello, will ya?"

"I'd be happy to, but I need to know how to get there."

Ben finally gave him the directions along with his three dollars change. "Ask her if she remembers the footprints in the jello. She'll know what you're talking about."

"Footprints in the jello. Got it. Thank you."

He doubted he'd get the chance to ask about this seeming non sequitur, he thought as he pulled back out onto route 7. She'd been pretty clear on the phone she had no interest in speaking to him. It had been a brief conversation:

"Hello. I'm looking for Ingrid Monahan."

"Speaking."

"This is James Riordan. We met on the beach yesterday. Your brother wanted you to—"

"There is nothing I or my brother can do for you, Mr. Riordan. Do not call this number again."

Click.

But this had gone beyond mere visions—echoes. His sanity was on the line. The fact that he'd written about ten thousand words that he—even after rereading them—had no recollection whatsoever of writing had frazzled him in ways the visions had not. The visions were sensory. External. But the writing was one-hundred percent internal. Having the mother and daughter hijack his brain as opposed to just his eyes and ears was far more invasive. He needed answers. Edgar Monahan had them.

And besides, Ingrid told him never to call again, she'd said nothing about stopping by.

Ravenwood Lane was on the west end of town, the farthest possible point from the ocean within the town limit of Sewall. It was a completely different world out here, the oceanfront mansions and salty cottages replaced by rundown homes with rusted out cars on the lawns. The pine trees were so thick they interfered with the signal from Cool 89.9, the occasional puff of static interrupting Jerry Lee Lewis and the whole lotta shakin' he had going on.

James would have known the Monahan home even if it didn't have the house number posted on the mailbox. He started to feel a trace of the sickness the moment he turned down Ravenwood Lane, which continued to get stronger until he reached a white,

169

paint-chipped ranch house. Edgar was in there. He knew it just as certainly as Edgar had known James was in the Seagull's Nest when he'd walked past on the beach the day before. And that being the case, Edgar surely had to know James was here now.

No sooner had James stepped out of the car, Ingrid stepped out of the house. She wore overall jeans and a thick green sweater. Her hair was ratty. James had a difficult time imagining her doing the Freddie or the Shake at the Sewall High dance with Ben Nosek.

"I told you to leave us alone."

"Ms. Monahan, please. I'm desperate here. And your brother can help me."

"No he can't. Please go."

"He knows things. He knows what's happening to me. Please. The visions—the echoes. I just want an explanation. I'm afraid I'm losing my mind."

"And how do you think Edgar feels, Mr. Riordan? He's in poor health as it is. Every time he talks to one of you he feels the sickness. I don't know what causes it, and neither does he, which is one of the many reasons you need to stay away from him. It's an untested poison that gets activated whenever he's near one of you."

"What does that mean? One of you. What are we?"

"I keep telling you, Mr. Riordan, but you refuse to listen: I don't know. And neither does my brother. No matter how many of you he talks to, he never gets closer to the answer. Something dark is at work, and I'd prefer Edgar lean away from it, not into it."

"You prefer, but what does Edgar want?"

"He wants the same."

"I don't believe that. He wants to help. That's why he sent you to talk to me."

"Mr. Riordan, we live a simple life here, but a happy one, all things considered. There are no echoes here. But every now and then we venture out and he experiences one, or he comes across somebody like you, and the obsession starts. He becomes consumed with whatever it is that's happening to him. Our simple but happy life is interrupted by this… thing. We have talked to doctors, priests, spiritualists, so called experts in psychic phenomena. We have talked to a small handful of others like you. And I keep telling you, Mr. Riordan, though you refuse to believe it, we have learned nothing. The echoes persist, and we are no closer to understanding them than we were ten years ago when they started."

"Which is exactly why we need each other, Ms. Monahan. Edgar and I. We are alone in this. Even if just to commiserate, even if we don't get any answers, just to be able to share our experiences, to compare notes. It could be cathartic."

"And yet, whenever two of you are near each other you feel a crippling sickness, as if whatever devil afflicted you doesn't want you to commiserate."

"It isn't crippling. Just unpleasant." James was feeling the sickness quite strongly. Not as strong as when he was face to covered face with Edgar in the grocery story, but stronger than when Edgar was a distance away on the beach, proximity definitely playing a role in the severity of the feeling. But like he said, it wasn't crippling, just unpleasant. In fact, the more he felt it, the more he noticed that, like everything else having to do with this affliction, the sickness felt a little disconnected from reality, like an amputee who feels "phantom pain" where their severed limb used to be.

"But unhealthy just the same," said Ingrid.

"Please. Ten minutes. Let me talk to him for ten minutes. We're alone in this, Ms. Monahan. Just like you're alone."

"I'm not alone. I have Edgar."

"You take care of Edgar. It's a duty."

"I assure you, we are perfectly happy. Most of the time."

"I'm sure that's true. But it can't be easy. Nobody knows what you go through. Nobody knows what you gave up."

"I haven't given up anything. My brother needs me. That's all there is to it."

"I talked to a man named Ben Nosek today."

"Hmph. A gas station attendant. So what?" Her words were dismissive, but there was a glint of fondness in her eye, the first hint of warmth James had seen in this woman since he'd met her.

"Nothing particular. He just said he knew you. That he used to take you to dances. He wanted me to say hello to you. He told me to ask if you remember the footprints in the jello."

Her mouth twitched, as if it wanted to smile but hadn't in so long in was molded in place, like a bowed piece of lumber.

"Look, Ms. Monahan. We're all alone in our own ways. It may not be any of my business, but I don't expect this is what you wanted your life to be. It's noble and admirable, but I don't believe the beautiful girl who used to go out for burgers and milkshakes with Ben Nosek thought this is what she'd be doing in 1980. Just like I never thought I'd be haunted by echoes. If I could just talk to your brother, even for ten minutes, just to know I'm not completely alone here, there's somebody else who understands."

"How do you know when an elephant's been in your refrigerator?"

"I'm sorry?"

"It's a joke. How do you know when an elephant's been in your refrigerator?"

"I don't know."

"Because of the footprints in the jello."

"I don't get it."

"It's absurd. That's what makes it funny. Certainly there would be more demonstrative evidence of an elephant having been in your refrigerator than footprints in jello. Not only that, an elephant's foot wouldn't even fit in a dish of jello."

"Oh. Not really my sense of humor I guess."

"They were popular with kids in the sixties, elephant jokes. Perhaps a little after your time. There were dozens of them, all equally absurd. Ben Nosek had a whole catalogue of them in his head. He could rattle them off for days. I don't know what it was about the footprints in the jello one, but when he told it to me I laughed so hard that chocolate milkshake shot out my nose."

James could see it, a younger, softer version of Ingrid—no, *Ing* Monahan—sitting shot gun in Ben Nosek's father's Chrysler at the drive-in, laughing at silly jokes, no idea that in a couple years her older brother would have his face literally blown off in southeast Asia, and she'd become his caretaker, never to laugh at another elephant joke again. "Sounds like you had a lot of fun in those days."

"You can't go back to the time before the echoes, Mr. Riordan. Edgar has been trying for a decade. He's learned to live with them, but you can't go back. Do you understand?"

"No. I take your word for it, but I understand almost nothing about this."

"Yeah, I expect you don't. Come in, Mr. Riordan. You can have your damned ten minutes."

They sat across from each other at a round table in an immaculately clean kitchen, James on one side, the Monahans on the other, Edgar with the usual white drapery over his missing face. The sickness, if he focused on it, was almost unbearable, but there was also the layer of reality in which he felt no sickness at all, and he was becoming increasingly better at separating the two spaces and living in the preferred one.

"Your time is short, Mr. Riordan. If you have questions you'd best start asking them."

"Well, I guess the most obvious place to start is by asking what they are, the echoes. At least as he understands them."

Ingrid signed into her brother's hand. Ingrid translated as Edgar signed back to her.

"As I've told you several times, he doesn't know. What he believes is that they are echoes of the past. He thinks past events, if powerful enough, can leave something of a stain on the fabric of reality that only people like yourselves can see. But it's always tragedy. He's never seen the echo of the birth of a child or an individual winning the lottery. Usually it's death."

"Are they dangerous?"

"He says no, just upsetting."

"And there's no way to stop them?"

"I've already answered that repeatedly, Mr. Riordan."

"I'd like to hear it from him if I may."

Ingrid signed into his hand. "He has learned to cope with them, he says. There are no echoes in this house, and he doesn't get out much. When he encounters one in the wild he's often able to ignore it, or at the very least keep it quiet. Sometimes, he'll encounter a particularly brutal and violent echo that catches him off guard, and those are quite upsetting, but in general he coexists with them. But no, as I've said, there is no way to stop them. Not that he's found."

"Has he spoken to a professional?"

"A professional what?"

"Well, I don't know. A doctor. A psychiatrist."

"My brother is not sick or crazy."

"No, that's not what I'm suggesting."

"Then what are you suggesting?"

"Just… I don't know. This thing is happening, and it's happened to others. I just figured, maybe, I don't know, medical science might be able to explain it if given the opportunity."

"Medical science would commit you to a psychiatric ward— and just imagine how many terrible echoes exist in a place like that. And supposing you did find a doctor or scientist who was willing to believe you—do you wish to spend the rest of your life as a lab rat? Poked, prodded, studied?"

"But maybe they could cure it."

"Go that route if you choose, Mr. Riordan, just be sure to leave my brother out of it. If anyone in a lab coat shows up asking questions we will claim my brother has never witnessed any such visions and we'll unequivocally deny ever having met you."

"Okay. I see your point. Does he know why it's happening to us? Me, him, the others—do we have anything in common?"

Brother and sister exchanged signs. "You've recently had a medical incident."

"I have."

"you were dead for a length of time, then brought back."

"That's right."

"And you visited the white place, as he calls it?"

"I did." James wasn't as astonished by this display of psychic ability as one might expect, having already figured on his death, resurrection, and visit to the white place as being very much related to his affliction.

"It's always the same story. He believes it has something to do with the white place. When he had his accident in Vietnam he was declared dead for several seconds, a time during which he spent in this white place. The doctors brought him back, and that's when the echoes started. Others like you describe the same phenomenon. A white place. My brother thinks it's some sort of virus one occasionally picks up on the other side, like catching malaria in South America."

"I touched one last night. An echo. And it sent me back to the white place. I thought I was there for a matter of seconds, but when I came to it was hours later."

Ingrid relayed this to Edgar. "He says he's done the same. Only once, years and years ago, and never ventured to try it again."

On the one hand, James felt elated. While the prospect of living with the echoes was not one that filled him with joy, it was comforting to know he wasn't alone, that others were having the same experience. He wasn't crazy. Still, he didn't feel like he was learning anything he hadn't already figured out—or at least assumed—on his own. None of what Edgar was telling him was much of a revelation.

James pulled his Pall Malls out of his breast pocket. "Mind if I smoke?"

"No." She stood up and retrieved an ashtray from a kitchen drawer. "But when your cigarette is done it's time to go. Edgar downplays the sickness, but I don't trust it. I don't think it's safe for two people like yourselves to spend too much time near each other."

James had almost forgotten the sickness. It was becoming increasingly easier to compartmentalize the layers of reality caused by the White Place Virus. "What can he tell me about my cottage?"

Ingrid signed, Edgar signed back. They went back and forth several times, their signs brief but increasing in aggression with each exchange, like they were arguing.

"Is everything okay?" asked James.

"He smells your cigarette."

"Oh. I can put it out if it's bothering him."

"It's not that. He wants one." Brother and sister went back and forth a couple more times before Ingrid finally said out loud, despite the fact that he couldn't hear her: "Fine. Go ahead and kill yourself. See if I care." She looked at James. "Would you mind?"

James slid her the pack of Pall Malls. She shook one out, put it in her mouth, lit it, took an experienced drag herself, then handed it to Edgar.

Edgar took the bottom of the veil covering his face and lifted it, laying it over his head, exposing the grotesquery beneath.

He signed into his sister's palm.

"He's asking me if you're horrified. Are you horrified, Mr. Riordan?"

Where Edgar's face should have been was a featureless crater of tumorous grooves and bulges. His forehead was mostly intact, but beneath that was a mass of scarred, stitched-together flesh with no discernible shape or logic—smooth in parts, lumpy in others, ranging in different shades of pink, like a raw pork shoulder. There was nothing to indicate where his eyes should have been. He had two long, asymmetrical, teardrop shaped nostrils near the spot where they would be on a non-deformed human face, but no nose to speak of. His mouth, is it were, was a lipless slit on what one would call his left cheek, about an inch and a half long, into which he stuck the cigarette. A slurpy rasp came from his throat as he inhaled. His neck bulged as if he were swallowing the smoke. He exhaled out one nostril with a sinusy wheeze.

"Tell him I'm very sorry for his accident." It would be rude to convey the truth—that the side of raw ham that was Edgar Monahan's face indeed horrified him, but it felt almost more rude—insultingly placating—to say it didn't.

"To answer your question, he doesn't know anything about your cottage."

"But yesterday—you told me he said I needed to leave there. That is wasn't good for me."

"All he knows is the house echoes. He's never been close enough to witness what the echoes are actually saying. Over the years my brother has developed the ability to sense them from far away, that way he can avoid them by not getting too close."

"It's a little girl. I think her mother may have—"

"Tut!" She put up a stifling palm. "My brother doesn't need to know the details. He has visions of past horrors of his own, he doesn't need to take on yours."

"Okay, but, I'm a writer. A novelist. And I've been working on a novel while I'm staying at the cottage. It's about the failed promise of the hippie dream."

"Sounds riveting."

"Well, the thing about it is, I've been going into trances when I write. Today, I reread what I'd written so far and, while a lot of it is the story I set out to write, there are whole chunks I don't even remember writing involving a mother and a daughter—the same I've been seeing around the house. Has Edgar ever had anything like that happen to him?"

"My brother is not a writer, Mr. Riordan."

"Just the same, could you ask him?"

Ingrid relayed the information into Edgar's palm. He put the cigarette into his lipless mouth slit while he signed back to her. Neck-bulge, slurpy-rasp inhale. Sinus-wheeze exhale out one elongated nostril. James had conflicting urges to shield his eyes and intensely study the grotesquery between Edgar's neck and forehead—stitched together grafts of skin from Edgar's own arms, thighs, buttocks, like patches of a macabre quilt sown together by Satan's grandma.

"Again, he's not a writer, so he wouldn't know, but he does say he often dreams about the lives of his echoes beyond what he sees in the visions. And sometimes those dreams occur while he's wide awake. You have time for one more question, Mr. Riordan, then I'm going to insist you leave my brother in peace."

James felt like he had a million more questions, but at the same time, he was hard-pressed to come up with one. As bizarre and otherworldly as this affliction was, it was also kind of straight forward: something bad happens, it leaves a mark—an echo—that only folks with the White Place Virus can see/hear/feel. Most of his questions at this point had to do with the hows and whys of it all, but Edgar was as in the dark about that as James was.

"Okay. The little girl in my visions. Something bad happened to her."

"I told you, Mr. Riordan, we don't need to hear about the specifics of your visions."

"No. It's not about that. It's just, I've been seeing the same girl on the beach. Not as an echo—I can tell the difference now—as a real girl. I talk to her. She's actually there."

"And what exactly is your question?"

"Well... I guess... how is this possible?"

179

Ingrid signed, Edgar responded.

"My brother has already answered this, Mr. Riordan. The visions are echoes of tragedy—usually death, but not always. Whatever terrible ordeal this little girl went through—and please, again, do not tell me, I do not want to know—she survived it. The girl you see in your visions is an echo, the girl you see on the beach is real."

"I think she's still in trouble. I think the abuse is still—"

"Mr. Riordan, please. In how many ways must I tell you I don't want to know. There is tragedy everywhere. Just look at my brother's face if you need convincing. At this very moment, countless people are suffering, starving, in pain, dying. It's the way of the world. The fact of it is bad enough, but having to actually witness it—the terror of knowing every time you turn a corner you might stumble into a photo-realistic vision of somebody else's past tragedy… I'm sorry this is your life now, Mr. Riordan, and I'm sorry for whatever is happening to that girl. If you'd like to make helping her your crusade then God be with you, but our plate is full of our own tragedies here, and I thank you for not heaping your own onto it. Now I think we've been more than generous with our time, Mr. Riordan."

Edgar slurped the last drag of his cigarette, stubbed the butt in the ashtray, and pulled the veil back down. The conversation was over.

He found himself desperate to help Elizabeth. If he took his visions for fact, both the physical echoes and his psychic novelization, it seemed as though mother and daughter are bouncing around from place to place, on the run from someone. Elizabeth—or Alice as he'd renamed her in the novel—suffers from extreme migraines and tinnitus. Mother, due to deep religiosity and probably some mental illness, is denying the poor girl the medical care she desperately needs, believing her ailments to be not a medical condition, but the work of demonic possession. Mother's home remedy is to strap the girl to a table and attempt her own amateur exorcisms. They are currently living somewhere on Sewall's Beach, where Elizabeth slips out every day at high tide to listen to the rocks sing, the only thing that gives her any respite from the pain in her head and the ringing in her ears.

He didn't know where to begin. The girl herself wasn't exactly forthcoming with information. He could go knocking on the door of every beach house looking for them, but even if he found them, what then? If he were to call social services, what would he say? *I believe this woman is abusing her daughter. – How do you know that, sir? – Well, I picked up the white place virus in the afterlife and now I can see echoes of past tragedies layered just above the surface of reality.*

And why was he so desperate to help her in the first place? He wasn't a heartless monster, but he wasn't exactly a crusader in the fight to help those who can't help themselves either. He did possess sympathy and empathy, but he also tended to mind his own business. Perhaps it was the intimacy—the fact that Elizabeth was occupying space in his mind, his eyes, his ears. She was a part of him. Her story was inside him. He'd literally written it.

But the more likely answer was Kelly. Elizabeth reminded him of Kelly. Kelly who died wearing the roller skates he'd bought her for her birthday. Who died while he was in his office sleeping with his student—a fact that continued to fill him with guilt. It wasn't so much the adultery or the age difference, but the nagging feeling, irrational as it was, that his activities somehow caused Kelly's death, like if he'd just gone home when he was supposed to the accident never would have happened. This was ridiculous of course. Kelly would have been out roller skating around the pond whether James was sleeping with a student, sitting in traffic, or playing Twister with the Pope—but tragedy has a dulling effect on rationality, and James continued to blame himself with as much conviction as if he'd been behind the wheel of the Saab that ended her life.

But if he could save Elizabeth…

It wouldn't bring Kelly back, he was still rational enough to understand that, but perhaps some of the goodwill from rescuing one adolescent girl would counterbalance some of the guilt he felt about the death of another.

Next time he saw her he'd be sure to get more answers out of her. But if her patterns were to continue, that wouldn't be until high tide the next day.

Of course, there was another way to learn more: he could write it.

As soon as he returned to the Seagull's Nest he went straight upstairs to the leisure room, sat down at the Smith Carolla, and waited for the spirit muse to take over.

And waited.

And waited.

His fingers didn't move, didn't type a single letter.

When this had worked in his past sessions it had been automatic. He'd sat down at the typewriter, started to write his radio DJ story, and at a certain point he fell into a trance and wrote the mother daughter story. But it wasn't working this time. He was trying to force it. He needed to forget about mother and daughter and write the DJ story. Then, when he was distracted, the spirit muse would sneak in.

When he'd last left Susie, she'd just been offered a permanent slot at the radio station and celebrated by necking with her supervisor. He knew he wanted to make a temporal jump here to the end of her senior year. It's May of '66. *Rubber Soul* and *Highway 61 Revisited* are all the rage. The underground press is emerging. Hippies are cropping up. Folks are burning their draft cards. Grass is becoming commonplace. Susie is the hottest thing in college radio, but it's the day before graduation; tomorrow she'll be moving back to the small town in Ohio where she comes from, having to say goodbye to the radio station and Professor Mitch, both of which she is madly in love with. It's the night of her final show.

Great set-up. Now type.

I said type, dammit!

That morning his fingers moved so quickly sparks were coming off the typebars. Now, nothing. Not a word. Not even a *the* to get him started. Blank paper.

It was because he'd read the manuscript. It worked when he was unaware it was happening, now that he knew about it—now that he was trying—he could no longer access that magic. It was like needing to give a sample at the doctor's office but being unable to go because you're thinking about it too much.

Okay. No big deal. Don't try to force it. Walk away. Do something else. Read a book. Go for a walk. At a certain point he was sure he'd suddenly snap out of a trance with twenty-five freshly typed pages next to him with no recollection of even having sat down at the typewriter.

He tried to read Dickens but he couldn't focus. All he could think about was Elizabeth. He put down *Bleak House* and went for a walk, but the weather had become unpleasant, dipping below forty degrees with a light rain and ocean winds whipping that cold rain around such that it felt sharp when it hit your skin. He returned to the cottage and sat at the typewriter again, but the result was the same: frustratingly blank paper.

So back to Dickens he went, no less distracted on his second attempt than he'd been on the first. However, this time around an idea struck him. Something about the labyrinthine trails of paperwork tying up the fictional Jarndyce v. Jarndyce at the novel's core inserted a small epiphany into his mind. Echoes being location specific, the attempted exorcisms he'd been seeing must have happened at the Seagull's Nest. That wasn't a new thought; he'd always assumed as much. He'd never gotten a great look at the girl strapped to the table, the room being dark every time he'd witnessed the echo, but he did get a good look at her in the crawlspace earlier, and she didn't look significantly younger than her alive counterpart he'd been talking to on the beach, meaning she and her mother had stayed at the cottage not too long ago. Judging from the meager means they lived by in his novelized recounting of their lives, he doubted they'd rented the place during vacation season, but they could likely have afforded the winter rental price. And if they were renters, they would have filled out the same paperwork Leslie had made James fill out a few days prior when he'd rented the place.

If nothing else, it was a place to start.

It was past dark now and bitterly cold. James walked across the property, holding up the cuff of his jacket to shield his face from the tiny chips of ice swirling in the brutal winds. He knocked on the door of the big house. He'd been up there only once before, on a rainy day during their vacation week when he was twelve or so. Leslie had invited him and Connie in to play boardgames: Jotto, Perquackey, Yahtzee, et al. He'd been amazed by how modern everything had seemed at the time, like something out of one of the stories he read in the *Galaxy Science Fiction Digest*. They even had their very own television set, the first one James had ever seen in the wild outside of Macy's department store.

Leslie answered the door in a royal purple aerobics leotard with matching leggings. "You're early," she said.

Had they made plans? James didn't recall.

"Come on in."

James stepped into the warmth. The place was nothing like he remembered it, except that it still felt new and modern—almost futuristic—every appliance, piece of furniture, artwork, accessory having been updated, probably several times, in the last quarter century. The television had the largest screen he'd ever seen, measuring a whopping twenty-seven inches.

"Who do you think did it? The smart money's on Sue Ellen, since her prints were on the gun and all. But I think that would be too obvious. I still think it was Dusty and they just did the whole fingerprint thing to throw us off the scent."

"I think I've missed something here, Leslie. I haven't the slightest idea who any of these people are."

"*Dallas*! We find out who shot J.R. tonight."

"Ah. Yes. Of course." One would have to be living under a rock—no, correction: *even if one were living under a rock*, it would have been impossible not to be aware of this phenomenon. The entire country was stumblingly inebriated with anticipation to find out who shot J.R. James, not a consumer of narrative television, had no idea who J.R. was, but even he knew somebody had shot him. But where James strayed from the rest of American society was he didn't give a baby rat's ass who done it. "Actually, that's not why I'm here."

"Oh?"

"I was hoping you might have some information. About some previous tenants of Seagull's Nest."

"James, I can't give you information on previous tenants. That's confidential."

"Oh. Right." Of course. He was surprised that hadn't occurred to him. "It's just, I think there might be a child in trouble."

"How so?"

"Well…" Man, he really hadn't thought this though. What was he supposed to tell her here? That he could see echoes of the past?

"See, there's this girl I've seen a few times on the beach and... well, I think her mother is abusing her."

"Oh, how awful. What makes you say so?"

"I don't know. Not for sure. But, well, she has a head injury. And she's evasive. And she always wears the same dress, with no coat or shoes. It's just... I have a daughter—*had* a daughter her age and... well, I just know something isn't right."

"And they stayed at the cottage?"

"I believe so. A mother and daughter. Maybe last winter."

"I didn't rent the place last winter. No takers."

"Hm. Winter before?" With the rate at which kids grew and changed at Elizabeth's age, it seemed unlikely the echo of her he'd seen in the crawl space was a two-years-younger version of the present one he knew from the beach, but not entirely impossible.

"No. That was a young couple, fresh out of college."

"Hm. Oh. Well, over the summer perhaps." Again, it didn't seem likely the mother from his novel would be able to afford the in-season price of a beachfront cottage, but he was grasping at straws.

"You're sure it was just a mother and daughter? No father? Siblings?"

"No. Just the two of them."

"I think the girl might be putting you on, James. At least about staying at the cottage. I don't remember every single person who's ever rented the place, but I don't remember any mother/daughter pair. That would have stuck out to me. It's always families or couples. Or single men who pretend to be novelists just so they can sleep with the landlady. Joking. Joking. But seriously, James, I'd have remembered just a mother and daughter."

It was possible he was wrong. Just because he'd only seen echoes of a mother and daughter didn't mean there weren't other family members around. But the novel. In the novel it was just mother and daughter. But who's to say that was accurate. There was a possibility his novelized account of Elizabeth/Alice's story was conjured solely from his own imagination, using pieces of information he'd gleaned from the echoes, then filling in a purely fictional backstory. Did he believe that? Not really. He was tuned in to the echoes in ways that couldn't be explained, like an extra sense beyond the understood five, and that sense told him he'd written the truth—he wasn't writing fiction, he was writing memory, though not his own.

"I suppose I could be wrong about some of the details. Like I said, she's evasive and vague. She's a curly red-haired girl. Pale-skinned. Freckles. Name's Elizabeth. Does that ring any bells for you?"

"Not particularly, no. Tell you what, have a seat, I'll be right back."

She left him alone in the living room. He took a seat on the L-shaped sectional sofa. There was a half-eaten mixing bowl of popcorn and a can of Hire's root beer with a straw poking out the hole on the coffee table. Next to the snack items was a *TV Guide* featuring a middle-aged, smiling, white-cowboy-hat-wearing gentlemen who James assumed to be the famous J.R. based on the cover caption: "How I Kept J.R. Alive" by Larry Hagman. On the TV itself was *The Dukes of Hazzard,* a program James was only aware of because his daughter often fought Linda to stay up past her bedtime to watch it. They would sometimes get into screaming matches over it. It seemed so trivial now. What difference would it have made to let the kid stay up an extra hour? It could have been one more hour each week she got to experience this life.

James heard Leslie re-enter the living room. He turned around, half-expecting to find her bare-ass nude, and a little disappointed to find she wasn't. She carried a plastic milk crate full of manilla folders, which she set on the coffee table. "Okay, this is everybody who's rented the place since my dad started renting it out thirty years ago."

Each folder had a tab with the year written on it. The more recent folders were crisp and fresh, gradually getting more faded and frayed as they went back in time. His eye fell on the weathered tabs of the earliest folders, containing the documentation of the residents who'd stayed in the Seagull's Nest in the early to mid-fifties. His family was in there. He felt a nostalgic pang to see it, though he couldn't explain why—it wasn't like looking at an old photo, it was probably just a form with his father's name on it. But still.

Leslie pulled out 1980. "I'm not going to give you any personal information, mind you. That's illegal. But I can't see the harm in finding out if they at least stayed here." She opened the folder and flipped through pink and yellow carbon copies of rental agreements. "No… no… Oh, the Burlingtons. Nightmare. Loud. Messy. Never again. They were from New York City." She said the location with disdain, the way a televangelist might say Hell. She continued flipping through the file. On the TV, an orange Dodge Charge did a donut on a dirt road while fast, finger-picking bluegrass played on the soundtrack. "No… Nope… No… No… That's all of them, James."

"Can you check nineteen-seventy-nine?"

She put 1980 away and pulled out 1979. "No… no… no… Wait a minute. Here we go. Walter and Marlene Littlefield. Three kids: Connor, Wayne, and Elizabeth."

Okay. Promising. It wasn't out of the question the Elizabeth he'd seen in the cottage could be an echo from the previous summer. It was less than a year-and-a-half ago. And besides, it had been relatively dark when he'd seen her in the crawlspace. He hadn't gotten that clear of a look at her. It was certainly possible she was a year-and-a-half younger than present day Elizabeth from the beach. But where were Walter, Connor, and Wayne Littlefield while Marlene was upstairs performing an exorcism on Elizabeth?

"Oh. No. Couldn't be them."

"No? Why?"

"I remember the Littlefields now. You said your Elizabeth was pale-skinned with freckles, right? The Littlefields were a white couple who adopted three black kids. Elizabeth Littlefield was no redhead—and she certainly wasn't pale-skinned."

"Is there any single mother situation in there at all? Perhaps they changed their names."

"Don't see how that's possible, unless these were some real grifters with all the fake identity bells and whistles. You need to show your driver's license."

True. Leslie had taken down James's license number when she filled out this very paperwork for him. The mother in his novel—if he was still going by that version, which he was increasingly beginning to doubt the reliability of—was a desperate woman of little means who likely wouldn't have the feintest idea how to go about procuring a false identity complete with fake driver's license.

"You want me to flip through seventy-eight? We've still got another ten minutes before *Dallas*."

"Might as well." But he was losing hope. His theories were dissolving. And why should he have trusted them anyway. He was seeing visions of the past for Christ's sake. There were forces at work here he couldn't possibly understand. Hell, Edgar Monahan had been dealing with it for over a decade and barely understood it more than James, who'd only been afflicted for a matter of days.

Leslie flipped through the file. "No… No… No kids… Ooh, the Philbricks. Nice people. No… No… That's all of them. Should I check seventy-seven?"

She went ahead and checked 1977 and 1976 after that. Finally James stopped her. Elizabeth would have been barely older than a toddler in the mid-70s, and the echo he'd seen of her was an adolescent. Could he have been wrong about the girl in the crawl space being Elizabeth? No. The likeness was too great. A sister perhaps? Maybe the girl from the echoes was Elizabeth's older sister, and the events he was having visions of did indeed take place earlier in the decade. Possible.

His head was starting to hurt. He couldn't think about it anymore. Elizabeth—the echoes. He needed a break. Hell, even sticking around to find out who shot J.R. would be better than spending one more second thinking about this.

"I'm sorry we didn't find your girl, James."

"It's okay. I must have made a mistake." And really, even if Leslie had found a file of a mother with a daughter named Elizabeth, what would he have done? What would have been the next steps? Leslie wasn't going to give him any private information. Plus, it was extremely unlikely there'd be any usable information in the file anyway. If mom and daughter were on the run, certainly they wouldn't leave a forwarding address—at least not a real one.

Which raised the question: since they were supposedly bouncing around from place to place to avoid being found, if they'd stayed at the Seagull's Nest, why would they move to a new place right down the beach? Shouldn't they be in East Timbuktu?

Stop! Stop thinking about it! He was going to drive himself crazy.

Ha. Drive himself crazy. Hard to do when you're already batshit fucking nuts. He'd entered the town limit of crazy back in the hospital when he'd seen Nurse Oona—who hadn't worked there in ten years—hurry out of the room across from him with blood all over her uniform.

"Those go back to when you first starting renting the place, do they?" asked James.

"Back to the late-forties."

"So my family would be in there."

"I assume. My father kept meticulous records and taught me to do the same."

"Could I see?"

"Sure. Mid-fifties, yes?"

"Yeah. Final year was '57, cause the Ford plant closed in '58 and we couldn't afford it anymore. I don't remember the first year we came. Five or six years before that I'd guess."

Leslie pulled out a random file from that time period. Nineteen-fifty-two. She flipped through the files. "Ah. Lookie here. I guess there's no confidentiality breech if I show you this one, since your name's on it." She handed him the form.

James read the information, written in neat handwriting he assumed belonged to Mr. Pettigrew. Renters: William and Angela Riordan. Children: Constance (11) and James (10). Permanent address: 2349 Medford st, Somerville, MA 02145. Rent received: $40. His father's familiar, highly eligible scribble of a signature at the bottom. There was nothing new or interesting on the page—

save for the fact that once upon a time a family of four could rent a beach cottage in July for $40 per week—but he still felt as if Leslie had just unearthed a reel of 8mm home video of his family. He'd been flooded with memories and nostalgia since returning to Sewall's Beach a few days prior, but there was something about holding this tactile sheet of paper in his hand. Memories are abstract. Distant. Disconnected to the present. But this sheet of paper…

"Oh! Well, isn't this interesting," said Leslie. She had another form from the 1952 file in her hand. "My father did a winter rental that year. A single mother and her daughter. Mother, Juliet Marner. Daughter, Elizabeth. How's that for a coincidence?"

For the first night since his arrival, he didn't experience the echoes. It wasn't that the echoes were silent, it's that he didn't sleep in the cottage where the echoes lived. He'd stayed with Leslie, disinterestedly watching *Dallas*—along with every single other human from Maine to Hawaii—having absolutely no reaction when it was revealed that sister-in-law Kristin Shepherd had pulled the trigger. Leslie, however, was particularly charged up after the show, and she released that energy by tearing off her leotard and straddling James. He was inside her before the final credits finished rolling.

He spent the night in her luxurious king-sized bed, making love a couple more times in between her incoherent rantings—or possibly ravings, he wasn't exactly sure what her take was about the J.R. saga, just that she had one, and it was enthusiastic. James didn't care about anything she was saying, but he didn't mind listening to it. In fact, he liked it. It kept his mind off his own problems. It reminded him there was a world out there where people's biggest concern was who tried to murder a fictional oil baron. It was stupid, but comforting, taking him back to his childhood days, watching adventure serials before the double feature at the Nickelodeon, having to wait all week to return for the conclusion to find out if the hero was able to pull himself up from the cliff he was hanging from by his fingernails. A time before dead daughters. A time before echoes.

She finally settled down around 2 a.m., according to the glowing blue numbers on the digital clock radio on her side of the bed. Her ramblings about the Ewing family slowly petered out, ultimately being replaced by rhythmic inhales and exhales just a couple degrees south of a snore. They weren't cuddling, but their bodies were touching, he on his back, she on her side facing away from him, back pressing against his side, her cushy buttocks against his hip. He liked the way her doughy body enveloped his, welcoming him, like resting one's head on a fluffed pillow. He'd been judgmental of her body at first (if he were to be honest with himself, he was judgmental of all women's bodies) but it had really grown on him. He found himself musing on how arbitrary it seemed that society had chosen the Marilyn Monroe type figure as the benchmark against which to measure attractiveness. Was that preference inherent, or had he and everyone else fallen for a sales tactic? He wasn't sure. Either way, he liked Leslie's body, and he liked that Leslie was comfortable in it. That adjective summed up everything about her: comfortable.

James was not falling in love with Leslie, nor did he think she was falling in love with him. They were simply two single adults who got along well enough, were living in close proximity, and had decided to fulfill each other's physical needs. Everything was easy and natural with Leslie—comfortable—and this element of the relationship was no different. When he left—whether he made it to the end of his hiatus or if the echoes chased him away tomorrow—they'd embrace, tell each other it was great to reconnect after all these years, and likely never see each other again. And that would be okay. And should they ever bump into each other on a random sidewalk in the future, they'd be perfectly happy to see each other—no awkwardness.

"James?"

He was slightly startled; he thought she'd fallen asleep. "Yeah?"

"I just thought of something. The girl. Elizabeth."

Elizabeth. While he hadn't fully vanquished her from his thoughts, the last few hours had been full of enough distractions to keep her in the distance. "What about her?"

"Not your girl from the beach—the one from the fifties, who stayed at the cottage."

He'd been trying not think about that. If one accepts the reality of echoes, it's perfectly plausible that the mother and daughter James had been seeing in the leisure room was an echo of something that happened in 1952. But if that were the case, how then would one explain the very real Elizabeth he'd been seeing on the beach in 1980?

"What about her?"

"I actually remember her. Just came to me as I was falling asleep. I was eleven, and she was about the same age. I remember being excited when they moved in, thinking I'd have somebody right next door to play with. But the mother wouldn't let her play with me. Said she was sickly or something. She wasn't very friendly, the mom. And the girl, Elizabeth, I hardly ever saw her at all. Eventually it came to be like there wasn't anybody living over there at all, at least as far as eleven-year-old me was concerned. That's probably why I forgot about them till now. But here's the thing: she was just like you described. Fair-skin, curly red hair. Weird, right? Maybe your Elizabeth is the daughter of that Elizabeth or something."

"Hm. Maybe." James's brain was so scrambled by all this he didn't even know where to put this information or what to do with it even if he found a spot for it.

"I remember something else though. You know how at high tide the waves push the rocks around and it makes that clacking sound?"

James certainly did. And he knew exactly where this was going as well.

"Well, sometimes the girl, Elizabeth, she'd stand out there on the beach, just above the reach of the surf, and put her hands around her ears and listen to the rocks. She'd stand there like a statue the whole time it was happening. Once the tide went back out far enough it wasn't moving the rocks around anymore, she'd go back inside. I went out there once and asked her what she was doing—this was early on, back before her mother told me to stay away from her. She said something weird, like she was listening to the rocks make music or something."

"Everything's okay when the rocks are singing."

"Yes! James, that was exactly it. Everything's okay when the rocks are singing. How did you know that?"

"Because your Elizabeth and my Elizabeth are the same Elizabeth."

"That's obviously not possible."

"I would have thought so too a few days ago, but the rules of what is and isn't possible have blurred for me since then."

"James, what the hell is going on here?"

He told her. Everything.

Not surprisingly, being the easy and agreeable person she was, she believed him.

In the morning, Leslie called her father, who'd moved to a retirement community in Florida five years prior. His short term memory was lacking, but his long term memory was solid. He remembered Juliet and Elizabeth Marner. He hadn't liked the idea of renting to a single woman—and Leslie's mother was most certainly against it as well—but off-season renters were tough to come by, and it was already late-September when Juliet had answered his ad in the classifieds. It was either take a chance on this woman or likely have to shut the place up for the winter and lose the income. So he took a chance. Juliet ended up screwing him over. She was two months behind on the rent when she and Elizabeth up and left in the middle of January. The emergency contact number she'd left was a fake, connecting to a Chinese restaurant in Augusta.

"If you find her," said Walter Pettigrew, "tell the tramp she owes me two-hundred-and-fifty bucks. Plus interest."

After the phone call, James and Leslie sat drinking coffee in what she aptly called the sun room, which jutted off the ocean-facing side of the house, three of its walls comprised almost entirely of windows looking out over the beach. While Leslie was on the phone with her father, James had hopped next door to grab his manuscript. They now combed through the mother and Alice sections, looking for further clues—though the questions were so numerous and vague it was unlikely they'd be able to match them up with the answers should they find any. The whole situation was a snake eating its own tail in a mirror maze.

Adding to the problem was that James—or, more accurately, whatever force James's subconscious had tapped into—had fictionalized parts of the story. Changing Elizabeth's name to Alice, for example. His descriptions of the Seagull's Nest were to a tee, but the cottage in the story was called the Sand Castle and was located in York Beach, not Sewall's Beach. The Stardust Diner in Lewiston, where Mother worked before being chased away by whoever was stalking her, did not exist, at least according to the Lewiston Chamber of Commerce.

"The good news is you're a pretty good writer," said Leslie. "The bad news is that means you're really milking the flow of information, giving the reader the bare minimum to keep up the mystery and suspense. Great for a novel, not so great when you actually need information. You're sure if you go back and sit at the typewriter again you won't be able to keep going?"

"I could try again, but I really don't think so. It worked because I wasn't aware it was happening. If I think about it, I can't tap into it. And it's impossible not to think about it. It's like trying to look at shadow by shining a light on it."

"Well, I'm at a loss, James. I say we just get ahold of a phone book for every region of Maine and call every single Marner in there till we find them. Joking. Joking."

"Hold on. That's not a bad idea."

"No, it's a terrible idea. Not only would that take a month, but the long-distance charges would be up the wazoo."

"I'm not saying we literally call all of them. But Maine isn't that big. And Marner isn't as common as Jones or Smith. We could look for Juliet. Or Elizabeth. Or even just J or E. There can't be that many."

"It was twenty-seven years ago. And who's to say they even stayed in Maine?"

"All I'm saying is it's worth a shot. What else have we got right now?"

Leslie drove. Black 1980 Mazda 626. They listened to the *Coal Miner's Daughter* soundtrack on 8-track cassette. Leslie sang along—pretty well—to Beverly D'Angelo's version of Willie Nelson's "Crazy."

The library was a centuries-old stone building on Main Street, wedged between the historical preserved Old Gaol (jail) and the crumbling headstones of a colonial graveyard, containing the buried dust of bodies nobody in town had any connection to anymore. James had never been to this section of Sewall. The beach in the summertime was a zoo. The beach in the winter was a wasteland—at least the residential section he was staying in. But the center of town had a whole different vibe all together—the type of place Normal Rockwell could set down a canvas facing any which direction and get a perfectly-fitting addition to his oeuvre.

The library was small; square-foot wise you could fit at least twenty of them inside the main library at the university. But it suited the purpose of the research they were there for: on a low shelf in the reference section was every phone book for the state of Maine.

They sat at the large wooden table and went through them one at a time. James was right, Maine was a relatively small state population-wise, and Marner wasn't the most common last name. Within twenty minutes they'd perused every listed Marner in the state, listing possible matches on the back of receipts Leslie had in her purse.

"I got an H and E Marner in Saco," said Leslie, "but that probably isn't her. If the E stands for Elizabeth the H has got to stand for her husband, right? In which case Marner wouldn't have been her name when she was a kid. But I wrote it down anyway. I got an E Marner in Kittery. Two J Marners in Bangor and another in Portland. I got an A Marner up in Macchias, could stand for Alice, you never know."

James had a similar collection of E and J Marners from around the state. He also had an actual Elizabeth Marner, but similar to Leslie it was listed next to a Martin, likely her husband, which would mean the Marner name was given to her in adulthood. It was a disparate collection of loose possibilities spread all throughout Maine.

But there was one outlier.

"This is the one." James slid his list in front of Leslie, tapping his finger on a name in the middle.

"Isaac Marner? You never mentioned an Isaac."

"I know."

"So…"

"I don't even remember writing this down. It's like the trance I'd slip into when I was writing the novel, only in extreme microcosm. This is the one. I know this is the one." That indescribable extra sense he'd developed for all things pertaining to echoes was as sure of this truth as his eyes were sure of Leslie sitting in front of him. Isaac Marner knew something.

They used a payphone outside a Cumberland Farms a little ways down Main Street. James broke a dollar in the store and fed the change into the slot.

"Hullo?" said a gruff voice after three rings.

"Isaac Marner?"

"This is."

"I'm calling for Elizabeth Marner."

"You got the wrong number, kid."

"How about a Juliet Marner?"

There was a long pause—so long James thought the man had hung up.

"Hello?"

"Elizabeth and Juliet, you said?"

"That's right."

"Who is this?"

"My name's James Riordan. I'm trying to track down Elizabeth or Juliet Marner."

"How'd you get this number?"

"Phone book."

"How do you know Lizzy and Jules?"

James gave Leslie a thumbs up. Bingo. "They once stayed at a beach cottage my wife's family owns. Years ago."

Leslie looked at him quizzical and mouthed: *wife?* James responded with a shrug that communicated: *Hey, I'm winging it here.*

"How many years ago?"

"Quite a few. It was the early fifties."

"Ayuh."

"So, you know them."

"Ayuh. Did."

"But no more?"

"Ayuh."

"Did they... have they passed?"

"Couldn't tell ya. They cut out, oh, I guess about thirty years ago at this point."

"What was your relationship to them?"

"I'm sorry, who are you again?"

"Name's James Riordan."

"And why are you looking for Liz and Jules?"

"It's a private, financial matter."

"Well, you ain't getting a cent out of me. Juliet was no blood relation of mine. I guess that kid's got some of the Marner blood, but I got no legal ties to either of them."

"I assure you, Mr. Marner, nobody wants any money from you. I just want to find Elizabeth and Juliet."

"Well, good luck and God speed to you on that, kid. My brother looked for them for years after they took off. Never caught up to 'em."

"And your brother is?"

"Alistair Marner."

James took particular notice of the name Alistair. Not far from Alice. Could James have plucked that out of the ether when naming his fictional version of Elizabeth? Maybe. Probably. The names were too close to be a coincidence, and echoes didn't trade in coincidence. "And Alistair was Juliet's... husband?"

"Ayuh."

"So Juliet is your sister-in-law and Elizabeth is your niece."

"That's how it usually plays out when your brother marries a gal and has a kid with her, ayuh."

"And you're saying they ran away? Thirty or so years ago?"

"They disappeared. Maybe they ran away. Maybe they fell in a well. Maybe they got taken by space aliens. Couldn't rightly tell you. But if I was a betting man, ayuh, I'd put my money on them two running away."

"Could I trouble you for your brother's number?"

"You can trouble me all day but there ain't no number gonna reach him. Unless they have phones in Hell."

"I see."

"I'll be honest with you, kid, whatever they owe you, I'd kiss it goodbye at this point. They're long gone. But if you do find them, tell the girl to give her uncle Isaac a call. Jules I was never crazy about, didn't seem quite right in the head if you're asking me, but I liked the kid. Jeez, if she's alive she's gotta be, what, forty? Not much of a kid now, I guess. But you can go ahead and tell her to give me a call. Let her know her daddy's dead and gone and she don't have to worry about him no more."

"He mistreated her?"

"You with social services?"

"No. I just—sorry, that was none of my business."

"My brother was an asshole. I don't mind saying it. But I ain't the judge. He's dead now, and whatever sins he committed in his earthly life he's paying for now in the afterlife."

"Is there anything else you could tell me to help me find them? Juliet's extended family, anything like that."

"You don't think my brother tried all that back when the trail was still warm? Got him nowhere. And I wouldn't have the information anyway. He picked Jules up during the war in some naval port down in... I don't even know. Philadelphia maybe? Baltimore? I never met her family. Couldn't even tell you her maiden name. I got nothing for ya, kid. Honestly, I hadn't thought of them in so long that when you first asked for Elizabeth Marner it didn't even ring a bell. Now is there anything else I can do for you?"

"Just to be sure we're talking about the same Juliet and Elizabeth Marner—"

"How many could there be?"

"Still. Elizabeth. Curley red-haired girl. Pale skin. Freckles."

"Ayuh. That's Lizzy."

"Okay. Thank you for your time, Mr. Marner."

"Don't mention it. And like I said, if you do find them, longshot though it is, ask Lizzy to give uncle Isaac a call. She was a good kid. I hope everything worked out okay for her."

James strongly doubted everything worked out okay for Elizabeth. It was time to accept a glaring fact: If Elizabeth Marner was twelve years old in 1952, she obviously couldn't possibly be twelve years old in 1980.

Which meant the Elizabeth James had been seeing on the beach was her ghost.

Elizabeth was dead.

And in all likelihood her mother had killed her.

James still intended to call all the other names on their lists, knowing full well the unlikelihood Juliet and/or Elizabeth Marner, if even still alive, would have a listed phone number. They clearly didn't want to be found. But James had little else to go on. Making all those calls from a pay phone would have added up, so Leslie, who was quite enjoying the experience, saying it was like a supernatural episode of *Hart to Hart*, offered to let him make the calls from her home phone. "Don't worry about the charges," she'd said, "just consider it payment for services rendered. Joking. Joking. I will let you buy me lunch though."

James used the leftover change from his call to Isaac Marner to grab a *Portland Press Herald*. He wanted to be sure to be back at the Seagull's Nest before high tide, hoping to catch Elizabeth—or her ghost—listening to the singing rocks. According to the paper, he still had a couple hours, plenty of time to stop for lunch.

"Well, if it isn't Stephen King," said Helen, stepping up to James and Leslie in their booth at the Seabreeze Diner, little green notepad in one hand, pen in the other. "Against the Wind" by Bob Segar and the Silver Bullet Band played on the juke box.

It took James a second to remember who she was and why she was referring to him by that hack horror writer's name. The last time he'd been in here he'd just arrived in town and had a bit of small talk with the waitress about his plans to write a novel. That had been, what, three day ago? Jesus, it seemed like three decades. That had been just moments before he saw the falling body at the Lobster Lodge. Before Elizabeth and Juliet Marner. Before echoes.

"Hey, Les," continued Helen. "I see you've met the famous writer."

"I'm hardly famous," said James.

"He's renting the cottage," said Leslie.

"Isn't that nice," said Helen. "You gettin' the usual, Les? Chocolate milk and a doughnut?"

"It never gets old," said Leslie. Then to James: "Helen's worked here since the Lincoln administration."

"How dare you," said Helen, playfully. "But I do go back to Roosevelt. That's Frank, not Theo. I been waiting on Les ever since she was a little kid. Chocolate milk and a honey-dipped doughnut, every time. I don't think I ever saw you eat an egg till you were in your twenties." She looked at James. "How's the book coming?"

"It's been an interesting beginning," understated James.

"I've read it," said Leslie. "He can write."

"I hear that's prerequisite if you're trying to create a novel," said Helen. "Just cause you didn't end up taking my advice and staying at the Lobster Lodge—I'm still expecting a copy when you're done."

"Count on it."

James ordered coffee, Leslie root beer, cheeseburgers with shoestring fries for both. James lit a cigarette. Bob Segar ended, giving way to Anne Murray's "Daydream Believer." James told Leslie his most recent theory about what Elizabeth from the beach was.

"A ghost?" Leslie was incredulous.

"You don't believe in ghosts?"

"Of course I do. I'm just surprised that you do."

"I didn't until recently. But after what I've seen…"

"Still. The echoes, as you call them—I don't know, I can talk myself into those still being based in science in some way. There's all kinds of ways the past can leave things behind. A shadow on the wall where a painting used to be hung. Or looking up and seeing a star that burned out years and years ago. Or an actual echo, bouncing back a sound that's not being made anymore. Which I suppose is exactly why Edgar Monahan calls it that. I'm not saying most people would believe you if you tried to explain it to them, I'm just saying I can see a rational person convincing themselves something like that is rooted in some sort of scientific reality, even if they don't fully understand it. But ghosts—that's a whole other realm."

"I'm not a hundred percent on it. I'm not even a hundred percent any of this is happening at all. Seems just as likely that I'm lying in the hospital right now in a quaalude coma and this has all been a dream."

"Take my word for it, it isn't"

"Which is what Dream-Leslie would say."

"Touché."

"I just can't think of any other explanation for it. I'd considered maybe Beach Elizabeth is Echo Elizabeth's daughter—but it's more than just a familial likeness. The girl I saw in the crawl space was the spitting image of the girl on the beach. I mean, I suppose it's still possible they look identical, but she also had on the same exact dress."

"Could be a hand-me-down."

"Could. But then what about the singing rocks?"

"Could be a habit passed down from mother to daughter."

"Could. But do you think all that's likely?"

"Not at all. I think ghost. I'm just making conversation."

Helen dropped off their burgers. Michael Jackson crooned "Rock with You" on the jukebox.

"Imagine working the same job as long as she has?" asked James.

"I can't imagine working any job period," said Leslie. "These women's libbers want to burn their bras, put on pants, go to work—have at it. Me, I'll stay home and live on Mr. Kilgore's dime, thanks."

"She said since FDR, right? So that's, what... at least thirty-five years ago? And he was in office for three terms, so it could be a lot longer than that."

"Mr. Kilgore sends me a nice, fat check every month. Think how bitter he must feel as he fills those out. I can't stop smiling just thinking about it." She dragged a cluster of fries through a pool of ketchup on the side of her plate and put them in her mouth.

"Are there any other diners in town?"

"Nope."

"What about when you were a kid?"

"This town can't sustain more than one diner. Not year-round anyway. It's always been just the Seabreeze." She opened her mouth to chomp down on her burger but stopped. "Hey, wait a minute. I know what you're thinking. Smart. Real smart. But Juliet Marner only stayed at the cottage for a couple months. And that was almost thirty years ago. You know how many waitresses have probably come and gone since then?"

"Worth a shot."

James got Helen's attention with eye contact and a raised finger. She shuffled over. "How're the burgers?"

"Delightful," said James. "Random question for you."

"Shoot."

"I'm wondering if you might remember an old employee. Relative of mine. Might have worked here in the fall and winter of '52."

"Fifty-two! I couldn't even tell you who worked in '72. Not any of the transients anyway. We've had a handful of long-timers over the years I might be able to recall, but a few months in '52? Fat chance."

"Fair. Anyway, on the off chance: her name was Juliet Marner. I don't suppose that rings any bells."

"You could tell me her name is Ladybird Terwilliger and I wouldn't remem — Wait. Juliet?"

James and Leslie shot each other a hopeful glance. Did Helen actually remember? "That's right," said James. "Juliet Marner."

"Yeah. Yeah. I think that girl's name was Juliet. Could that have been '52?" She looked up and thought, as if there was a calculator on the ceiling to help her with the math. "Jeez, I guess so. You never feel quite so old as when you realize something that feels like it happened just a few years ago was actually twenty-eight years ago."

211

"But you remember her?"

"Yeah, strangely enough I do. I mean, if it's the same girl I'm thinking about. Pretty sure her name was Juliet. Only here a few months. And I don't remember the specific year, but early-50s sounds about right. She's your aunt you said?"

"Yeah." His family tree was really growing. In the past hour he'd claimed Leslie as his wife and now Juliet Marner as his aunt.

"How funny is that? Juliet. Yeah. Of all the people you should mention. Like I said, so many people have come and gone through here, I don't remember five percent of them. Even your aunt, all due respect, I'm sure she's a lovely lady, but I wouldn't remember her a bit if it wasn't for this one incident."

"You mind sharing?"

"Sure. Strangest thing. It all started with a missing apple corer."

James had forgotten all about the apple corer. With everything else he'd been seeing and hearing in the cottage, finding an apple corer on the floor, then subsequently losing it, hardly seemed notable.

"Louise, that was the owner's sister," said Helen, "she was the baker, from the time the place first opened—back in '33, which, believe it or not, was even before my time—till she died just a few years ago. We still use all her recipes. Her daughter took over and hasn't been off by a teaspoon of flour, not a once. Anyway, Louise was throwing an almighty fit one day cause she couldn't find her apple corer. She was trying to make the apple pies, see. She had all these apples peeled and needed to core them and get them into the pies before they started to brown. Without a corer, that was gonna be a challenge. Had the whole staff looking for that damn thing.

"Anyway, she eventually got all the apples cored with a paring knife, muttering curses under her breath about it the whole time. Never did find the corer. But then, later that afternoon, I'm out back in the office, end of my shift, counting my tips. Juliet's back there with me, counting her own tips. Nothing unusual. Just two waitresses counting their haul. But then Juliet takes off her apron and folds it up, but as she does so, something falls out of the pocket and clatters to the floor. It's Louise's apple corer!

"We both look down at it, then back up and lock eyes with each other for what seemed like ten minutes but probably wasn't more than a second or two. I imagine I just looked confused, meanwhile she's looking at me guilty as sin—a real hand-in-the-cookie-jar type moment. She reaches down, snatches it up, stuffs it in her purse, and she's out of there. Left in such a hurry she didn't even take her pile of tips with her.

"And that's it. She never came back. Never saw her again. All over an apple corer—at least that's why I assume she left. Seems like such a small thing, no? I mean, who's to say that corer hadn't just ended up in her apron by accident, right? Maybe she didn't even know it was there. She could have said that. I would have believed her. I'm sure everybody would have. Louise would have been irritated to the moon and back that she went through all that trouble with a paring knife while the corer was in Juliet's pocket all along, but she'd have gotten over it. I mean, it's an apple corer, for Pete's sake. Who'd want to steal an apple corer? If she got caught with a stack of twenties from the till that would be one thing, but an apple corer? Could have been an honest mistake.

"Of course—and with all due respect to your aunt—I'm not sure I believe that. That look she gave me when it fell out of her pocket… guilty. Her aim was to take that apple corer. I'm not judging, mind you. I'm not trying to say nothing from the old

Seabreeze has never ended up in my kitchen at home. It was just bizarre is all.

"I wished I'd had a chance to talk to her. To let her know I wouldn't have told anyone. She could have stuck around. If I remember right, I think she had a kid. Is that correct?"

"Yes," said James. "Elizabeth."

"Mm. And the husband wasn't around, I think. Korea maybe?"

"Yes. My uncle would have been in Korea at the time."

Leslie raised her brow and smirked at James, a look that conveyed: *Well, well, Mr. Pants on Fire, aren't you good at this!*

"Poor woman. It always seemed like she was having a rough go of it. Couldn't have been easy, husband overseas, trying to support herself and a kid. I always hoped she landed on her feet. Did she?"

"She did. My uncle came home from Korea after the war and they all moved down to North Carolina. I get down there to see them every few Christmases. They're doing great. Happily ever after."

Leslie had to look away while she stifled a laugh, highly amused at the speed with which James could prevaricate on the spot.

"Oh, I'm so happy to hear that."

"Next time I see her I'll be sure to ask her about the apple corer incident."

"Oh, please don't. It was so awkward. I'm sure she doesn't want to relive that." But if James ever did find Juliet Marner, he had every intention of asking her about the apple corer incident.

"I might be rewriting history," said James, as Sissy Spacek sang Loretta Lynn's "You Ain't Woman Enough (To Take My Man)" on the 8-track player, "but when I think back on it, that apple corer had an unreal quality. It was there, it was solid, I held it. But similar to how the echoes I see and hear are both there and not there at the same time, this was the same thing, just the tactile version. I just didn't know enough about the echoes at the time to recognize it. But again, I could be rewriting history to fit what I know now."

"I saw you in the kitchen the other morning," said Leslie, "looking through the drawer for that thing. There's nothing worse than not being able to find something when you're absolutely sure you put it in a particular place, then it's not there. But I'd say you were disproportionately affected by it. You seemed more freaked out than frustrated. Then again, maybe now I'm the one rewriting history to fit what I now know."

They pulled into the driveway and got out of the Mazda. It was dismal out. Not just the sky but the very air seemed grey. There was a light sprinkle that seemed to hover more than fall. It was only mildly chilly, but it was the type of chill that found its way under the surface of your skin and into your veins, like ice cubes in your blood.

There was still a good half hour before high tide, so James went with Leslie to the big house to start calling the numbers on their lists. They weren't optimistic about their success, and that attitude proved correct. The E Marners turned out to be Eric, Erin, Edward, et al. The J Marners were John, Joe, Jessica, et al. The Elizabeth Marner on James's list, as suspected, was a Marner by marriage. There were a few who didn't answer, but James didn't have high hopes. He was almost certain Elizabeth Marner was dead, and if Juliet was still alive, she could be anywhere in the world, and likely not in the phone book.

Shortly after 1:30 p.m., they heard the first disparate clacks as the tide finally reached out and grabbed the front line of the strip of beach rocks. And there, like clockwork, was Elizabeth. James had been keeping an eye out for her through the window of the sunroom, where he and Leslie sat making the calls, but he hadn't seen her coming—hadn't seen her arrive. The beach had been deserted one second, he blinked, then there was Elizabeth, hands behind her ears, wearing that same beige dress—because of course she was, ghosts don't have wardrobes.

"There," said James. "Do you see her?"

"Where?"

The fact that Leslie had to ask said everything he needed to know. Elizabeth was right there, not a hundred yards away on the beach in front of them, plain as day. "Right down there. Standing in front of the staircase to the cottage."

"James, I don't see her." For the first time since James let her in on the mystery, Leslie seemed spooked. She'd jumped on board without skepticism, as easily as if James had simply asked her to help him look for his missing cat, as opposed to solve a decades old mystery, the accumulated evidence of which came exclusively from hallucinations. Up until this point she'd sat in the seat next to him on the rollercoaster with an *ooh-isn't-this-fun* demeanor about the whole thing. He wanted to believe she believed him, but there was also a part of him that felt like she was just humoring him for her own entertainment, like they were a couple kids playing pretend. But if that was the case, the Isaac Marner phone call and the apple corer revelation had pushed her to genuine belief. And if she genuinely believed, that meant James was looking down at the beach at a young girl Leslie couldn't see. And that was fucking spooky as hell.

"Nothing? You really don't see anybody down there?"

"Just empty beach."

In a way, James was relieved that Leslie couldn't see her. He'd already gotten over the intellectual obstacle of accepting the possibility of ghosts existing. Elizabeth—beach version—being a ghost fit nicely into his theory of what was going on. If Elizabeth wasn't a ghost, then nothing made sense, at least as far as any of this made sense in the first place.

"How do you know she's not just another echo?" asked Leslie.

"I don't. Not for sure. But there's a difference. I can't put it into words. Echoes feel like they're layered on top of reality. Elizabeth, down on the beach, she doesn't feel that way. She's uncanny, but not in the same way echoes are. Plus, she talks to me. Echoes don't do that. I can see them, but they can't see me anymore than J.R. Ewing can see you watching him on the television."

This metaphor delighted Leslie.

"Of course," continued James, "there's always the possibility I'm completely off my nut and there's nothing down there at all, ghost or otherwise."

"No. She's down there. How else could you have possibly known about her line: Everything's okay when the rocks are singing."

That was a great point. Elizabeth had said that to him, and she'd also said it to Leslie in 1952. They hadn't compared notes on that, and yet they both knew the quote.

"I'm going to go talk to her."

"Should I come?"

"I don't know. You're welcome to."

They put on their hats and jackets, left the house, walked across the driveway and behind the cottage. Leslie stopped on the patio. "Aren't you coming?" asked James.

"I... no. No, I don't think so. I feel weird. James, this is... I don't know. Is this really happening?"

"Is what really happening?"

"This. I mean, digging up the past, investigating, that was one thing. But am I now really supposed to believe there's a girl down on the beach that I can't see? That you're heading down there to talk to a ghost?"

"How do you think *I* feel?"

"I can't imagine."

The tide continued its ascent up the shore, grabbing more and more rocks with each successive wave, the singing rock choir building in intensity with every verse.

"I need to talk to her," said James.

"Do that. I'll stay here."

James descended the stairs. The winds had picked up, the light drizzle now whipped around, peppering his face with icy droplets. Elizabeth, in her light dress, didn't feel a thing. Ghost don't feel cold. Ghosts don't get wet.

"Me again," said James, stepping beside her. "Remember me?"

"Yes," said Elizabeth. She'd been standing on the beach, exposed to the elements, for several minutes. Her hair should have been wet and matted down, her dress soaked and sticking to her skin, but she was dry as dust.

"I have a friend with me today. She's up there." He pointed to Leslie up on the patio. "I have a question for you, Elizabeth. Can you see her?"

Elizabeth turned to look at Leslie, keeping her hands cupped behind her ears. She looked incredulously at James. "Of course I can see her."

"Do you want to know something interesting? She can't see you."

"Why is that interesting?"

"You don't find it interesting that a person can't see you? That doesn't strike you as at all strange?"

Elizabeth thought for several seconds. "Maybe once it would have. In the before-times. But not now."

"The before-times? Before what?"

"I don't like to think about the what."

"Okay. You don't have to. Were you happy in the before-times."

"Sometimes, I think. Usually not."

"You know, I know a little about your before-times."

Elizabeth studied him for a beat. "I don't remember you from the before-times."

"No. We never met. But I knew your mother a little bit. Juliet, right?"

Elizabeth bristled at the name.

"I don't talk about her."

"But that was her name, right?"

"I don't talk about her."

"Okay. We won't."

"How about your father. Alistair. Do you remember him?"

"The demons took him."

"Excuse me?"

"Please, mister." A trickle of blood dripped from beneath her curls. James didn't say anything this time. Alerting her to the blood is what had sent her sprinting down the beach in their last encounters. He needed her to stay. He needed to talk to her. "I don't like to think about them."

"Okay, I'm sorry." He tried a different avenue. "Do you know what year it is, Elizabeth?"

"Year?"

"Yeah. Like, nineteen-so-and-so."

"Oh. I did once. I don't think it matters anymore." The trickle of blood settled in her eyebrow and stopped.

"That lady up there, she met you before. In the year 1952. She lived in the big house next door when you stayed in that cottage."

"I don't remember her."

"Well, that's the thing, she was your age back then. See, it's now the year 1980. Twenty-eight years have passed. She's all grown up now, but you're still the same."

"I don't have any use for years."

"No? Why?"

"They don't matter anymore."

"Do you mean time itself doesn't matter?"

"I guess not. I haven't thought about it since… the before-times."

"And do you find any of this strange, Elizabeth? Before-times. After-times. Time itself having no meaning. People not being able to see you. Do you think about what any of it means? Why things are so different now than they were in the before-times?"

"I don't think much of anything at all, mister. I just come out to listen to the rocks singing, then I go back."

"Go back where?"

"To the white place."

"Is that where you live now? In the white place? I've been there, you know. But only for a visit. I came back."

Elizabeth looked at him curiously. She took her hands away from her ears. "I didn't know people could do that."

"Well, I won't pretend to understand how it works."

"I wouldn't want to come back. Not to the before-times."

"No. But maybe you don't have to be stuck in the white place either. Maybe there's a way to pass through it. To, you know…"

"Where?"

"Someplace better." He didn't say Heaven. He didn't think Elizabeth understood she was dead, and he didn't want to be the one to break that upsetting news.

"How?"

"I'm not sure, exactly. But I'd like to try to help you. But to do that, you need to talk to me about the before-times."

Another trickle of blood leaked from beneath her bangs, tracing the path of the previous one, which should have become rinsed into a diluted pink smear on her forehead in this rain, but remained an unmolested, dark red trail. She returned her hands to her ears and turned back to the rocks. "I don't talk about the before-times."

"I know. You don't like to talk about the before-times. But the thing is, I believe the reason you're stuck where you are is because... well, some things from the before-times have been left unresolved. Somebody hurt you, Elizabeth. I believe it was your mother. And I think it happened right upstairs in this cottage. I think—"

"Stop!" She whirled toward him, again dropping her hands from her ears. Another trickle of blood dripped down her forehead. Then another, though this next was more of a stream than a trickle. Then more. And more. Blood was now flowing in a pulsating cascade down her face, soaking her features like a wave rolling over the beach rocks. It soaked her bangs, covered her eyes, coated her nose, flowed over her lips.

James stood frozen as the river of blood became a geyser, no longer flowing but erupting from her forehead, steadily blasting through her bangs like a swarm of bats flying out of a cave. It was an impossible amount of blood. Within seconds she was covered, forehead to fingertips and toes, beige dress now a wet maroon. And the blood kept coming.

"Jimmy!" said a voice some part of him recognized, but he was paralyzed—the blood casting him into a dark hypnosis.

Elizabeth stood stalk still, blood continuing to shoot out of her, a sanguine fire hydrant with a loose seal.

"Jimmy!" A hand on his shoulder. He turned. At first he saw nothing but a blurry mass of pink, brown, and grey, like the focus knob on a television had been turned all the way. The image in front of him slowly came together, the colors differentiated themselves, the lines of the image sharpened, as if that same focus knob was creeping back to its sweet spot.

"What the hell are you doing, standing down here by yourself in the rain like an ignoramus?"

"Connie?"

"Well, it ain't Farrah Fawcett."

James turned to look back at Elizabeth, but she was gone.

"Do you remember that time we told him he got stung by a jellyfish?" asked Connie.

"No," said Leslie.

"Ugh," said James, "give it a rest, Con. Yeah, yeah, we all get it, I was a gullible kid."

Connie ignored him. "This was great. So, Jimmy scrapes his toe in the water, right? Who knows on what. Barnacle or something. We look at it, and you tell him it looks like a jellyfish sting."

"I did?" asked Leslie.

"Sure did. We really gave it to him, telling him jellyfish stings were fatal. Scared the crap out of him. Then we tell him the only way to cure a jellyfish sting is to pee on it."

"That's true, you know," said Leslie.

"So, Jimmy starts running up to the cottage, but I tell him there isn't time, he's gonna be dead before he gets up there. So, Jimmy sits down in the sand, pulls his little wiener out of the side of his trunks, and pees all over his own foot, right there on the beach!"

Leslie belted out an operatic wail of laughter. "I don't remember that at all!"

"True story. Right, Jimmy?"

"Forever and always my tormentor," said James.

They were bunched around the yellow Formica table, empty plates of what minutes ago had been piled with beef stroganoff. Betty on the Beach warned of potential thunderstorms overnight before spinning Paul Anka's "Diana."

"Thanks again for dinner, Leslie," said Connie, standing up. "You didn't have to do that."

"Don't mention it."

"It's a good thing you're around; my brother can barely cook spaghetti."

"Oh, I've seen him try. 'Barely' is a gross overstatement. Joking. Joking... Actually, no, I'm not joking at all."

"Gee, it's fun being ganged up on by two women." But he was indeed enjoying himself. The surprise visit from his sister was a welcome distraction. He'd been swallowed by Elizabeth Marner the last several days; it was refreshing to have a piece of his actual life around to somewhat ground him back in reality.

"Aww, poor Jimmy." Connie finished her can of Pabst Blue Ribbon, then excused herself to the bathroom. Before closing the door behind her she poked her head out and said, "Got any jellyfish stings that need tending to, Jim? Now's the time. Going once... Going twice..."

"Your talent for milking untold amounts of hilarity from the teat of the same story is unparalleled," said James.

Connie stuck her tongue out at him, a gesture she'd directed at him countless times as a bratty child. Connie's exterior was hardened by decades of cold winters, smoky bars, and shitty boyfriends, but in that moment James saw the seven-year-old she used to be, breaking through her weathered face—a non-supernatural echo.

"What happened on the beach?" asked Leslie before the bathroom door had even fully closed behind Connie. This was the first moment the two of them had been alone since Connie arrived. Leslie was dying for the details.

"Definitely a ghost."

"I thought the fact that I couldn't see her had already confirmed that. Did she talk to you?"

"A little. Mostly just more vagaries. She won't talk about her mother or anything else that happened in what she calls the before-times."

"The before-times?"

"I think she means before her death, but she won't say it. Honestly, I'm not even sure she knows she's dead. She has no sense of time or logic. She says she mostly lives in the white place. She called it that, just like me. It's gotta be the same place I was in."

"Purgatory."

"Sure, if you're Catholic. But regardless, some kind of liminal space between life and death, yes. Seems she's trapped there."

"Her soul needs closure."

"That's exactly what I was thinking. I just don't know how."

"Justice. We need to find Juliet and expose what she did. The old spirit-can't-rest-till-its-killer-is-exposed story."

"Assuming it was Juliet. Yeah, I thought of that. Could also be a situation with her body. Maybe she's buried in a shallow grave somewhere, and we need to find her. Bury her right. Bless the ground. Something like that."

"The old spirit-can't-rest-till-its-earthly-remains-are-given-a-proper-burial story."

Danny and Juniors' "At the Hop" was playing on the radio, a stark juxtaposition to the conversation they were having.

"So, what do we do next?" asked Leslie.

"I don't even know where to begin. Clearly we need to find Juliet Marner, which at this point seems impossible. And who's to say she's even still alive. And if she is, do we expect her to just come right out and admit what she did? Tell us where she disposed of the body?"

In the bathroom, the toilet flushed. Seconds later, the water started running.

"Are you going to tell her?" Leslie nodded toward the bathroom door.

"Connie? She'd have me committed to the nut house. Quite frankly, there's still a big part of me that thinks I might belong there."

The high-pitched hiss of the faucet ceased. Connie emerged from the bathroom. "You know what they say: you don't buy beer, you just rent it." She went to the counter and plucked another can of Pabst Blue Ribbon out of the plastic six-pack ring. "And I'm signing another lease."

Connie eventually finished off the whole sextet. James nursed the same glass of red wine while Leslie polished off the bottle. Ashtrays were filled. Stories were told. Reminiscences were recounted (ideally ones making James look silly if Connie had her way). Betty on the Beach spun music by Lloyd Price, Rusty Draper, Cathy Carr.

"You're sleeping with her," was the first thing Connie said after Leslie left around 10:30.

"Why would you say that?"

"You're a real shit, Jim."

"What did I do?"

"What the hell is the matter with you? Your wife leaves you for balling some teenager—"

"She was twenty."

"—and the next day you're doing it with the landlord of your rental house. She's not even your type, Jim. Far from it. Will you just do it with anybody, you frickin' sicko?"

"Who said I was sleeping with her?"

"You think I'm a goddam moron, Jim? Easy math: you're you and she's a woman."

"What's that supposed to mean?"

"You're a user. A user of women. You don't have real relationships with them, it's all about what you can get from them. You got her over here cooking for you, doing the dishes…"

"Oh, come on with this. I didn't take you for a Gloria Steinam disciple."

"Name one woman in your life who's not just there to fill some kind of need for you."

"You. Unless you consider being an enormous pain in my ass a need."

"That's different. I'm your sister. And I'll argue I do fill a need for you. I keep you in check. Without me you'd be lost."

"Let's test that theory. Get out of my life and let's see how I fare."

"Ha. You'd be crawling back to me within days."

"And yet, you're the one who drove up to Sewall's Beach."

"Yeah, my point exactly. You think I came up in the middle of November to work on my suntan? I'm here to check on you. You're up here thinking you're seeing people falling off balconies. That's what happens when you don't have big sis around."

"You're only ten months older than me."

"I can still kick your ass."

James laughed. If it ever actually came down to it, Connie probably could kick his ass. Physically she was a wee little thing; he wouldn't break a sweat beating her at, say, arm wrestling. But in an actual claws-out scrape? Smart betters wouldn't put money against her if she stepped into the ring with George Foreman.

"You don't really think I use women, do you?"

"Tell me one thing you like about the teenager, other than the fact that her tits stay where they are when she takes her bra off."

"I wish you'd stop calling her a teenager. It makes me sound disgusting."

"Got it. Day before her twentieth birthday, pervert. Day after, two adults having a consensual good time."

"I realize it's arbitrary, but the language affects the optics."

"You should have thought of that before you fucked a teenager. And you haven't answered the question. Name one thing other than her supple little body you like about her."

"She's smart."

"She's smart."

"Yeah, she's smart."

"Smart how?"

"What do you mean smart how? Smart in her brain."

"Okay. Take the same brain, but put it inside a middle-aged man's head instead of the head of a hot babe who's a few days older than a teenager, would you still be saying that? Would this be a guy whose brain you found so intriguing you'd go out for lunch with him a couple times a week and discuss literature?"

"Sure. Maybe. I don't know." He thought back to that last afternoon in his office, tangled up naked with Susan on the sofa. She'd told him about her idea to compare *Macbeth* to *The Wizard of Oz*. That idea had excited him, but had it really stimulated his intellect? No. It gave him a hard on is what it did. If Connie's imaginary middle-aged man with Susan's brain had pitched that idea, what would James have thought? He'd have thought it was juvenile, that's what he'd have thought. Susan was smart, but she wasn't an intellectual peer. She was smart for an undergrad—for a girl a few days older than a teenager.

And it wasn't just sex he used women for. Connie was right, Leslie not only took care of his sexual needs, but she cooked and cleaned. Even going along with him on the Elizabeth and Juliet Marner investigation was filling a need. The need to bounce ideas off another person. The need to not feel so alone in this crazy situation. The need for confirmation that he hadn't totally lost his mind. It was an all take and no give relationship.

"Jesus. Is that who I am? Am I just some chauvinist asshole?"

"Yes. You're a real shit. But the good news for you is so is every other man on the planet, so you don't really stand out. And now, in the long tradition of women catering to your needs, I have to ask: how are you?"

"Fine."

"Fine? That's it? I drove all the way up here for some beef stroganoff and an *I'm fine.*"

"That was an excellent beef stroganoff."

"Yes, your maid is a terrific cook. But I'm being serious here, Jim. You call me two days ago and tell me you're seeing and hearing shit. I've been worried about you. I don't know why cause you're a big dumb idiot who doesn't deserve my energy, but I'm your big sister and it's my job to worry about you, whether I want the damn job or not, which I don't, but I'm stuck with it. So, I ask again: how are you? And if you tell me you're fine again I'm gonna give you a reason not to be fine and an expensive emergency room bill."

He contemplated telling her for a moment, but a fleeting one. She'd hung on to a story about him believing an old wives tale about urinating on jelly fish stings for over thirty years and still pulled it out to embarrass him in front of company, imagine what she would do with this! *Hey, did I ever tell you about the time Jimmy thought he made friends with the ghost of an eleven-year-old girl? Okay, so it all started when the big dummy washed down half a bottle of quaaludes with half a bottle of Maker's Mark...*

"I'm good. Really. I think you were right. It was nerves getting the better of me. That and side effects from the overdose."

"You sounded shaken on the phone. It was unbecoming."

"Sorry to disappoint you."

"You didn't tell anyone, did you?"

"Tell anyone what?"

"What I told you. About the birds. On Storrow."

"Who the hell would I tell?"

"I'm just making sure."

"Nice to know this has been all about you this whole time."

"Yeah, I drove all the way up here just cause I was scared you'd tell somebody I once saw imaginary birds. I was just asking is all. We got a reputation to uphold, Jim. It's bad enough you talk about *Wuthering Heights* for a living. We don't need all of Boston thinking the Riordan kids are a bunch of sissies."

"You seem to have left your priorities somewhere back on the streets of Somerville."

"You can take the girl out of Winter Hill…"

"We lived in Magoun Square."

"Two blocks up. Same diff." She helped herself to one of James's Pall Malls. Buddy Holly was singing "Everyday." "And how's it going with the other stuff?"

"What other stuff?"

"What other stuff do you think? The whole reason you're here."

"Oh. As well as can be expected I supposed." A brick of guilt landed in his stomach. He hadn't been thinking about Kelly nearly as much as he should have been. She was never far from his thoughts, but under the circumstances, shouldn't she have been at the forefront of his mind at all times? He hadn't been his best self back in Boston, living in filth, barely eating, barely moving— but at least it felt like an appropriate reaction. A proper tribute. His daughter had just died; it felt like a betrayal to do anything but grieve as completely and purely as possible. But how long should that have lasted? Surely he needed to get on with his life at some point. Wasn't that what the whole trip to Sewall's Beach was supposed to have been about? Why then did he suddenly feel so horrible about doing just that?

He realized something. The first time he'd seen Elizabeth he made the connection immediately: she was around the same age as his daughter. This was undeniably a major factor in his obsession with the mystery—perhaps the sole reason he'd stuck around when things started going off the rails here at the Seagull's Nest. The moment he started seeing visions, ghosts, echoes—any rationale human being would have high-tailed it out of there. It wasn't like he'd just invested his life savings in an old house that happened to be haunted and now he was stuck there. It was a winter rental. Month to month. He could have left any time. But he didn't. He stayed. Because a young girl—a girl his daughter's age—was in trouble.

He harbored a misplaced feeling of responsibility for Kelly's death. But it happened. He couldn't crumple up those pages and rewrite them. That story had gone to the presses. But Elizabeth. For a while he'd believed she was alive, living somewhere along the beach, suffering abuse at the hands of her mother. He'd wanted to help her. Now he believed she was beyond that kind of help. She was dead. But she still needed help—perhaps more imperatively than when she'd been alive. Her very soul was trapped between worlds, and James might be the only person who could guide her into the eternal light.

James had transferred his energy from Kelly to Elizabeth. He'd failed the former, but if he could just save the latter... He knew it wouldn't bring Kelly back, but in some strange way it felt like it would provide some sort of closure.

But he was faced with a major problem: He had no idea how to save Elizabeth's soul. Figuring how to do that felt as unrealistic as figuring out how to time travel back to the morning of September 28 to warn Kelly not to go roller skating that afternoon.

"Houston to James. Houston to James. Time to land the space shuttle."

"Huh?"

"I just asked you three times if you had any plans to come back for Thanksgiving and you were floating off in orbit somewhere."

"Oh. Sorry. I was thinking."

"So?"

"So what?"

"Thanksgiving, space cadet. You coming to Uncle David's?"

"When?"

"Tuesday. They decided to change it up this year. Carter's last executive order before he leaves office. He thought Turkey Tuesday had a nice ring to it. Thursday, you idiot!"

"I know that. I just meant… is it this Thursday?"

"Yes. You coming or what? Aunt Carol wants a head count."

"I don't know. Maybe."

"I don't think you're getting the concept of a head count."

"Can I think about it for a night? You just sprung it on me."

"Yes. Or course. Apologies. Sorry to have blindsided you with a major national holiday. I should have prepared you for this by, I don't know, having it happen at the same time every year since the frickin' pilgrims."

They chatted for another half-hour, smoking cigarettes, Betty on the Beach spinning the music of their youth. James set Connie up in the bedroom she used to sleep in as a child, which didn't strike her as having seemed much bigger back then because her body had been the same size since she was twelve. They said their goodnights, Connie suggesting tomorrow morning they should "eat at that diner we used to go to that had those great doughnuts. That is, unless your maid usually comes over and makes you breakfast."

James laid down in his own bed but it was immediately clear he wouldn't sleep, despite it having been a long, full day and him not having much sleep the previous night. He couldn't stop thinking about Elizabeth, going over all the things he knew or thought he knew, trying to piece them together, fill in blanks with possibilities. But there was very little to go on. Nothing, really. There was Isaac Marner, who had nothing but stale information. Leslie possessed documented proof Elizabeth and Juliet had stayed at the Seagull's Nest for a few weeks twenty-eight years ago. There was a waitress who remembered Juliet stealing an apple corer. That was it. That was all the hard evidence. And all it did was prove they existed; it supplied no leads for tracking them down, dead or alive.

There was little hard evidence, but what about the soft evidence? He had a psychic connection to the Marners. When he could tap into it, it made him the world's greatest private investigator, with access to surveillance equipment that allowed him to literally time travel—to monitor his subjects in the past. The problem was he couldn't tap into it at will. It happened when he wasn't paying attention. When he tried to force it, it wouldn't cooperate.

With one exception: the manifestations in the leisure room. The exorcism. He'd witnessed some duration of it every night he'd slept in the cottage. In each case, he'd stopped the performance, either by turning on a light or touching the echo and sending him to the white place. But what if he didn't interrupt it? What if he just stood there and let it play out before him to its conclusion? He wondered how much and for how long these echoes actually reverberated. If he didn't interfere, would he be able to watch everything that happened? Supposing Juliet really did murder Elizabeth on that table, could James then continue following her to wherever she stashed the body?

James went up to the leisure room. All was quiet, save for the patter of rain—which had gotten heavier as the evening wore on—against the spider web window. His typewriter and manuscript sat on the table. He flipped through the pages, half expecting to find some new material, either that he'd written unawares or perhaps had simply written itself, but alas it was the same manuscript, ending at the same point in the story.

He sat down at the typewriter. He knew he couldn't force the writing, but perhaps if he could distance his mind—think about something entirely different—it would start flowing through him again. Of course, the harder one tries not to think of a purple giraffe the more one is going to think of nothing but a purple giraffe.

A couple years ago, Linda had become obsessed with transcendental meditation—T.M., as she and all her drippy friends called it. She'd tried to teach James how to do it, but it hadn't taken with him, due in no small part to the fact that he didn't take it seriously and had only tried it to humor her (and, if he was really being honest with himself, he'd hoped his trying it out would finally get her to shut up about him trying it out). They sat Indian style on the floor, backs of their hands resting on their knees, thumbs lightly pinched to their index and middle fingers, eyes closed. There was some kind of chant—a mantra—that they were supposed to say in their heads. What was it? Some word for love or peace or something or other in an ancient eastern language. Shira? Shirim? Something like that. The idea was to say it over and over, focusing on just the mantra. Other thoughts might intrude, but if they did, you were just supposed to let them float by, like debris in a river.

He'd been terrible at it. His intrusive thoughts would not float by. They'd stop, come ashore, and set up camp. Minutes would go by before he'd remember, *Whoops, I'm supposed to be chanting some kind of mantra here, aren't I?* He'd return to the mantra for maybe seven seconds before: *Shirim. Shirim. Shit, I still have all those* King Lear *papers to grade. Oops. Shirim. Shirim. Man, reading fifty papers by first-years on* King Lear *is a special kind of torture. Really anything by first-years is a special kind of torture. I wish the damn humanities department would spring for a teacher's assistant for me. Whoops. Mantra. Right. Shirim. Shirim. Shirim. I think I'll have a roast beef sandwich for lunch...*

But Linda really swore by it, and so did her friends, kooks though they were. And so did half the college, both student and faculty. In fact, transcendental meditation had been huge across the nation. Surely there had to be something to it, right? If he could figure it out—if he could clear his mind—maybe the portal to the Elizabeth's story would open.

He placed his fingers lightly on the keyboard and closed his eyes. *Shirim. Shirim. Why the hell did Juliet Marner steal that apple corer? Shirim. Shirim. Shirim. I wonder what Leslie's doing right now. I wonder if she's up. I wouldn't mind a quick screw right now. Shirim. Shirim. I can't believe Connie drove all the way up here just to check on me. She's always looked out for me. Ha. I remember the time Mark Napier stole my yo-yo at Sunday school. Connie gave him a bloody nose. Couldn't have weighed more than fifty pounds at the time. Or the time we were all playing street hockey and Frankie McQuaid tripped me with his stick. It was an accident—we were on the same team! But Connie still came at him and chipped his tooth with—oh shit. Shirim. Shirim. Shirim. Maybe she buried her on the beach. Right out front. Right underneath where Elizabeth's ghost is always standing. Are there any proximity rules with ghosts? Are they only allowed to lurk within a certain radius of where they died or…? Ah! Mantra. Shirim. Shirim…*

He cycled through this process for several minutes, never managing to string together more than a dozen consecutive *shirims* before the intrusive thoughts took over. The more he tried to focus on not letting in intrusive thoughts, the more not letting in intrusive thoughts became an intrusive thought in and of itself.

He gave up. The writing wasn't going to happen. Deliberately trying not to force it was just another way of trying to force it. He'd just have to wait for the echoes of Juliet and Elizabeth Marner to start their nightly performance.

He sat on the sofa. The copy of *Bleak House* he'd started reading the other day was still open on the cushion. Dickens wasn't speaking to him just then, so he perused the bookshelf for something else, something lighter—literary candy. His eye fell on *The Shining* by Stephen King. Hmph. He'd been a detractor of the golden boy of horror since he'd burst on the scene a few years ago. Every lowest-common-denominator reader on campus that spring was lying under a shady tree in the quad reading a paperback copy of *Carrie*. Just the year before, that same crowd was walking around with Vonnegut's *Breakfast of Champions* in their backpacks, now they were reading about a cranky teenage girl who throws a psychic tantrum at prom. The downfall of intelligent society was truly nigh.

In fairness, however, he'd never read a single word that destroyer of intelligent societies had written.

All right, King, he thought to himself, let's see what you got.

He devoured close to a hundred pages before he drifted off to sleep with the book still in his hands.

He was only out for a few minutes before he was awoken by a crack of thunder. With the accompanying flash of lightning he saw the silhouette of Juliet Marner, leaning over the head of the table, framed by the spider web window.

The echo was reverberating.

"No!" shrieked Elizabeth.

"Hold still," said Juliet.

Elizabeth was bound with rope by the wrists and ankles, tied to the legs of the table, splaying her body like a starfish. Many yards of duct tape were looped several times around the middle of the table and the girl's torso, between chest and waist, further limiting her movement. She thrashed, but her body was held firmly in place by the restraints.

Juliet was stuffing something into Elizabeth's mouth—a dish towel? A sock? "No! No! No. no…" The protests became muffled as Juliet succeeded in stuffing whatever crumpled up ball of cloth into her mouth.

The *sharp peel* of duct tape as it *unstuck* itself from the roll. The *tearing off* of the freshly unspooled piece. Elizabeth's *muffled cries* as the duct tape went over her mouth, securing whatever gag had just been inserted.

Juliet released another few inches of duct tape from the roll but did not tear it. She stuck the end of that piece to the edge of the table, adjacent to Elizabeth's head. She proceeded to unspool the tape over Elizabeth's face, just below the eyes, to the other side of the table, then passed the roll underneath, back up over the origin of this long strip of tape, and around again, once more over the face—this time across the girl's chin, back under the table, and around a third time, passing over the girl's mouth this time. All the while that awful peeling sound mixing with muffled hysterics of the poor child.

James knew it was an echo. He knew what he was seeing had already happened and there wasn't a thing he could do to stop it. But the paternal urge to jump in and stop it was strong—to rush at Juliet, perhaps push her right out the spider web window, sending her plummeting to the patio in an explosion of broken glass. But that wouldn't happen. He knew if he touched her everything would disappear and he'd end up back in the white place.

"It's for your own good," said Juliet. "Do you want the demons to take you? Like they took him?"

Outside, in the present reality, thunder rolled. A flash of lightning illuminated the horrifying scene. James saw the terrified eyes of Elizabeth.

The girl continued to thrash, but it did little more than shake the table. In doing so, however, she caused an item that must have been lying close to the edge to spill over and rattle to the floor.

James looked down. The apple corer. It landed in the exact spot he'd found it the other night.

"It's the demons making you resist," said Juliet. "You need to fight them. They know what's about to happen and they're scared." She leaned down to pick up the corer. From where James was standing, he could have given her an explosive kick to the face, launching her head across the room like a punted football. But again, that isn't how it would have played out. Any contact would send him to the white place. But his foot was itching. That bitch. That monster. Doing this to her own daughter. Doing this to *anybody*.

Juliet set the corer back down on the table and picked up another item, which James couldn't identify in the darkness, though his eyes had adjusted well enough to discern most of what was happening in front of him.

"Please, hold still, darling," said Juliet, maternal tone harshly juxtaposed against her actions. "It will be so much easier if you hold still."

Thunder. Lightning.

In the flash of electric blue that momentarily filled the room James saw what was in Juliet's hand: a straight razor.

With one hand she brushed Elizabeth's red bangs off her forehead and held them back, with the other she put the blade to the girl's brow.

Jesus. This was never an exorcism — it was an operation.

Elizabeth's scream pierced through the gag as Juliet dragged the razor from Elizabeth's brow to her hairline, creating a two-inch gash that remained bloodless for what felt like far too long considering the severity of the cut.

But when the blood came, it came in buckets.

Down each side of her head, into her eyes, soaking her hair, covering the table in the very pattern James had found his typewriting sitting in the other day.

Elizabeth screamed and thrashed.

"I know, honey, but it's necessary to release the demons."

Juliet picked up the apple corer. With one hand she spread open the gash in her daughter's forehead, with the other she put the cylindrical blade of the apple corer on the exposed skull.

Then she started twisting back and forth, grinding a circular rivet in the bone.

James had seen enough. His paternal reflexes overwhelmed everything else. He charged at Juliet.

Everything disappeared.

He was back in the white place.

The white place faded back to reality, like a dissipating fog, and he saw the face of his sister hovering over him, shaking him. Grey daylight filled the room. He was uncomfortable. His face hurt.

"You are definitely not fine" said Connie. "This is how I used to find Patrick every Saturday morning."

"Who?"

"Patrick. We were going together for two years, thanks for noticing."

"Oh. Right. Patrick." James didn't remember him. Connie had had lots of boyfriends. And, being Boston, more than one of them had been named Patrick. Also being Boston, more than one of them were the types to wake up in a compromising position on the floor on a Saturday morning.

"You only had half a glass of wine. Did you go into my purse and steal another handful of quaaludes?"

James sat up. He was surrounded by—and on top of—dozens of books. He grazed the back of his hand over his throbbing cheek and found a sticky crust there: dried blood. When he'd charged at Juliet, his soul had entered the white place, but his earthly body must have kept going and crashed face first into the bookcase.

"I wasn't drunk," he said.

"Then how the hell did you end up like this?"

The events of the last week hadn't exactly been garden variety, but his response to Connie's question might have been the most surprising of all: he started to cry.

Connie stood up quickly. One might almost say she recoiled. She'd have been less surprised to see beetles come out of his eyes as opposed to tears. Riordan men don't cry. The last time she'd seen James cry was when he was six years old. He'd come home in tears after Mark Napier stole his yo-yo at Sunday school. Her father smacked him in the face and called him a sissy. She never saw James cry again.

"Jesus, Jim, what the fuck is going on with you?"

James sniffled and wiped the tears. The crying only lasted seconds before he stifled it. It had crept up on him, caught him unawares, sucker-punched him. But he was quickly able to fend it off. Getting smacked in the face and being called a sissy at a tender age has a way of teaching you to control certain things. "Sorry. I—I have no idea where that came from."

Connie was uncomfortable. She always had something to say. Always had an opinion. Always had a solution. But a grown man crying—she didn't know what the hell to do with that. "You're scaring me here, Jim."

"I'm scaring myself." He hadn't even cried when Kelly died. He hurt. Soul-crushingly so. He gave up all semblance of living to the point of *literally* dying. But he hadn't cried.

He stood up. His body ached, but he hadn't sustained any real injuries. He went to the sofa and lit himself a Pall Mall. "I have to tell you some things."

Connie helped herself to one of his cigarettes and took a seat facing him. "I'm listening."

"I've been seeing things."

"Still?"

"This isn't just imaginary birds on Storrow, Con."

"Hey! You promised you wouldn't ever bring that up."

"No, I promised I wouldn't tell anyone."

"Well, I'm someone."

"Connie, I'm serious here. Something is going on with me."

"No shit."

"Just please listen. Keep that mouth shut for once and just listen to me. Something is going on. I'm falling apart here. And it's not grief or stress or drug side-effects. Or, hell, maybe it is, I don't know. I just need you to listen. Keep your opinions and your judgements and your witty quips to yourself for a few minutes and just listen."

"Jesus, Jimmy. What's going on?"

"I'm trying to tell you. It started with those fucking quaaludes…"

He told her. All of it. The white room. The imaginary medical emergency he'd seen in the room across the hall at the hospital. The falling man. Elizabeth on the beach. The apple corer. The blood on the table. The voice on the radio. Juliet and Elizabeth in the leisure room. The psychically-written novel. Edgar and Ingrid Monahan. Isaac Marner. Helen the waitress. Right up to Juliet digging into Elizabeth's skull with a stolen apple corer and him charging into a bookcase.

Connie's face was a portrait of horror, increasing with every new turn—not because she was listening to a scary ghost story, but because she was witnessing her baby brother unravel before her eyes. It was like that fight between Muhammed Ali and Larry Holmes a couple months back, when she and the patrons at the bar watched in horror as the once incomparably great Ali got his ass royally dominated. The fight had to be stopped and the whole world had to reckon with the fact that the mighty had truly fallen. The same thing was now happening to James's brain.

Even James himself was feeling the slip. When he'd recounted this same story to Leslie—what existed of it at the time—she'd received it with total openness, giving him a sense of credibility in the telling of it. But Connie's glaring incredulity made him feel foolish—made him realize how utterly ridiculous all of this was. Psychic visions of the past. Ghosts. Supernatural viruses contracted during a visit to the afterlife. It was absurd, all of it. Even though he knew it all to be true, he didn't believe any of it as it came out of his own mouth.

"Here's what we're going to do," said Connie, when he'd finished. "We're going to get you packed up and you're going to leave this place. We're taking you straight back to that hospital and marching you into the neurologist's office and finding out what the heavenly fuck is happening to your brain."

"I know. You're right. I mean, you're probably right. This whole time I never fully believed it myself—there was always a part of me that thought maybe I was crazy, living some sort of delusion. But I don't feel delusional, Con."

"Delusional people don't feel delusional. That's part of the delusion."

246

"Yes. Sure. I know. But, Con, let's say the visions—the echoes—all the things I've been thinking I'm seeing and hearing, let's say that's all in my head. Fine. But there's so much else that can't be explained away as delusion. Edgar Monahan, for example. He knew exactly what was happening to me. Or what about Leslie finding the rental agreement? Or her remembering Elizabeth saying the thing about the singing rocks? Or me picking out Isaak Marner's phone number. Or the waitress remembering the thing about the apple corer? All of that happened, Con. And it wasn't my imagination."

"James," she almost never called him James, "you need to get your face washed and pack up your stuff. I'll tidy up here while you do that. Then you're going to get into your car and—"

"But how do you explain that stuff, Con? I mean, an apple corer! A random kitchen tool. I don't think I've seen or even thought about one in… I don't know, thirty years. And then the waitress just happens to remember Juliet Marner working there and stealing an apple corer? Explain it, Con. I know how crazy it all sounds. I do. I hear myself. But how do you explain that?"

Connie chose her words carefully, as if negotiating with a deranged man with a gun to a hostage's temple. "Okay. Let's say it's all true. Everything. All true. This woman killed her daughter trying to cut demons out of her head. Okay? It happened. So what? What now? What business is it of James Riordan's?"

"I need to help her."

"Why? And, more importantly, how?"

"I don't know. But I can't just… do nothing."

"Kelly's dead, Jimmy."

"What? I know that."

"She's dead and you couldn't have done anything about it. It happened quick and she—"

247

"Stop."

"It happened quick and she didn't feel a thing. She was good kid, Jimmy. A great kid and a horrible accident happened to her. She's not trapped between worlds. She's in Heaven with God and she's happy."

"I know all that. I didn't make up Elizabeth because I feel guilty about Kelly." He wasn't entirely sure he hadn't. He'd had similar thoughts himself.

"I didn't say you did."

"You're implying it."

"What I'm implying is no good can come from you staying here another minute. Either way. Maybe your imagination is running wild, maybe you're being called upon by a ghost child to expose a thirty-year-old murder. Doesn't matter. It's time to go, Jimmy. You woke up on a pile of books with a bloody face."

"Well, you've always known I'm an aggressive reader."

Connie laughed. It was rare that she ever laughed with him as opposed to at him. "Come on. Get cleaned up."

For the first time since Kelly died, James actually felt free. He still grieved, of course. And there was a small matter of him perhaps being in the middle of a psychotic break from reality. But Connie had given him permission to let go. He felt like he'd been walking around with a couple hundred-pound sand bags hanging over each shoulder for weeks, and he'd finally cast them off.

Kelly was with God in Heaven.

Elizabeth, if she existed, wasn't his problem.

He stubbed his cigarette out in the ashtray and went downstairs to wash the blood off his face and start packing.

Time to leave the Seagull's Nest.

Time to go back to Boston and get himself right.

Leslie opened the door seconds after he rang the bell. "Oh! Good morning." She wore a navy blue with white stars aerobics leotard with red and white striped leggings. "Listen, I went ahead and called the rest of the numbers on the list. Didn't lead to anything, as we suspected. What about you? Any echoes last night?"

His instinct was to tell her everything he'd seen. How Juliet Marner had strapped Elizabeth to the table, cut her forehead open, and bore into it with the apple corer. But he resisted, like a recovering alcoholic passing up an offered drink. Connie was right: no good could possibly come from travelling one more step down this road. "I'm leaving," he said.

"What do you mean you're leaving?"

"Just that. I'm going back to Boston."

"For good?"

"For good."

"Just like that?"

"Yes. It's not good for me here. This thing with Elizabeth is… I can't do it anymore. It's unhealthy for me."

"But what about… you know."

"There's nothing I can do for Elizabeth."

"I was talking about us. What about us?"

"What do you mean?"

"You and me." She clarified by pointing at herself then him, as if she could have been talking about any two other people. "Us."

Us? James hadn't realized there was an us. He liked Leslie. He enjoyed sleeping with her. But he'd considered "us" to be a relationship of casual convenience between two single adults. He had no romantic feeling toward her. He never stopped to consider whether she had romantic feelings toward him. Had he really expected to just pop over here on his way out of town and say goodbye with a transactional handshake? Connie was right: he was a real shit.

"Well, I was always going to leave at some point, right?"

"Yes. That you were."

"It's just happening a little earlier than originally expected."

"Mm. Well, that's your right." She was clearly hurt. James hadn't been prepared for this. Leslie was so agreeable about everything else, he'd just assumed she'd be agreeable about this. But of course that wasn't taking into account the notion she might have, you know, feelings.

"Well. Um. Thanks for everything. You can just keep the rent for the rest of November. It's okay."

"Yes, that was my biggest concern: not having to prorate the rent and refund you eleven dollars."

"I'm sorry. I don't know why I said that. I'm just feeling awkward, I guess. I didn't expect this to go this way."

"And how exactly did you expect it to go? Did you think we'd slap five and say 'good game' like a couple little leaguers?"

Honestly, she wasn't that far off. "No. I just… There's a lot going on right now, that's all."

"Ok. Fine. There's a lot going on. You're leaving. Wonderful. Drive safe. Is there anything else I can do for you? Can I whip you up a batch of pancakes before you go."

"No. Thank you. I really think I should just go."

"Oh, James, did you for one second think I was serious about making you pancakes?"

To his great shame, he actually did. Here he was, unceremoniously breaking it off with a woman who'd done nothing but cater to his needs for a week, and he didn't even recognize it as biting sarcasm when she offered to reward his callousness with pancakes. "I'm sorry, Leslie. My head's not right."

"Understatement."

"Well…" There was nothing left to say. He handed her the key to the Seagull's Nest. "Here's the key."

She snatched it from him.

"I'll call you," he said.

"Great. I'll go wait by the phone."

"Leslie, I—"

"Goodbye, James." She closed the door.

"I remember you used to just nibble the glazed surface off and leave the rest of the doughnut," said Connie. "It was disgusting. There'd just be this cakey brown circle left all lined with teeth marks."

"I remember you used to blow into your milk with your straw till it bubbled over the surface.," said James. "You'd try to get the bubbles to rise up as high as possible without spilling over. You always took it just a bit too far though."

"Dad used to get so pissed."

"Talk about crying over spilled milk!" He took a bite of his doughnut, wiped a dollop of jelly from the corner of his mouth with the back of his hand, then wiped his hand on his napkin.

"Why do you do that? Wipe your mouth like that."

"Would you prefer I have jelly all over my face?"

"No. But you wipe with your hand first, then wipe your hand on your napkin. You've done that since you were a kid. It's inefficient. Why not just skip the middleman and wipe your mouth with the napkin directly?"

"Why don't you stop picking on me for two seconds for once."

"Do you wipe your ass that way too."

"Disgusting."

Doubling down on her potty humor, Connie took a dramatic bite of her chocolate cruller and chewed it with her mouth wide open.

"How's it going over here?" Helen sidled up to refill their coffees.

"Terrific," said Connie. "These doughnuts haven't changed a bit since I was seven years old."

"Neither has my sister's sense of humor," said James.

"Oh, this is your sister?" said Helen. "Did your brother tell you I worked with your aunt for a little while?"

"Carol?" said Connie, confused.

"Juliet," said Helen. "Back in the early fifties."

Connie pieced it together. "Oh, right. Auntie Jules, of course."

"I felt kind of bad after you left yesterday," said Helen. "I had no business telling you that story about the apple corer. I'm sure your aunt is a very nice lady."

"On the contrary," said Connie. "We had to stop inviting her over for holidays because whenever we did, half the kitchen utensils would disappear."

"She's kidding," said James.

Helen sauntered off to serve other customers. James looked out the window, watching a bundled up old man throw a stick to a chocolate lab on the beach across the street. Rupert Holmes sang "Escape (The Piña Colada Song)" on the jukebox.

"You don't think it's even a little weird?" said James.

"Jimmy, don't."

"How do you explain it? How do you explain how this waitress knew Juliet?"

"Wow, call the local news. Woman named Juliet once worked at local diner."

"And rented the cottage at the same time. And stole an apple corer. And had a daughter named Elizabeth. And on and on and on."

Connie gave a dramatic sigh. "There are a million possible explanations for all of this, Jim. Not the least of which being: you're out of your fucking mind. Leslie's dad rented the cottage to a woman named Juliet in 1952. Fine. Woman named Juliet works at the diner around the same time. Maybe it's the same woman, maybe it isn't. Either way, the woman in your fantasies was never named Juliet until Leslie found that rental agreement, right? In your book she was just Mother. In your hallucinations she doesn't have a name. You've latched onto her as having some sort of importance just because she was a single mom with a daughter who rented that cottage. But your friend had to go through thirty years of rental agreements to find her. Obviously over thirty years of rentals she's gonna eventually find a single mother and daughter."

"And the daughter just happens to be named Elizabeth?"

"Wow. Such an uncommon name."

"And what about Isaac Marner?"

"What about him?"

"He knew them."

"Yeah? So? That only proves they existed, which you already knew from the rental agreement. You called every damn Marner in the phone book. You don't think it's likely you'd eventually come across a relative?"

"And the apple corer?"

"Waitress tells you somebody named Juliet stole an apple corer thirty years ago, that night you dream about a lady hurting a kid with an apple corer. Seems simple to me."

"No. I found an apple corer on the floor days before the waitress told me about Juliet stealing one."

"So you say."

"You think I'm lying about that?"

"No. I believe you believe it. I know you wouldn't tell me such a cockamamy story if you didn't actually believe it. But I also think, given your mental state, you could be retroactively inserting false memories into the story—convincing yourself things happened that didn't actually happen."

"But I told Leslie about the apple corer when it happened. She remembers it."

"Does she?"

"Yes."

"You don't think she might just be going along with all this just to placate you?"

"Why would she do that?"

"Cause she's in love with you."

"What? No, she's not. She barely knows me."

"She's forty and divorced, Jim. I realize for you that just opens up the door to screw a bunch of teenagers—"

"She was twenty."

"—but for women there's a certain amount of desperation that comes with that situation. She'll tell you whatever you want to hear. For God's sake, Jimmy, let this thing go. I'm gonna tell you something right now, a compliment, and you know that's not easy for me to do, but here goes: You're a total idiot—"

"Thank you. I know how hard that must have been for you."

"Let me finish. You're a total idiot in the little brother sense, but you've also always been one of the smartest people I know, in, like, an academic sense. I need you to tap into the smart side and tell me what's more likely: a psychotic break or ghosts."

"If it's ghosts that means there's nothing wrong with me. If it's a psychotic break, I'm fucked."

"Well, yeah, but you've always been fucked. Let's get you to the neurologist before we decide you're *fucked* fucked. They got lots of pills nowadays. You'd be surprised."

"Would I? It was your stupid pills that started all this."

In fairness to quaaludes, it was the wheel of a roller skate hitting an acorn that really started all this, but the pills had played no small role in the escalation of his psychotic break.

"You got a quarter?" asked James.

Connie dug around in her purse and found one.

"I'll be right back." James went to the jukebox, inserted the quarter, made a selection, and returned to the table as the opening chords of Olivia Newton John's "Magic" rang.

"You remain forever and always an enigma," said Connie.

James shushed her, then sat silently and listened through the first chorus. "This song really is terrible," he finally said.

"If I'd known this is what you intended to do with my quarter I would have as soon thrown it into the ocean."

"Kelly loved this song. She loved the whole record. She could sing every single word."

"I adored that girl, but I would never accuse her of having good taste. She was eleven. Eleven-year-olds are dumb."

"I was supposed to take her to see this movie the night she died. Her and her friend Michelle."

"I know."

"It's the last thing in the world I wanted to do. I was complaining about it all day to my colleagues. In the end, I guess I got my wish: I didn't end up going. I always felt guilty about that. Like I'd somehow manifested her death to get out of taking her to the movie."

"Jesus, Jim. That's the stupidest thing I've ever heard."

"I know that now. And I knew it as I was thinking it. But I couldn't help it. Losing a child—it fucks with your mind in ways you could never imagine."

"So I've seen."

"The first day I pulled into town I stopped to eat here and this song came on. I had to leave. Threw down a bunch of money and ran out like the place was on fire."

"In fairness to you, I think this song would have that effect on lots of people, even without the association you have to it."

James smiled. "I can listen to it now. Awfulness notwithstanding, of course. I think about Kelly singing it around the house and... well, it makes me sad, but not in a devastating way. In a way that kind of feels good. Like lightly pushing on a bruise. What does that mean?"

"It means it's time to go home."

"I agree. Let's go home."

Connie took a left out of the parking lot, which was the more direct route to I95 north. James chose to take a right, which was a longer and more circuitous route, but it allowed him to drive along the strip—spending another few minutes breathing in that salt air and nostalgia. He doubted he'd be returning to Sewall's Beach anytime soon. Maybe not ever.

It was a warm day for the season and he was able to drive with the window down relatively comfortably. It was nearly high tide, which meant the ocean was quite close, the sound of the waves crashing felt almost as if they were a part of the composition of the Four Lads' "Standing on the Corner" that played softly from the speakers.

He drove past closed-up shops, restaurants, and beach houses, trying not to think about Elizabeth, but it was nigh impossible. There was just too much about everything that had happened that couldn't be explained away by happenstance and coincidence. Even a psychotic break didn't feel like a satisfying explanation for something like, say, anything having to do with Edgar and Ingrid Monahan. But then again, if he was indeed having a psychotic break, he wouldn't be the best judge of what was or was not a satisfying explanation. He couldn't trust his own judgment—his thoughts and memories were suspect.

Best not to think about it at all. When he got back to Boston he'd see the neurologist and take it from there. In the meantime, he needed to push Elizabeth Marner and all things having to do with the echoes as far from his mind as possible.

"Standing on the Corner" faded out and the smooth voice of Betty on the Beach spoke. "That was the Four Lads with 'Standing on the Corner' from 1956. That song was originally written for a Broadway musical from the same year called *The Most Happy Fella*. And if you didn't happen to be in New York City in 1956 to catch the show, you can currently see a filmed production of it on PBS's *Great Performances*, so check your listings for that. Well, it's almost high tide, which means just about time for the rocks to start singing—"

(James coughed out the lungful of smoke he'd just inhaled. It was a good thing it was the off-season because he veered into the wrong lane, which would certainly have resulted in a head-on collision were there any oncoming traffic with which to collide.)

"—and if you live by the beach you know exactly what I mean by that. And if you don't know what I'm talking about, let me just assure you of one thing:

"Everything's okay when the rocks are singing."

James stood on the edge of the bluff looking down into the rocky alcove that housed the little shack from which Betty on the Beach broadcast. Standing in front of the shack, on the beach, just past the point where the tide was pushing and pulling the singing beach rocks, was Betty herself. She wore a heavy sweater over a flowing white dress, the skirts of which fluttered in the ocean breeze. Even from this distance James could see she had fiery red hair.

He could also see she held her hands cupped behind her ears.

Betty. Short for Elizabeth.

Was it possible?

But Elizabeth was dead. James had seen her ghost.

Or had he?

He made his way down the rickety wooden staircase that zig-zagged down the rock cliff wall. The alcove was small, barely larger than a tennis court, and completely enclosed by cliffs on either side. To the north you could see nothing but ocean beyond the cliff wall, to the south you could see Sewall's Beach stretching around the distance, lined with beach houses, one of which—though it was impossible to pick out in the blur of structures—was the Seagull's Nest. In front of it, James knew, a younger version of Betty on the Beach was standing in the exact pose as her older counterpart.

A wooden walkway led from the base of the stairs to the shack, but other than that the ground was entirely made of rocks and pebbles. The Rock'n'Roll Dance Party was especially raucous down here, the area being made up of a much larger percentage of rocks, not to mention the acoustics from being surrounded by stone cliffs on three sides.

James walked toward the woman. There was no way to do it stealthily, each step rattling and shifting myriad rocks under his feet. Betty heard him approaching and turned around.

Good God! It was Elizabeth! A forty-year-old version, but unmistakably Elizabeth. Same freckle pattern, same curly red bangs, same lost eyes.

She started slightly when she saw him.

"Sorry, I didn't mean to startle you."

"Who are you?"

"I'm James. I'm…" He had no idea how to introduce himself in this context, so he simply said: "I listen to your radio show."

"I appreciate that. Was there something I could do for you? I don't mean to be rude, but I'm not crazy about visitors. Especially unannounced ones."

This was a delicate moment. How does one approach a conversation like this? Where does one even start? "This is going to sound crazy, but if I could just convince you to give me five—maybe ten minutes of your time to listen to what I have to say. After that, you can tell me to get lost. I'll go away and never bother you again. But if you could just hear what I have to say."

"What's it about?"

"The past."

"Who's past?"

"Yours."

"I think I'd like for you to leave."

"Please. If you could only just listen."

"I can't. I've got a reel running inside. When it runs out there will be dead air."

"Are you Elizabeth Marner?"

A look of fear spread across her face. The very look her eleven-year-old version made when James told her she was bleeding. "No. That isn't my name. I have to go. Please leave." She started for the shack, brushing past James.

"Please. I'm not here to threaten or expose you or anything. I just—"

"Please go." She did not turn around.

"I know why you do that. I know why you say *everything is okay when the rocks are singing*. You have tinnitus. And migraines."

Betty stopped.

"And when you cup your hands around your ears like that it's soothing. It's the only thing you've ever found that gives you any relief."

Betty turned around, astonished. She took a few steps back toward him. "Who are you?"

"I'm just James. I'm a literature professor from Boston. But who I am has nothing to do with how I know the things I know. I can't sum that up in a few words. But if you'll give me just a few minutes of your time…"

Betty looked hard at him for several seconds, then said: "I need to get back on the air." She turned and headed back toward the shack. After a few steps she stopped, turned, and said: "Come on."

He followed.

The shack had the impossible quality of being larger on the inside than it was on the outside—like a magic trick. Not only did it serve as a radio station, but it was also her home. It was one large room with a disheveled kitchen in one corner and an unmade bed in the other. The majority of the room was occupied by the radio station. There was a work space consisting of a large table full of gear, most of which—save for dual record players and a reel to reel tape player—James couldn't even begin to guess the function of. Every wall was lined with shelving stuffed with record albums, 45s, 8-tracks, cassettes, and meticulously labeled canisters of tape reels.

The Kingston Trio's "Tom Dooley" was playing in the room, as well as on dozens of radios around the town of Sewall. Betty poured herself a mason jar of water from the tap and offered one to James. He declined. She sat down at the chair in the workstation. She cleared off a stool, piled with *Rolling Stone* magazines—the top issue featuring Bob Segar lying on a motorcycle in a pose more appropriate for a Playboy model—and offered it to James. He sat down.

"What I'm about to tell you," he began, "you're not going to believe. I'm telling you that right up front. But I need you to suspend your disbelief long enough for me to get through it, then you can decide how much of it you want to believe. At the very least I think you'll find it fascinating."

"I'm listening."

"About a week ago, I had an accident. I had a… let's call it a bad reaction to some medication. My heart stopped. I was legally dead for several seconds."

"Oh my God."

Pat Boone's "Don't Forbid Me" took over for the Kingston Trio.

"While I was deceased, I found myself in a void. A nothingness. A white place, as I've come to call it."

Betty's already pale face dropped several shades.

"Your reaction," said James. "Have you ever been to a place like that?"

"Keep talking."

"Ever since then I've… seen things. Hallucinations. Visions. I don't rightly know what they are scientifically. I've been fortunate enough to meet another with the same affliction. He calls them echoes, which I think is an apt word. Because they're visions of the past. Echoes of things that have happened before." He searched her face for any clues she might have experienced the echoes herself, but there was nothing there. If she'd been to the white place, which James believed she had, it didn't appear as though she'd picked up the virus while she was there.

"Pardon me a moment. I need to change the reel." She went to the shelf, perused the cannisters for a moment, then made a selection. She removed the reel and set it up on the player below the one that was already playing. Just as Pat Boone was fading out, she hit play, and Tab Hunter's "Young Love" faded in.

"There. This will play for the next forty-five minutes. Please, continue."

"These echoes, they're always echoes of tragic events. Things so horrible they leave an unwashable stain on the very fabric of reality.

"I see how you're looking at me. I don't blame you. Again, I just ask you to hear me out.

"I've been staying at the Seagull's Nest, just down the beach over there. Are you familiar with that cottage."

The look on her face said indeed she was, but she confirmed it: "I'm thinking you already know that I am."

"You stayed there with your mother. Juliet."

She bristled at the mention of Juliet.

"I saw what she did to you there. In a vision. I saw it echoed."

"I... don't know what you're talking about."

"My intention here isn't to drudge up past trauma, though I realize that's exactly what I'm doing. I'm sorry if it's painful, but you do know what I'm talking about, and I think if you were to brush the hair back from your forehead there'd be a scar that proves it."

"How can you know about that? I've never told anybody. Nobody. Ever." She looked away from James, talking to herself now. "She must have. She told someone. No. That isn't possible. She couldn't have."

"I saw it. I watched it happen."

"This is impossible. Who are you?"

"I told you it was going to be difficult to believe. But I am who I say I am, and I know the things I know because I saw them happen. Psychically. Supernaturally. Magically. I don't even know myself. I know how crazy this all must be to you. I haven't fully accepted it myself if I'm being honest. But I swear on the soul of my deceased daughter I'm telling the honest truth. I might be delusional. I might be experiencing a psychotic break. But this is the truth as I've experienced it. That's all I can tell you."

"Okay. Fine. Let's say I were to believe you. Let's say you can see into the past. Why come here. It happened. It's over. What is it you want from me?"

"I don't know."

"Wonderful."

"There's another element to this I haven't told you about yet. I've also seen you on the beach. In front of the cottage. Every day at high tide, listening to the singing rocks. The eleven-year-old version of you."

"Well, if you see into the past, as you say, I don't see what should make this odd."

"She's not an echo, this other version. I can tell the difference. Echoes only replay tragedies. Your younger self just listens to the rocks on the beach. There's no tragedy attached to it. Also, she talks to me. Echoes don't do that. I thought she was your ghost. I thought you died on that table and this was your ghost. But here you are. Unless, of course, you're not actually Elizabeth Marner."

Betty put her hand to her forehead and brushed her hair back. There, in the very spot James had watched Juliet cut Elizabeth with a straight razor, was a deep scar.

"I'm so sorry," said James. "I can't imagine."

"It was a long time ago. I turned out okay. Mostly."

The girl on the beach... When James thought Elizabeth was dead, everything followed a kind of logic—given a certain level of belief in the supernatural of course. The girl was a ghost. But now... "If you're alive, then this girl on the beach... I'm sorry to come here and put all this on you. Honestly, I don't know what I expect from you. Maybe I never should have come here."

"She is a ghost."

"I'm sorry?"

"The girl on the beach. She is a ghost."

"I don't understand. A twin? Is that it?"

"No. She's me. I've always known she's there. I didn't *know it* know it until you came by just now, but I've always sensed her."

"But… you're alive. I mean, aren't you?" He wasn't sure of anything anymore.

"My ears rang constantly when I was a child. And I suffered murderous headaches. But you already know this."

"Yes."

"I inherited it from my father. He suffered from the same thing. But when his migraines would come it made him rageful. He'd beat on my mother and me."

"I'm so sorry."

"It was a long time ago. My mother finally couldn't take anymore. We ran away. Bounced around the state. Staying in boarding houses, cheap apartments—her waitressing at diners and truck stops and such."

James already knew much of this, but he let her talk.

"We didn't stay in one place too long, cause she was worried dad was gonna find us. The thing is, she wasn't much better than he was. Oh she wasn't physically abusive like he was, but she wasn't right in the head, my mother. I don't know if she was always this way or if all the abuse made her so, but she believed my dad was the way he was because he was possessed by demons. She thought the ringing in his ears was demons speaking to him. And when he'd get his headaches, she thought that was the demons taking over. And considering he used to beat the shit out of us every time he'd get those headaches, she may have been right in a certain kind of way."

The Champs' "Tequila" was playing. It added an awkward juxtaposition to the tragic story Betty was telling. She eventually turned the volume all the way down.

"Well, because I had that same ringing and those same awful migraines, mom thought I was possessed too—thought I'd inherited dad's demons. She tried a steady regimen of prayer, but once she realized that wasn't doing any good she started looking at different solutions.

"You ever heard of trepanation?"

"You mean trepidation?"

"No. Trepanation. It's a medical procedure. Goes back centuries. Back to a time when the idea that a chronic headache being caused by demons was more acceptable. Certain cultures believed if you drilled a hole in the skull of the possessed individual, the demons would escape and that person would be cured."

"Jesus."

"You're telling me. What you saw—or claim to have seen—was my mother trepanning me. Opening up an escape hatch in my skull to set the demons free.

"Interesting thing about having a hole bore into your skull: it's painless. The skull doesn't have pain receptors. Having my forehead sliced open—that hurt. But the hole in the skull was surprisingly pain free. Which didn't make it any less horrifying. I'll never forget the scraping, the grinding, as she twisted that tool back and forth, back and forth, carving out a circular rivet in my head, closer and closer to my brain with every awful turn of that retched tool. It reverberated through my whole skeleton. I could feel the grinding in my toes."

James put his hand to his own forehead, as if to block an imaginary apple corer from cutting into his skull.

"I'm sorry to be so graphic."

"Please. I should be apologizing to you for making you relive it."

"It feels good to talk about it, honestly. I've held this in for close to thirty years. This is releasing demons more than that cursed trepanation did.

"I passed out during the procedure. I went to the white place you described. I felt like I'd only been there for seconds, but it must have been a day or two. I woke up on a cot mattress on the floor in a little room somewhere—I could see out the window that we were in a big city. Turned out to be Boston, though it could have been Shanghai for all I knew at the time. My head had been stitched up with just regular old thread and hurt like a fire was burning there.

"I didn't leave that room for days. No radio. No books. Nothing. Just a mattress on the floor and me, mom, rats, and cockroaches. She'd go out every so often and come back an hour or two later with a stale loaf of bread and a dented can of green beans or something that we'd ration out over a couple days. She kept asking me if the ringing and the headaches were gone and I didn't dare tell her they weren't for fear she'd cut into my skull again. But then one day I had a migraine so bad I couldn't even sit up. I tried to pass it off as something else but mom knew. She didn't try anything. Didn't even really say anything about it. But she cried herself to sleep that night.

"I woke up the next morning and found her in the bathroom. Blood everywhere. She'd cut her wrists. Dead."

"Oh my God."

"I left that room and went down into the streets. Just an eleven-year-old girl with nobody to look after her and nowhere to go, out in the big city. Still had that regular old sowing thread in my forehead. I eventually got picked up by a policeman. I didn't say anything. Nothing. I thought if they found my mother dead on the bathroom floor of a rooming house that I'd somehow get in trouble. I didn't even tell anybody my name. Nothing. Cause I didn't want to get sent back to dad either.

"Long story short, they cleaned me up, got me to a doctor and fixed my head right, then put me in the system. They let me choose my own name since I swore up and down I couldn't remember what my actual one was. I went with Betty. I knew another Elizabeth back in school and everybody called her Betty. I liked it. I bounced around to a couple different foster families. Turned eighteen and went out on my own. Cleaned hotel rooms. Waitressed. Secretaried. Etcetera, etcetera. Lived simply, saved my money. Now here I am."

"That's absolutely harrowing."

"Tell me about it."

"And the girl on the beach?"

"All my life—by which I mean my post-mother life, I'd been drawn back to Sewall's Beach. The intuitive thought would be that this would be the last place I'd ever want to return to, I know, given what happened here. But I could never shake it. I've suffered this tinnitus all my life. I've seen doctors, acupuncturists, masseuses, hypnotists—nothing has worked. The only thing that ever soothed it was the singing rocks. Cupping my hands behind my ears and listening to the ocean drag those stones over each other. I would dream about it—a siren song beckoning me back here.

"But it was more than just that. The rocks only sing at high tide after all. I felt like I'd left something behind back here. I wasn't the same person I was before I'd left.

"Now, that might seem obvious. My mother had strapped me to a table and drilled a hole in my head. No Novocain. No anesthesia. *Of course* I wasn't the same after that. But it wasn't that. It was deeper. I was incomplete. It was as if I'd left a piece of myself behind when I left. Wherever I went, whatever I did, I could always sense there was a missing part of me back on Sewall's Beach, Maine.

"I can feel her over there. At high tide, when I come and listen to the singing rocks, I know she's over there doing the same thing.

"I think I died on that table, if only briefly. I think I died, and when I was dead I became a ghost. But then I came back, but the ghost remained behind. That piece of my soul never reunited with my body. I've always known it—or, at the very least, I've sensed it. I knew there was a missing piece of me over there, I just didn't understand how and in what form. Not until today. Not until you came by."

James tried to wrap his head around it. A person dies, leaves behind a ghost, but then that person is revived, but the ghost remains behind. Was that possible? Of course it was. Just as possible as anything else he'd been forced to accept over the course of these last few days.

"I want to help," said James.

"With what, specifically?"

"Elizabeth—you—younger you, she doesn't understand who or what she is. She just exists. Or, kind of exists. I think if she knew what she was—if she knew she—you—was still alive... well... I want to help you get that missing piece back."

271

The first rock moved shortly after midnight—a lone tap against another rock, unnoticeable unless you were really listening for it, which James and Betty were. With the next wave, a few more rocks moved, creating a small smattering of clicks and clacks. It was beginning.

It was relatively warm for the middle of the night in late November. The sky was clear; big, bright stars; bigger, brighter moon; blue light of the vibrant cosmos speckling the ocean and illuminating the beach.

"I don't know for sure that she'll come," said James. "I only ever saw her during the day. I never looked out here during high tide at night."

"She'll be here," said Betty. "She's on her way as we speak."

James didn't ask how she knew this. They—Betty and Elizabeth—were the same person; Betty knew the whereabouts of Elizabeth as surely as James knew the whereabouts of his own self.

James looked up at the big house next to the Seagull's Nest and imagined Leslie asleep inside. She'd been so amenable—so willing to believe in echoes, psychic phenomena, ghosts. Or was Connie right? Leslie was only going along with it because she was in love with him. No. He didn't believe that. Was she in love with him? It was possible he supposed, but he also felt like she was genuinely interested in the mystery. She'd have loved to have been involved in everything that had happened in the last twenty-four hours, and James found himself disappointed that she wasn't. Part of him wanted to run up to the house, wake her up, and fill her in. He'd taken her for granted—used her—and now he missed her.

"She's here," said Betty.

James turned around. Sure enough—barefoot, beige dress. Elizabeth. Only she wasn't cupping her hands behind her ears listening to the singing rocks. She was staring at Betty. And Betty was staring back at her. To see these two together in the same space! It was an uncanny feeling—like time itself had become corporeal and was being bent like hot metal. The same person, twenty-eight years of life separating them, staring at each other.

"You can see her?" asked James.

"No," said Betty. "I can feel her."

"Elizabeth," said James, "this is…" James doubted anyone in the history of the world had ever had to introduce two people the relational dynamics of which existed between the two women in front of him. "…Betty."

Elizabeth didn't say anything, just stared at her older self, mouth agape, confused. It was like watching a person try to solve a riddle, knowing the answer is right there but not quite being able to reach it.

"Do you recognize her, Elizabeth?" asked James.

She didn't respond. Couldn't. A malfunctioned machine.

"I've been looking for you," said Betty. "I lost you. Twenty-eight years ago. Upstairs in that house right there." She gestured to the Seagull's Nest. Each pane of glass in the spider web window reflected the moon. "Do you remember what happened up there twenty-eight years ago? What mother did to us?"

"She doesn't like to talk about the before-times," said James.

"I remember," said Elizabeth.

"She says she remembers," said James.

"I heard her," said Betty, not looking at James.

"You can hear her?"

Betty ignored him. "We got separated when that happened, you and me. We went to the white place, do you remember?"

"Yes."

"I came back, but you stayed."

"I live there now. I only get to come out when the rocks are singing."

"Why?"

"I don't know. That's just how it is. I'm in the white place, then the rocks call me and I come here. Then back to the white place. Over and over and over and over."

"What happens if you try to leave?"

"There is no leaving the white place. There's nowhere to go. Just white. Until the rocks sing. Then the door to here opens. Sometimes, when I'm here, I run, but I always end up back in the white place."

"I want you to come back with me."

"Where?"

"Life."

"Life…" She said it like it was an idea she hadn't considered in so long she wasn't even sure she could define it anymore. "How? If I try to go with you, I'll just end up back in the white space."

"I don't know."

James knew. He could do it. He could recombine them. He was the conduit.

"Take my hand." He held a hand out to Betty. She looked at it, not understanding. "Trust me. Take it." Betty took his hand. He held his other hand out to Elizabeth. "Take my hand."

Elizabeth took a step back. "I don't think I'm supposed to touch the people from the after-times."

"It's okay, honey," said Betty. "Take his hand."

Elizabeth trepidatiously reached for his outstretched hand.

The moment of contact sent a surge of psychic energy through James. His body seized and stiffened, his jaw clenched, his back arched. The world became a flickering merger of the beach and the white place.

Elizabeth dissolved into a smokey mist. She entered James's body through his hand, then traveled up his arm. The feeling was similar to the sick feeling he got when he was near Edgar Monahan, that full body nausea, but it only existed in the parts through which Elizabeth was flowing. She crossed his chest, though his heart, down his other arm, out his hand and into Betty's.

Betty's body trembled. Her head hung back. Her eyes clenched shut.

Elizabeth was out of James's body, completely transferred to Betty. Their hands separated and she fell to her knees. The white place disappeared and only the natural environment of the beach surrounded them.

Elizabeth was gone. Except, she wasn't. She was next to James, inside Betty.

"Are you okay?" he asked.

Betty was kneeling on the beach. The whole event had lasted a matter of seconds and involved almost no physical movement, but Betty was breathing heavily, as if she'd just finished a 200-meter dash. She looked up at James and smiled. Yeah, she was okay.

Betty stood up, faced the ocean, cupped her hands behind her ears, and listened.

James stood next to her and did the same.

Neither spoke for the entire duration of the performance.

The rocks were singing, and everything was okay.

Just like Edgar Monahan had, James got used to it. He could sense when he was in the vicinity of an echo and avoid it. If one did happen to sneak up on him, he could usually close his eyes—the physical ones as well as his mind's eye—and miss the worst of it. He might see the truck veering off the road but stop the echo before the collision, or see the old man clutch his chest but squeeze his eyes shut before the heart attack.

Every now and then he'd be blindsided by one. Like a few months ago when he'd gone to New York to meet with his agent and saw the man being beat to death with a tire iron on the subway platform. But for the most part he'd become adept at navigating them. After the Elizabeth/Betty affair he understood why Edgar and Ingrid Monahan were so insistent on not digging into the echoes. He was pleased with how that affair ended, but he certainly didn't want to go down that type of rabbit hole again.

He reached the end of Perkins Street where it intersected with Pond Street. It was the first time he'd been there in nearly a year. He'd sold his house in Jamaica Plain and moved to a small condo in Back Bay. With both Kelly and Linda gone, he didn't need all that space. Plus Back Bay was a much easier commute across the river to the campus in Cambridge.

But the real reason was the echo. Kelly's echo. It was nearly impossible to live where he lived and not have to traverse the section of Pond Street where the accident occurred. He didn't know for sure that Kelly had left an echo behind—not all tragedies leave an echo—but it was a risk he wasn't willing to take.

But now he was about to find out.

The light changed and the WALK sign lit up. He crossed the street and headed down the path toward the pond. He found Linda on a bench by the boathouse, right where she said she'd be. She held a bouquet of flowers. "You're late," she said when she saw him.

"Orange line. You know." He hadn't seen her since she left him. She looked a thousand years older. But so did he.

"Well, I appreciate you coming anyway."

"Of course I came. Did you think for a second I wouldn't?" Truth was, a huge part of him didn't want to. Even now he had an urge to sprint back to the Jackson Square station and get back on the northbound T. But he had to face this.

"I honestly didn't know."

"Look, Linda. I need you to know how—"

"No. Don't do that. Don't apologize. It happened, it's over, and things are the way they are. I've accepted it. I've moved on. I don't hate you, but I certainly don't want your apology either. Let's please not do that."

"Okay."

"You look well."

"No I don't."

"Okay. That's true. You don't. Neither do I. And don't insult me by saying I do. I have mirrors at home. I look fifty-five years old."

"We've been through some shit."

"Are you doing okay otherwise?"

"Not terrible. I finally wrote a book. I got a New York agent shopping it around."

"Good for you. The sixties one? The failure of the peace and love generation, or whatever?"

"No. A horror novel, believe or not. It's about a guy who can see visions of past tragedies. My agent is trying to sell it as a Stephen King comp."

"You hate Stephen King."

"Hate is a strong word."

"You said he farts out supermarket paperback diarrhea."

"I'd never read him when I said that. I've since reconsidered my stance."

"Well, congratulations, I guess. On the book."

"Thanks. How about you? How are you doing?"

"Under the circumstances, fine. Trying to stay busy. Meditating a lot."

"You seeing anybody?"

"Romantically? You've got to be kidding me. I can't even think about that right now. Why, are you? Wait! No. Don't tell me. I don't want to know. Yes I do. Are you?"

"Nothing serious."

"Jesus, Jim, not the undergrad. No, don't tell me. Yes, tell me. Is it the undergrad? Wait, no, don't tell me."

"It's not the undergrad. That was a mistake. Mid-life crisis kind of st—"

"Please don't justify it."

"Sorry."

"And don't apologize. So, who's the new flame?"

"Again, nothing serious. She doesn't even live around here. I took a trip to Maine to gather myself after the accident and I struck up a little friendship with the woman who owns the cottage. Once a month or so I drive up there for a weekend or she comes down here. It's no big deal."

"Well, I'm happy you've been able to move on so quickly."

"You're the one who left me."

"Not without reason."

"Which you refuse to let me apologize for."

"Let's not do this, James. Not today. That's not why we're here."

"She would have been thirteen today."

"A teenager. Can you imagine? Sometimes a swear it was only a week ago that she was in my belly."

James took her hand. She looked down at their conjoined hands—suspect at first, like she might yank hers away, but ultimately decided to allow it. They sat in silence for several minutes watching joggers, cyclists, dog walkers, a family of ducks.

"I guess we should do this," said Linda.

"I guess we should."

They got up from the bench and headed up the path back to Pond Street, to lay flowers and say a prayer at the site of Kelly's death. They continued to hold hands, though there was no romance in it—just two parents supporting each other through a tragedy.

They headed up the sloping sidewalk along Pond Street, cars whizzing by them.

Then he felt it. That buzz, that hum, that vibration he felt when he was about to experience an echo.

Suddenly, there she was. His daughter. Just as he'd last seen her, one year ago.

She was roller skating toward them, chatting and giggling with her friend Michelle. It seemed as though something quite amusing had just passed between them.

God, she looked so happy.

They were going way too fast.

Her skate hit some obstacle on the sidewalk.

She lost control.

Her arms flailed.

She careened toward the grass median between the sidewalk and the oncoming traffic.

James closed his eyes, silencing the echo.

ENDNOTES:

Thank you so much for reading *Echoes*, the 1980 entry in the "Grody to the Max Series." I hope you enjoyed it. Feel free to let me know how much you loved or hated it by contacting me though my website: **www.nealwritesthings.com** (QR code below).

While you're there, I encourage you to sign up for my monthly newsletter. You'll receive all the latest news and updates regarding all things Grody, as well as info on my other books, films, podcasts, etc. You'll also receive promotions, discounts, and other freebies. And as if that wasn't enough, I always include a cat pic or two. Seriously, go sign up!

One last bit of business before I let you go: reviews. It's incredibly difficult in the current landscape to get noticed out there in Internetland (especially now with the rise of AI content threatening us hardworking humans). Reviews and—to a lesser degree—star ratings are extremely important in the publishing world to boost visibility. At this time I humbly ask that you might be so kind as to consider leaving *Echoes* an honest review on either Amazon or Goodreads (or both!). I can't tell you how grateful I am that you've already spent the amount of time you have on *Echoes*, but if I could just squeeze another five to ten minutes out of you to write a quick review (or five to ten seconds to click a star rating) I would be beyond grateful.

That's it! Thanks again for reading, and I hope to see you back here soon for the 1981 entry in the "Grody to the Max Series": a classic 80s summer camp slasher cheesefest called *Three Fingered Willy*.